The Man in the Seventh Row
(The Movie Lover's Novel)

and Related Stories of The Human Condition

By Brian Pendreigh

Reaction on the initial publication of The Man in the Seventh Row: The Movie Lover's Novel

"A strange and beguiling novel about films and those who love and live them." Ian Rankin

"A most unusual novel, proving emphatically that life is possible both inside and outside the cinema! It's a very nice blend of the real, the fictional and the dream world and I really don't think I've read anything quite like it before." Barry Norman

"I loved it... a terrific read, definitely one for fans of film." Janice Forsyth

"Mad metaphysical genius" Donna Moore

"Hugely enjoyable, pacy, sharp and witty... It is a novel that baby boomers and film buffs will strongly relate to, and all enthusiasts of unusual – of original – fiction will take great pleasure in." – Andrew Marr

"Strange, he thought, how so much in life connects, so many disparate elements come together, and make some sort of sense in the end."
"The Man in the Seventh Row is not particularly easy to summarise. Indeed, just as the story's protagonist, Roy Batty, observes in the quote above, both the novel and its plot can be described as 'many disparate elements come together'. And while it does, for a time, seem as if these elements might run the length

of the novel in parallel lines, it is to tremendous effect that they do ultimately find each other.

"In the '60s, young Roy experiences a fully realised and vibrantly elucidated childhood. The reader is treated to rich, detailed prose which leaves little doubt that there is some of the author in these stories. When the story returns to Roy's present, we find a shell of a man, shattered by a tragedy to be revealed in due time, certain that his fate draws nearer with every torn ticket stub.

"The novel remains thoroughly compelling throughout, so powerful is the author's ability to craft each narrative. Though admittedly a somewhat challenging read... the culmination of the author's efforts is truly breath-taking... The reader is likely to find the occasional swelling of the throat, eyes filling slowly with a threat of tears. Pendreigh's infectious love of cinema and brilliant wordcraft combine to make for a singularly enthralling tale." James La Salandra, Literally Jen website

The Man in the Seventh Row first appeared in 2011 as a standalone novel, but I never felt it was quite finished. With some tweaking and the addition of the three additional chapters, it is complete.

The Man in the Seventh Row: The Movie Lover's Novel was originally published by Blasted Heath, 2011
Soul Music and Sometimes She'll Dance, originally published by Blasted Heath, 2012
Hommage, originally published by Boxtree, 2001
The Man in the Seventh Row and Related Stories of the Human Condition, published by Brian Pendreigh and John Lennox Publications, 2020
All copyright Brian Pendreigh

Note on Sometimes She'll Dance: William Wallace was obviously a real person. I always thought his story could make a great movie. The first version of Sometimes She'll Dance was written in the 1980s, long before Braveheart was made, though Wallace and Braveheart are largely incidental. The character of Sam Murdoch was partly inspired by the early life and literary career of the Scottish novelist and screenwriter Alan Sharp, who I met and interviewed some years after I had written the first version of the story.

The Man in the Seventh Row

1

Scotland, June 1962

Memories are elusive and unreliable things. You think you have them, and then, suddenly, they are gone, like tears in the rain. And like tears in the rain, you can never be sure they were there in the first place.

He was not sure if he remembered, or if he simply thought he remembered, because his mother had told him so many times that that was the way it happened, a long time ago. Either way, whether it happened or not, he knew it was true.

* * *

North Berwick is a chilly seaside town on the Scottish coast. Every morning commuters drive the twenty miles to work in the banks and insurance offices of Edinburgh. It is now a dormitory town, but not so long ago it was a thriving holiday resort. When he was a boy, his family spent their summer holiday fortnight there.

He was about four when they took him to the Playhouse cinema for the first time. The little boy sat transfixed among the packed rows of adults as the house lights dimmed and music exploded in his ears. His vision and imagination were filled with moving pictures of men on horses. He was swallowed up by the adventure, the action, the strange, exotic people and places. It sucked him in and he was no longer aware of those around him. The people around him now were Yul Brynner, Steve McQueen and James Coburn, though he knew them, not by those names, but as Chris, Vin and Britt. He had entered another world, the alternative reality of the cinema.

He sat open-mouthed, without a whisper - so his mother would tell him in later years - until Yul Brynner took off his hat. Then he screamed out in shock and horror:

'Look!' A finger thrust towards the man in black. 'He's got . . . no hair.'

Everyone seated around them laughed... or maybe tutted.

For the rest of the fortnight the boy rode the sand dunes, clutching imaginary reins, slapping his thigh until the flesh reddened. Sometimes he would draw his pistol and shoot a Mexican bandit or six. At first the pistol too was imaginary, then his father bought him a silver-painted toy Colt 45, which he kept in immaculate condition for years.

As the years passed, his attitude towards bald people changed. By the time he was 17 he shaved his head, and wore only black shirts, as Brynner had done.

He remembers quite clearly seeing 'The Magnificent Seven' as a small child. It is his favourite film. But it may simply be a romantic trick of memory that it was the first film he saw. The suggestion that he shouted out when he saw Brynner was bald may just be a fanciful notion. Surely it's obvious from the start that Brynner is bald?

As a man, he watched the film again and waited for Brynner to take off his hat. And he waited and waited. The audience learns a lot about Brynner in those opening scenes when he accepts the commission from the Mexican dirt farmers to defend their village and gathers his tiny force of mercenaries, adventurers and idealists. He is a man in total control. Everything he does is slow and deliberate. He never panics, no matter the odds against him, he never loses his temper, never rushes, hardly even breaks sweat. Which is probably why he doesn't need to take his hat off. We feel we know him, a role model, a hero, a comrade-in-arms, and yet he retains this incredible secret beneath his headgear.

Midway through the film Brynner is hard at work digging a trench beneath the burning Mexican sun when he finally removes his hat. And he does so only momentarily. Like Sharon Stone crossing her legs in 'Basic Instinct'. But it is long enough for Brynner to reveal that, unlike Sharon Stone, he has no hair. It is easy to imagine that a small boy might be unable to control his reaction to such a revelation.

It is a slight, inconsequential story. But the boy's exclamation upon the revelation of Brynner's baldness may be the man's earliest memory. Maybe. Maybe not. Maybe it is someone else's memory. Maybe it never happened at all. He does not know.

The picture house is gone now. The actors are dead, but the film survives. And that is the main thing. When you watch a great film nothing else matters. The man knows that. He knows that audiences refused to leave their cinema seats during the Blitz, as London crumbled around them, and he knows how the people looked for sanctuary from the Great Depression in the spectacle and extravagance of Busby Berkeley's musicals. The movies were the great escape long before Steve McQueen made his bid for freedom. The man knows that.

2

Los Angeles, March 1996

Everything is dark. A beam of light cuts through the blackness. It originates high at the back of the hall, hovers above two dozen scattered, shadowy heads and terminates in an explosion of Sixties Technicolor, an alternative reality in which colours differ from those in our own world. A classic film is playing.

A middle-aged man in a neat moustache that seems to have survived from the previous decade, heavy black sunglasses, sky-blue shorts and matching open shirt, calls for attention from the guests spaced around the edge of the pool. With all the enthusiasm of a children's television presenter he bounces over to the patio door through which he asks if the feature attraction is ready. From behind the door, a nervous voice makes a mumbled appeal for further discussion.

The speaker remains unseen. But the audience know who it is. They know the film, scene by scene. They have all seen 'The Graduate'. Everyone has seen 'The Graduate'. It came out in 1967, plays like a favourite old Beatles 45 and there is a temptation, not always resisted, to whisper some of the choicer lines before the actors do.

There is a ripple of anticipation as the man with the moustache attempts to coax the feature attraction from his sanctuary into the Technicolor, Californian afternoon. Practising Kissenger's art of shuttle diplomacy, he bounces from patio door to poolside, promising the guests a practical demonstration of the exciting 21st birthday present that cost over two hundred bucks and that is currently being worn by his son Benjamin Braddock.

A man shuffles along the seventh row of the cinema and sits down without once looking away from the screen, a warm smile of recognition on his face.

The patio door is thrown open to reveal a figure in a black rubber wet suit and flippers. It is wearing an air tank on its back and carrying what would appear to be a harpoon in its right hand. Its features are obscured by a mask and mouthpiece, connected by pipe to the tank. It slowly, hesitantly makes its way forward across the kitchen floor, slapping each foot down with a sound reminiscent of a seal clapping for fish. And all the time Mr Braddock Senior burbles on like the ringmaster at the circus, 'perform . . . spectacular . . . amazing . . . daring', as if he were indeed introducing a seal and might reward it with a halibut.

Through the mask we get the diver's/seal's perspective of proceedings: Mr Braddock clapping and waving his feature attraction towards the pool. His words remain silent. We hear only our own breathing from within the mask. It appears Mr

Braddock may walk backwards right into the pool, but at the last moment he stands aside. The diver looks down into the clean, clear, sparkling blue of the Californian dream lifestyle and turns away. His father, wearing a sunhat at a jaunty angle, and his mother, sporting white-rimmed sunglasses and a huge, white-toothed laugh, shout soundlessly and gesture excitedly towards the water. It is like watching 'The Muppets' with the sound turned down. Suddenly the diver drops into the pool. When he surfaces his two bespectacled parents are there, to greet his return with their smiles as permanent as the breasts of an aging Hollywood starlet. It is the sort of touching family moment of which only cinema is capable, as Ben shares his isolation with the general public and yet remains alone behind his mask. He retreats again below the surface. He stands on the floor of the pool, holding his harpoon, like Neptune, his sub-aqua reign dictated only by the number of bubbles in the tank on his back. There are a lot of bubbles. He can outlast his parents. He can outlast their guests. He can outlast the director's patience. While the camera lingers on the defiant figure at the bottom of the pool, the dialogue of the next scene begins on the soundtrack.

The light from the screen illuminates an expression of doubt on the face of the man in the seventh row. He knows the dialogue like the lyrics of a song, but the singer seems to have rearranged the verses. Ben is expressing some concern about his future to his father. This should not be the next scene. Not in the standard version of the film. The man thought he had missed this bit. But these days no one seems content to consider a film complete. This is the era of the special edition and the director's cut. Give Kevin Costner an Oscar for 'Dances with Wolves' and he will give you another hour of film. Give Ridley Scott cult status for 'Blade Runner' and he will give you a unicorn and a whole new meaning; possibly. Give George Lucas some new electronic technology and he will remake 'Star Wars'.

The man in the seventh row knows nothing of a new version of 'The Graduate'. Maybe the cinema just got the reels in the wrong order. And yet something else is different: unfamiliar and yet familiar. And a shiver runs down his spine, just as it had the first time he saw 'The 39 Steps' and Robert Donat explained to Godfrey Tearle that he did not know the identity of the villain but he did know that he had part of one finger missing. Tearle asks if it is this finger, and holds up his right hand to reveal a thumb, a forefinger, a middle finger, a ring finger and just half of a little finger. For a moment the man in the seventh row feels quite cold, as if Benjamin is holding up his hand to reveal it is not all there.

Ben's father's head partially obscures the audience's view of Ben. Ben's mother comes to encourage him to leave his room and meet their friends, including Mrs Robinson. Ben's mother walks directly in front of the camera, so the audience can see neither Ben nor his father.

Ben rises from his melancholy. He is neatly dressed in dark jacket, white shirt and yellow, red and black striped tie. A reassuringly conservative image of youth in a decade of revolution, just as the man remembers from previous viewings. The clothes are the same. The words are the same. The scene is the same, except for one small detail. Every other time that the man has watched 'The Graduate' the character of Ben has been played by Dustin Hoffman. This time Dustin Hoffman is not Ben. Ben is being played by someone else. The man in the seventh row recognises the features at once, but there is no smile of recognition now.

3

A gasp issues from the lips of the man in the seventh row at the appearance of this impostor in the role made famous by Dustin Hoffman. It hits him with all the unexpected emotional force of a child's discovery that his boyhood hero has no hair. He thought he knew the character, and now this. This Ben Braddock is taller than Dustin Hoffman, his hair is golden blond and his eyes are a blue twinkle, hinting at mischief and menace in unequal measure. It is a thin, angular face, with a sharp, aquiline nose and not an ounce of spare flesh, suggestive of a high metabolism, or maybe high anxiety. The man in the seventh row has seen a lot of films and read a lot of books about the cinema and he remembers reading that Robert Redford had been lined up for the role of Benjamin Braddock.

But the newcomer looks more like Jim Carrey than Robert Redford. His smile more Riddler than Graduate. Redford was closer than Dustin Hoffman to the original concept of the outstanding college athlete. It is now impossible to imagine anyone other than shy, uncertain Hoffman in the role; impossible to imagine anyone else, but not, it seems, impossible to see someone else.

Computer technology was now making anything possible. It was only three or four years since Steven Spielberg asked George Lucas to see if he could create convincing dinosaurs on computer, without any great expectation of success. Lucas showed the dinosaur stampede to Spielberg and the man in the seventh row remembered reading what Lucas said: 'When the lights came up we were all crying. We knew that nothing would ever be the same.' Back in the Seventies, Lucas had filmed a scene for 'Star Wars' with Harrison Ford and another actor who wore an unwieldy body-suit to represent the monstrous space slug Jabba the Hutt. Lucas was unhappy with the original scene and it never appeared in the finished film. Now he was working on another take, retaining Harrison Ford's original performance from 20 years earlier, while replacing the man in the funny outfit with a computer-generated image that was more to his liking. The end-result would look like a gigantic, talking dog turd. There is talk of computer-generated versions of James Dean and Marilyn Monroe in new roles opposite today's leading stars. Cinema is a place where illusion and make-believe are real.

Mrs Robinson persuades the blond, blue-eyed Ben Braddock to drive her home. He seems a little nervous. The man in the seventh row frowns. He shifts uncomfortably in his seat. Nervously he looks around to gauge the reaction of others to this unfamiliar version of the film. Eyes remain fixed to the screen as if nothing untoward has occurred. There is no sign of any representative of the cinema management coming to explain that it is all an unfortunate mistake, please accept your money back and complimentary tickets for another screening. The man had not expected that there would be.

Mrs Robinson, the wife of Ben's father's business partner, is a maelstrom of dark emotions, her hair piled up on top of her head, her eyes lined in black, beneath thick brows, a sensuous pale slash of mouth carrying a promise of passion and more than a hint of the bitter disappointment in her life.

She wears a cocktail dress that is striped like a tiger, shiny like a snake and blackly transparent in its sleeves like the veils of Salome. She has been drinking. Ben drives her home and she persuades him to come in for a nightcap. He is reluctant. He says he wants to leave, but this Ben Braddock lacks the conviction of Hoffman's performance. She tells him her husband will not be back for hours.

'Mrs Robinson,' he says. He is shaking his head and smiling to himself. 'Oh, Mrs Robinson,' he says, shaking his head as he realises the implications of their situation.

'What is it Benjamin?'

'If you're trying to seduce me, let's just cut to the bedroom, before Mr Robinson gets home.'

Sometime later Ben is sitting at the bar downstairs when Mr Robinson arrives home. He is a loud, friendly, rather inattentive individual. He insists on getting Ben another drink. Ben asks for Bourbon. Mr Robinson gives him Scotch and seems not to notice that his wife is still in a state of disarray as she comes down the stairs. Mr Robinson says he has only one word of advice for Ben.

The man in the seventh row frowns again for he knows that that is someone else's speech and that Mr Robinson is supposed to tell Ben to take it easy and sow a few wild oats. But Ben has already sown them.

'Plastics,' says Mr Robinson. 'It's the future.'

'Oh yes,' says Ben, with a mischievous smile and a twinkle in his blue eyes. 'I agree. I see a future in which plastic will replace money, people will pay restaurant bills with a small rectangle of plastic, have a bit of plastic with their picture on to prove who they are, and when they go to a hotel, to sow a few wild oats, they get a bit of plastic to open the door of their room instead of a metal key.'

Mr Robinson looks slightly disconcerted at the extent of Ben's enthusiasm. There is a murmur of laughter around the cinema.

'Plastic is the future, oh yes Mr Robinson, plastic is the future all right.' And as Ben rises to leave, he smiles and winks

16

in the direction of Mrs Robinson.

The man in the seventh row rises unsteadily to his feet and makes his way along the row, banging into the legs of a man at the other end.

'Sorry, sorry, excuse me.'

He stumbles up the aisle and into the brightness of the hall. He finds the men's room, fills a basin with cold water, cups his hands and splashes it all over his face. Alarm shows in his blue eyes as he looks at himself in the mirror over the basin. The fringe of his blond hair has fallen forward and is plastered to his wet brow. A drop of water falls from his nose.

The man from the seventh row stares into the mirror at the features of the man who is playing Ben Braddock in the film down the hall.

There is no twinkle in his eyes, the whites of which are bloodshot with fatigue and worry. There is no mischievous grin, none of the confidence and arrogance of the revisionist interpretation of Ben Braddock. He seems no more than a washed-out remnant of the man on the screen, but there is no doubt that he is, or was, the man in the movie. He presses his hands to his face and lets out a sound that is part sigh and part sob.

He returns to the cinema hoping Dustin Hoffman too has returned. But it is his own image that stares down at him as he makes his way along the seventh row once more.

Ben is explaining to Mrs Robinson's daughter Elaine that ever since he graduated he feels this compulsion to be rude. She says she knows how he feels. They go to the Taft Hotel for a drink. The desk clerk greets Ben as Mr Gladstone and asks if he is there for an affair, a question that had originally thrown Hoffman and had resulted in him ending up by mistake in a private function.

But the inquiry does not disconcert the new Ben.

'Good idea,' he says, 'I'll just check that the young lady's up for it.'

'Any luggage or just the toothbrush, Mr Gladstone?' asks the clerk.

'Just the toothbrush,' says Ben, patting his jacket.

Elaine asks why the hotel staff call him Mr Gladstone. He explains about her mother wanting him to drive her home and asking him in. He admits they were lovers and had assignations at the Taft, where he used the name Gladstone.

Ben and Elaine are silent. Both are clearly thinking about their situation. Ben eventually breaks the silence.

'Ever done three in a bed?' he asks.

The man in the seventh row grimaces.

Elaine is shocked and goes off to college in Berkeley. Ben tells his parents he is going to marry her. They are delighted, until he admits that not only has he not told Mr and Mrs Robinson, but he has not discussed it with Elaine. He drives up to Berkeley and takes a room in a cheap rooming house. The other residents include a young Richard Dreyfuss who has enrolled on the Shark Studies course, and will himself come into conflict with Mr Robinson when the latter refuses to close Amity's beaches just because a great white shark is eating the holiday-makers. By this time Mr Robinson will have changed his name to Mr Vaughn but is clearly still a very bitter man after his treatment by Mrs Robinson.

Mrs Robinson has told Elaine that Ben raped her. She wants Elaine to marry a rich medical student, whose peers include a young Ryan O'Neal. He looks puzzled when Ben says that he hopes Ali gets better soon. Ben looks momentarily sombre and shakes his head sadly as he walks away. Elaine tells Ben she does not care if he raped her mother; she loves him and wants to marry him. But, for some reason that is not entirely clear, Ben is late for the wedding. He does not know where they are getting married, his Alfa Romeo is out of petrol and when he starts to run the last few blocks he seems to be running without getting anywhere.

Ben is wearing a hooded jacket of the type that used to be called a windcheater. Underneath he is wearing a plain black shirt. There is a look of tremendous relief on Elaine's face as he arrives at the church. She is dressed in a traditional white wedding dress, including the usual crumpled-up net curtain on her head. He joins her at the altar and the priest begins the service.

In the original it had not been this way. Oh no, not like this at all. This is wrong, very wrong. Ben had an affair with Mrs Robinson, but there was no affair with Elaine. Ben followed her to Berkeley and discovered she was about to marry another student. He set out to track them down and ran out of petrol on the way to the wedding. By the time he reached the church the minister was concluding the ceremony. Elaine was married to someone else. He screamed her name. After a moment's hesitation, she responded with his name 'Ben'. Angry bitter faces crowded in on them. Mrs Robinson slapped her daughter's face. Mr Robinson tore a sleeve off Ben's windcheater. Ben grabbed a crucifix and swung it madly as he and Elaine retreated towards the church doors. They escaped together on a passing bus. That's the way it happened. That is the way it should be.

The man in the seventh row knows that in real life Anne Bancroft, who played Mrs Robinson, was only ten years older than Katherine Ross, who played her daughter. Anne Bancroft was 35, much the same as the man in the seventh row is now. Katherine Ross was never one of the favourite actresses of the man in Row 7. Pretty rather than sexy. She was a bowl of strawberries and cream to Anne Bancroft's bottle of rich red claret. Katherine Ross was the prim schoolteacher never able to lure Sundance away from the wise-cracking, kick-them-in-the-balls, let's-make-a-run-for-it Butch Cassidy. Butch was more fun. It was probably nothing sexual. That was the problem - nothing sexual. There was something missing between Ben and Elaine.

On screen, Ben turns to look at Mrs Robinson as the minister concludes the ceremony and the crash of the organ alerts Ben to what he has just done. He and Elaine are man and wife. He does not kiss the bride. For a moment he stands frozen. Then he shouts. The church echoes with his words, two words, loud and separate.

'Missis Robinson'.

She jumps to her feet and her response cuts through the shocked silence.

'Benjamin'.

Angry, bitter faces crowd in on them. Mr Robinson tears a sleeve off Ben's windcheater. Elaine slaps her mother's face. Ben grabs a crucifix and swings it madly as he and Mrs Robinson retreat towards the church doors. He uses the crucifix as a bar to hold the doors shut. Ben and his new mother-in-law dash towards a passing bus. They struggle onto it and make their way to the back seat. They collapse, exhausted, happy. Nothing is said. Ben's face is expressionless. A smile creeps across his face. It grows into a grin, a big mischievous grin, and then he winks.

* * *

The first time it happened, the first time Roy experienced this business of someone he knew being sucked into a movie, it was his father. He turned up in The Magnificent Seven. Or Roy thought he did. Roy wanted to join him, but he couldn't. He couldn't see himself up there on the screen, not at that time. It was just a fleeting appearance, one of the Mexican peasants, not one of Brynner's little band of gunfighters. His father was never really the sort of man who would ever have been so presumptuous as to take a starring part. He only really ever had a supporting role in life.

4

Woody Allen's 'Manhattan' opens with the sound of Gershwin and a black and white shot of an urban skyline fills the screen. The film the man in the seventh row is watching also opens with the sound of Gershwin and a black and white shot of an urban skyline. Well almost urban, not countryside anyway.

'Chapter one,' declares the voice-over with authority. 'He adored North Berwick. He idolised it out of all proportion.' The skyline of slate roofs and chimney pots, the clock on the council chambers and the modest spire on St Andrew's Church is succeeded by a series of evocative, haunting monochrome images. The caravan park in Tantallon Road. The bowling greens in Clifford Road. The square utilitarian library block that looks like a public toilet in Forth Street.

'Uh, no, make that: He... romanticised it all out of proportion,' says the voice. 'No matter what the season was, North Berwick always existed in summer, it always existed in the Sixties (at a push the Seventies) and it pulsated to the great tunes, not of Gershwin, but of Donovan, Marmalade and the Bay City Rollers.'

'Chapter One.' North Berwick is seen framed in the whale's jaw bone on top of Berwick Law, the hill behind the town. And Gershwin is replaced on the soundtrack by Donovan declaring that 'first there is a mountain'. The town's vernacular, individualistic buildings cling to the narrow strip of land between the hill and the grey waters of the Firth of

Forth.

'He was too romantic about North Berwick,' says the voice-over.

A small white motor boat carries visitors towards a gigantic plug of rock that rises sheer from the sea. Sunshine dances on the ruins of an ancient castle. Children build castles in the sand and watch the sea come in and knock them down, pulling away just a little more of the foundations with every incoming wave, until at last they collapse and are lost forever. Like tears in the rain.

'He thrived on the holiday crowds. To him North Berwick meant ice-cream cones and beach huts, games of putting on the sea-front, staying up late to go to the cinema, and pokes of chips afterwards.'

Rows of villas stare across the road at a long stretch of beach, empty but for one distant figure.

'Chapter One. He was as tough and romantic as the town he loved. Behind his blue eyes was the steely sharp edge of an easterly wind blowing in from the North Sea and sweeping down the High Street. North Berwick was his town. It was a metaphor. A metaphor for the way we were. North Berwick was his town. And it always would be . . .'

The narrator pauses. "Well, either North Berwick or Los Angeles."'

Los Angeles. Los Angeles was bigger. Los Angeles, the city where the man in the seventh row now sat. He had once calculated that Los Angeles was 1,500 times bigger than North Berwick, in population terms. Los Angeles, City of Angels, city of lights, city of dreams, city of nightmares. He felt a lump in his throat.

5

Los Angeles, March 1996

In the lobby of the Chinese Theatre, Roy pauses at the display of stills from 'Snow White and the Seven Dwarfs'. In his mind it takes him back to...

Scotland, Some time in the 1960s

Eight or maybe nine years old, Roy stood on the pavement outside the Playhouse in North Berwick, considering the large colour photographs depicting scenes from the film. Seven little men, with big noses, big eyes, big white beards and big, floppy colourful caps. Not at all like the Magnificent Seven, Roy thought. He preferred westerns to cartoons. At least he liked to pretend that he did. But 'Snow White' looked funny and he had heard it was a bit scary. It was from Walt Disney, who made 'Greyfriars Bobby', which was a true story that happened in Edinburgh in the old days, and 'One Hundred and One Dalmatians', with the spidery Cruella De Vil, who wanted to skin the little puppies for a fur coat, but who wasn't real, just a made-up character for the film. Disney also made 'Lady and the Tramp', with the fight between Tramp and the fiery-eyed rat to save the baby, and the injustice when Aunt Sara thinks Tramp is trying to harm the child. The dog-catcher takes him off to the pound, which has already provided the film's most poignant moment when one stray is led off on 'the long walk', wagging his tail, not knowing he will never come back. All these moments imprinted themselves on Roy's young memory. What his parents remember most about 'Lady and the Tramp' is having to move seats three times - once because a big man with a pipe sat right in front of Roy, then because his mother's seat seemed damp, and finally because Stephen's third seat seemed sticky. Stephen was much smaller than Roy and had difficulty in positioning himself to stop the seats tipping up with him in them. He said his seat was sticking to his legs. His mother could not feel anything sticky, but they moved again, with Roy complaining that he was missing the film.

And they remembered Roy asking if it was a true story, was it really all made up, how did they know it was all made up, and did people really take dogs away to be killed? His mother told him that they would never take a dog away to be killed unless it was a nasty, vicious brute that bit people or had those mysterious, menacing, invisible little beasties called fleas. Later, when his parents thought Roy was asleep in bed, Roy heard his father say to his mother that he couldn't understand why they had to pretend that innocent animals never got killed.

'After all,' he said, 'I'm a butcher.'

'Well,' said his mother, 'that's nothing to be proud of.'

Roy definitely wanted to see 'Snow White'. It was different from other Disney films Roy had seen, which were all about dogs. This one was about human beings. In one still outside the cinema Snow White was considering the red apple given to her by the evil witch. Roy knew she was an evil witch, because he had seen excerpts on television. Even so, he would have recognised her as a witch from the wart on her long nose. She looked a wee bit scary, with bony fingers and a black hood. Snow White on the other hand looked disappointingly dull and sappy. Maybe it was because she was a girl and she was wearing the weirdest dress with puffy shoulders and a white collar that stood up by itself.

'Next week,' said the sign, a special sign for this unusual week-long run. Roy would have to wait until the second half of the holidays to see 'Snow White'. But his parents had promised to take him to 'Batman' tonight. It had the Joker, the Penguin, the Riddler and Catwoman, all together in the one film. Of course Roy had a particular affinity with Batman. He was Batman. That was his nickname. Batty, hence Batman.

He quite liked being called Batman. As nicknames went, it was one of the better ones. 'Come on Batman.'

'Just coming.'

'Fats?'

'What about you, Minger?' And Minger would reply with the sound of a deflating balloon. 'Are you coming Spit?'

Spit was a very fast runner and 'Spit' was short for 'Spitfire'. When Miss Donaldson, their teacher, asked why Spit was called Spit, Fat Bob told her it was because he spat all the time and she gave Spit a stern lecture about what a disgusting habit it was. Years later there was a boy at Roy's secondary school nicknamed 'One Per Cent', not because he did badly in exams, but because Domestos, at the time, claimed to kill 99 per cent of all known germs.

Roy's nickname entitled him to the principal role when they played at Batman in the back green on a summer's day, with Roy in swimming trunks and a towel around his neck, held by a safety-pin and flapping behind him as he ran, going 'Dee-dee-dee-dee, dee-dee-dee-dee; dee-dee-dee-dee, dee-dee-dee-dee, Bat-man!'. Batman was a great influence for good on their lives. Not only did he represent law and order and justice, frequently summarised in brief on-the-job tutorials for Robin the Boy Wonder, but it was difficult for the game to get out of hand if you had to stop to say 'Pow' and 'Ker-unch' between each pretend blow.

Roy preferred the nickname Batman to his surname - a word he knew could be used to mean 'not quite right in the head'. When his family moved to Learmonth the local kids experimented with 'Nutty', but Roy told them he already had a nickname and that it was Batman and they stuck to it after that.

'What's the difference between Bing Crosby and Walt Disney?' asked a little, ginger-haired girl, who had appeared at Roy's side, gazing at the 'Snow White' pictures too. She was slightly younger than Roy and spoke with the harsh, intimidating Glasgow accent common to many of the children on holiday in North Berwick.

Roy knew about Bing Crosby. Crosby was his father's favourite singer. His father had a 78 of 'White Christmas', which Roy played over and over again on the old gramophone at his grandfather's house. Roy could hear Crosby's voice pouring over the words like honey. His grandparents had a television too and it was there that he had seen Bing Crosby in some funny films that always had the word 'Road' in the title. Bing Crosby and Bob Hope did a little routine, like a child's game, where they clapped their hands against each other and said 'Patty-cake, patty-cake' and then the last move was punching the baddies. Roy's grandfather sat in the grandest armchair chuckling and puffing on his pipe. In future years whenever Roy saw mention of the Road movies he would smell the rich aroma of tobacco that lingered in the house long after his grandfather.

'Walt Disney is the man who makes the cartoons,' Roy explained knowledgably to the little girl. 'And Bing Crosby is in films that aren't cartoons, and he sings songs.'

'Bing sings,' chirped the little girl, in apparent confirmation. She paused instinctively for dramatic effect. 'And Walt disnae.'

Roy looked at her blankly. She looked at him and smiled one of those big warm Glasgow smiles that can send a shiver down a middle-class Edinburgh spine.

'Bing sings and Walt disnae,' she repeated, sensing perhaps that he was a little slow on the uptake. Only then did he realise that it was a joke.

'My name is Roy Batty,' he said.

The little girl did not say her name. She turned and

walked away. Roy watched the little figure in the yellow summer dress hurry to catch the grown-ups who were ahead of her. Roy looked for her at the Playhouse the following week, when his parents took him to see 'Snow White'. But she was not there. Maybe it was too scary for her. Roy didn't find it scary, but he could see how littler children might be frightened. Some things in the film worried him.

'Is it a true story?' he asked.

His father assured him it was not.

'How would I know if someone had poisoned my apple, Dad?'

'No one will poison your apple, Roy.'

'But what if a witch got it?'

'There's no such thing as witches,' he said. 'Witches are just an old wives' tale.' And he laughed at his own wit.

Roy was far from reassured. 'But they burned witches down beside the swimming pool, Dad. They do exist. Definitely. There's a sign down at the swimming pool.'

'That was in the old days, Roy,' said his father impatiently.

'Do you believe in magic, Dad? Do you believe in ghosts? What's the difference between Bing Crosby and Walt Disney?'

Roy remembered the little girl and looked for her the following summer. And the summer after that. But he never saw her again. Sometimes he imagined that she had died after eating a poisoned apple. He saw her only once, but he often thought of her and her joke about Bing Crosby and Walt Disney.

He spent a long time just standing looking at the pictures in the display cases outside the Playhouse. Every time the family went along the High Street he would stop and admire the pictures, like an art aficionado reconsidering a favourite Van Gogh or Monet in the National Gallery.

Only occasionally did his parents take him to the pictures in Edinburgh - it was usually 'going to the pictures', rarely 'going to see a fill-um' and certainly never 'going to a movie,' which was an American term Roy started using only as an adult. On holiday in North Berwick, however, they would go two or three times in the fortnight. North Berwick is only 20 miles from Edinburgh, but the train took forever as it strained to pull itself free of the city's stony grip, across the green countryside and past the old villages with lazy green squares, tall-spired churches and Belfry Cottages taken over by lawyers and surveyors from the city. East Lothian is as close as Scotland comes to the Home Counties. There is something safe, permanent and reassuring about streets called Windygates Road, Station Hill and Quality Street.

Roy looked out of the window and ticked off different kinds of cows in the 'I Spy the Countryside' book that his father bought him every year at Waverley Station before they set off. His little brother Stephen looked at the pictures in his comic and told everyone he was going to be sick. He always was, somewhere near Drem.

North Berwick became a second part-time home, for two weeks every year. The family was not adventurous, though they were more adventurous than the previous generation. Roy's grandparents had holidayed at Portobello, not Morgan the pirate's haven in Central America, but a seaside resort just three miles and a half-hour bus ride from Edinburgh city centre. Roy's father asserted his independence when he got married and turned his back on Portobello in favour of North Berwick. He liked North Berwick and they went back every year for ten years. Ordinary, lower middle-class families did not go abroad in the Sixties. There was something safe and certain about North Berwick's red and white and grey stone houses and its gardens of green and red, pink and yellow.

'North Berwick suits me,' Roy's mother would say, as if the resort somehow complemented the blue of her eyes and she did not want to risk the colour clash that another resort might present.

Dave and Doreen Batty would have disputed any accusation that they went to the same place every year.

Although they went to North Berwick every year, they always went to a different guest house, sometimes on the east bay, sometimes on the west and sometimes in one of the newer streets up behind the town centre, staying with landladies called Mrs Brown, Mrs Hood and Mrs McGregor, middle-class, middle-aged women, whose sacred mission was to provide accommodation for paying guests and ensure no one ever learned their Christian names. Perhaps they did not have Christian names. Even their husbands would refer to them as Mrs Brown, Mrs Hood and Mrs McGregor.

'Did Mrs McGregor mention that tea is served in the television lounge, so Sarah can lay out the tables for breakfast?' Mr McGregor inquired. 'No? Ah well then. I'm sure she'll be doing just that.'

A TV lounge seemed an appropriate setting for tea. It should have been served with something beginning with V . . . tea and vegetables. But it was served with biscuits so perhaps they should have called it the TB lounge. They were always Rich Tea biscuits.

Bedrooms smelled of mothballs, and halls and stairs were heavy with silence, punctuated at regular intervals by the awakening of a stately old grandfather clock on the landing and shattered three times a day by the hammering of a gong as dramatic and significant as an air-raid siren. Children would congregate at the foot of the stairs prior to mealtimes and Mrs Whichever would choose one to thump the brass instrument with the little cloth-covered baton. Like the half-naked man at the beginning of the Rank films. Bong. Roy Batty Films Presents . . . 'Mince and Tatties' . . . A Meat and Two Veg Production.

Each summer the Batty family would deliver their stiff square suitcases to their new guest house, meet the new Mrs Landlady, change Stephen out of his soiled clothes and wander through the town centre before unpacking, just to see what had changed. Nothing ever changed except the programme at the Playhouse. It normally changed three times a week, but films might play for anything from a single night to a whole week, in which case Roy would feel short-changed unless he saw two or three double bills in the other week of the holidays. He fidgeted impatiently while his parents discussed meteorological trivia with Mrs B&B and then ran ahead of them to see the display cabinets at the entrance to the red sandstone cinema in the middle of the High Street, just beside St Andrew's Church, the most prominent building in the town. Apart from a few Disney films and TV spin-offs like 'Batman' and 'Dr Who and the Daleks', the titles were unfamiliar to Roy. 'The Lion of St Mark' and 'The Vengeance of She' suggested more excitement than 'Doctor in Love' and something called 'Sex and the Single Girl', which sounded really soppy. Anything with 'adventure', 'guns' or 'swords' in the title would be considered reliable, anything with 'love' was deeply dubious. Roy was not sure what 'sex' was, but he knew it had something to do with love. He relied on the posters and lobby stills to give him a true taste of what he might expect in the coming days. 'The Lion of St Mark' promised swords, costumes, pirates and action, while 'The Vengeance of She' offered adventure, danger and exotic settings.

'Bon Voyage'. What was a bon voyage? The pictures did not give much away, just a lot of people standing around. He had to dash round to the side of the building where there was another display cabinet with details of what was 'coming soon'. Cowboys. Four armed men in a line in a dusty, deserted street. Four men who clearly meant business.

'Gunfight at the O.K. Corral,' read Roy.

His father confirmed that it looked good, as if it needed confirming. The title was confirmation enough.

'It's the story of Wyatt Earp and Doc Holliday,' said his father, 'so it seems like a suitable film to see on holiday. Doc Holliday. Ha-ha-ha. And it's directed by the man who made "The Magnificent Seven", John Sturges.'

His father was unusual in those days in that he not only enjoyed westerns and could name the stars, but could name the directors as well. He even went to see foreign films at the

Cameo cinema and the film guild. Roy's mother went to the cinema once a week on a Wednesday with Betty, a friend from her single days, poring over the Evening News after tea to choose their film, largely on the basis of who was in it. Roy found out much later that Betty had gone out with his father before he met his mother. But obviously Roy's father could never have married Betty, otherwise she would have become Betty Batty.

At the Seaview Guest House, or maybe the Buena Vista, named after Walt Disney's distribution company no doubt, Roy's parents unpacked and folded away the clothes in the chest of drawers or hung them up in the heavy mahogany wardrobe, while Roy wrote the names of films on squares of paper and positioned them beneath his 'Monday-Tuesday', 'Wednesday-Thursday' and 'Coming Soon' signs. He took up half the bedroom floor with his display. 'Gunfight at the OK Corral' quickly progressed into the 'Monday-Tuesday' slot and he drew a picture of four men with guns and cowboy hats to accompany the title and heighten public anticipation. And, sure enough, he saw it on the second Monday and would have seen it again on the Tuesday too if he could have persuaded his father to take him. Roy had to content himself with re-enacting the film himself on the Tuesday, singing the catchy theme tune 'O. K. Corr-al; O.K. Corr-al' and attempting to accentuate the natural dimple in his chin to make him look more like Kirk Douglas.

The Batty family spent most days of their holiday on the beach, changing into swimsuits in one of the decrepit bathing huts that stood in limping file along the west bay. Dad would spend most of the morning erecting windbreaks while Mum complained the wind was coming from the other direction. Roy pretended he was Robinson Crusoe, whose adventures he followed on the black and white television serial with the wonderful music that would suddenly sweep across the lonely island, or Robert Newton, hopping along on one leg in 'Treasure Island', or a French foreign legionnaire in 'Beau Geste', which he had watched on the television with his

31

grandfather, and the windbreaks would become an Arab encampment. Roy was going to join the Foreign Legion when he grew up. Either that or be an artist. At noon his father would take the windbreaks down again and store them in the hut. Spades and buckets were shoved under the hut's bench seat, swimming costumes taken off.

They set off across the putting green in the direction of the Seaview or Buena Vista, Sergeant Dad leading the way with the lemonade, biscuits, newspapers, paperbacks, suntan lotion, half-written postcards, boxes of tissues, box camera and other essential supplies, bundled into a deep tartan shopping bag. He might seem rather old and plump for a special mission behind enemy lines. His fluffy white beard more readily brought to mind Santa Claus than Sergeant Stryker, John Wayne's character in 'The Sands of Iwo Jima'. But the jolly appearance masked a ruthless and highly experienced professional, a trained killer, nicknamed 'The Butcher'. Yards behind him came the tall, thin figure of Corporal Mum in black glasses, which suggested either a serious Mob connection or a serious eye deficiency, for there was no sun about. Ten yards behind her came Private Roy Batty, carrying a machine gun, cunningly disguised as a rolled-up windbreak. Behind him a tiny figure was crouched, with an inflatable rubber duck around his middle. Private (Second Class) Stephen would not last a week here. If Roy's father had known of the game Roy was playing in his mind he would have suggested Stephen was a sitting duck.

But Roy was the only one who knew what was going on. Roy Batty was young, but he was the real hero in the platoon. Ever alert, he scanned the putting greens for Japanese soldiers. Suddenly he dropped to the ground, with one arm flinging an unseen grenade in the air. 'Kah-pooom,' it went and sent two yellow-bellied Japs into the air. At the same time a fat man in a white Fred Perry shirt sent a one-foot putt five feet past the hole. Private Roy Batty smiled at him and hurried after the NCOs.

After lunch of mince and tatties, the family might go to

see the stuffed birds in the poky wee museum in School Road or visit the trampolines in the Lodge Gardens. Occasionally Roy and his father might climb the Law, the hill behind the town, or go to Fidra or the Bass Rock, where Messerschmidt-gannets dived-bombed their patrol boat with millimetre accuracy. They would meet Mum and Stephen back at the harbour and buy ice-creams, a plain slider for Dad, an oyster for Mum, a cone for Stephen and, for Roy, a black man: a slider with soft nougat built in.

It was just a question of filling in time until tea at 5.30 and then Roy and his father, and in later years the whole family, could be off to the Playhouse at the back of six to witness She's vengeance or Dr Who's battle with the Daleks. It mattered little that the battle for the future of the universe had begun just as the Batty family sat down to eat. As often as not, they would arrive in the middle of the film, sit through the trailers, a newsreel, a cartoon, adverts, and a supporting feature or a short with a title like 'Looking In On the Royal Navy', 'This is Jordan' or 'Exciting Times in Milton Keynes New Town', and when the excitement in Milton Keynes died down they would see Dr Who renew battle with the sinister exterminators or She revenge herself.

The Batty family were still at their mince and tatties when Sean Connery announced himself to the Playhouse audience as 'Bond, James Bond'. By the time Roy and his father got there Bond had arrived in the Caribbean, from which Ursula Andress was emerging, with a knife and some sea-shells, and little else.

Roy was already half way up the stairs by the time his father bought the tickets at the little booth in the middle of the foyer.

'An adult and a child for the circle, please.'

The circle was more expensive than the stalls. The cashier pressed the appropriate buttons and two tickets, like snakes' tongues, shot out from a slot in the surface in front of her. An usherette tore their tickets in two and shone a light on the carpet to guide them to their seats. Roy stumbled after her and his father, his eyes already fixed to the screen.

'That's Sean Connery; he's from Fountainbridge,' whispered Roy's father, as they sat down, as if the information that Bond was a neighbour of theirs was all Roy needed to know to make sense of the story.

Watching the second half of films first was by no means a practice peculiar to the Batty family. Every few minutes they were disturbed by others whose schedules were dictated by the landladies of the town rather than the manager of its cinema. Disney cartoons were easy to pick up half-way through and there was no difficulty differentiating good from evil in 'Dr Who and the Daleks': the baddies looked like giant pepperpots and had a vocabulary limited pretty much to the single word 'exterminate'. And in 'Dr No', shortly after Roy and his father came in, Dr No explained his plans to Bond in detail, as Bond villains are curiously wont to do, enabling the Battys to catch up on the plot and Bond to undermine the cold and ruthless German-Chinese half-breed with the false hands. Roy subsequently had to sit through a western before he got his first sight of Bond through a gun barrel to the sound of Monty Norman's twangy theme tune and saw Bond's cleverest trick of all, throwing his hat onto the hat-stand in Miss Moneypenny's office, something Roy would practice for hours.

Ursula Andress emerged from the sea once again with her knife and her shells, Bond introduced himself once more and Dr No's men strafed the beach.

'This is where we came in,' Roy's father said.

Roy said nothing, his eyes glued to the fire-breathing dragon that pursued them along the beach.

'Time to go,' his father said.

'Just another five minutes,' Roy pleaded as the evil Chinaman went over the plot one more time.

"Come on," his father said, rising from his seat. "I want my poke of chips."

They always bought chips after the film and ate them as they walked back to the guest house. Roy liked the little crispy ones that had a habit of sinking to the bottom of the steaming poke, and he relished licking his greasy fingers clean of salt and vinegar when the chips were finished.

Then one year something terrible happened. It was 1969, July 1969. Dave and Doreen Batty had decided to go somewhere different for their summer holidays, not just a different guest house, but a different place entirely, farther than anyone in the family had ever gone for their holidays before. They went all the way to the west coast and got a ferry over the Firth of Clyde to the seaside resort of Millport on the island of Great Cumbrae, where they stayed in the guest house of a Mrs McDonald. It started off alright. Roy imagined he was secret agent James Bond, travelling in disguise as a holiday-maker, to investigate what was happening on this strange unfamiliar island, run by the cold and ruthless Mrs McDonald and her sidekick, a German-Chinese dwarf using the unlikely alias of Mr McDonald.

It was not long before Roy had uncovered the extent of the villainy - a town hall was posing as a cinema and, worse, much worse, it was showing only two feature films in the entire fortnight. 'Ring of Bright Water' was a lovely story of a man and his pet otter Mij, with a very sad ending.

'Did the otter really die, Mummy?' Stephen asked.

'No, it's only a story,' said his mother.

'But it's a true story,' said Roy. 'So it must have died.'

Stephen looked as if he might burst into tears. 'But not the otter we saw in the film,' said his mother. 'It didn't die.'

'It was just acting,' said his father.

'You mean it wasn't really an otter at all?' asked Stephen, his eyes widening.

But the film that Roy really wanted to see was the other one showing. A war film. Men in combat uniform with grenades on their belts and machine guns in their hands spitting fire into the blackness like the dragon in 'Dr No'. One, two, three, four, five, six, Roy counted; seven, eight, nine, ten, eleven, twelve of them. In a line like the heroes in 'The Guns of Navarone'. Lee Marvin, one of his favourite actors was at the front, his features carved from rock. He had seen Marvin in the western 'The Professionals' in North Berwick the previous year. He was tough. And by his side was Charles Bronson from 'The Magnificent Seven'. With Marvin and Bronson at the forefront twelve should be enough to defeat Jerry.   'Damn them or praise them,' the poster said. 'You'll never forget The Dirty Dozen.' And Roy never did forget. He never forgot them, but he never saw them either. 'The Dirty Dozen,' the poster said, 'X.'

'What does X mean, Dad?'

'You have to be sixteen to see it,' said his father.

'How do you mean you have to be sixteen, Dad? 16 what?'

'Years old. You have to be sixteen years old to get in.'

'Why?'

'I don't know. Maybe they think there's too much fighting in it for children.'

'But there was lots of fighting in "The Magnificent Seven" and I got to see that.'

'Maybe there's too much blood in this.'

'But I see loads of blood every day. You're a butcher. I really want to see it. It's the film that I most want to see ever.'

'But they won't let you in.'

'Who won't let me in?'

'It's the law.'

'You could tell them I'm sixteen, but I'm very small for my age because I'm a dwarf.'

'No. You can see it when you are sixteen.'

'It won't be on then.'

'It'll come back.'

'OK,' said Roy, but he sounded most uncertain. He reckoned no one ever stopped Lee Marvin going to see a film he wanted to see. That was why he was leader of the Dirty Dozen.

Roy's father went off one night with another man from the guest house, without saying where he was going, but Roy knew. Neither Roy nor his father made any mention of dirty soldiers at breakfast next morning. Roy's father neither damned nor praised them. The family crunched their toast and said nothing. Roy looked at his lap and did not see the other guest approach their table until it was too late.

'Me and your dad saw a great film last night, Roy. You would have loved it.'

Roy could feel the tears well up in his eyes, but he did not cry, because men don't cry.

It was the next day, when they were on the beach, that Roy finally asked his father to tell him the story of 'The Dirty Dozen', deciding that hearing the plot second-hand was better than nothing. His father told him how Lee Marvin was an army officer who recruits twelve desperate criminals from a military prison for a secret mission behind enemy lines. The mission is a success, though nearly all the men are killed.

'Was Lee Marvin killed?' asked Roy.

His father assured him that Lee Marvin survived.

'Was Charles Bronson killed?' And over the next few days he renewed the conversation to clarify various details until he could recount the story better than many people who had seen the film.

Roy's father was of an age to have served in the Second World War, but the Army turned him down because he was asthmatic. Listening to his father tell the story of 'The Dirty Dozen' Roy imagined he was recounting his own war experiences.

'He doesn't like to talk about it much,' he told his friend Jumbo at school as they exchanged Commando comics, 'but my father was in the war. He dropped into France and had to kill some top Jerries. Most of his men were killed, but he got back alright.'

'You're dad's a butcher with asthma,' said Jumbo. 'And your story's mince. The only thing your dad ever dropped was sausages.'

Roy was hurt.

Because he didn't get to see 'The Dirty Dozen', his mother took him and Stephen to the pictures the following week in Edinburgh. They went to see 'The Wizard of Oz'. Judy Garland was not Lee Marvin, and the Tin Man, Cowardly Lion and Scarecrow presented little threat to the Third Reich. No self-respecting 11-year-old could admit to liking the Munchkins, with their silly squeaky voices and songs about yellow brick roads. But Roy did like them and for years to come, whenever he saw a rainbow in the sky, he would think of Dorothy and the place she dreamed of and wonder what the end of a rainbow was like.

It all seemed so innocent then, a little girl and her dream, before he found out about Judy Garland's drug dependency, her nervous breakdowns and her suicide attempts, before he read reports of orgies and rowdiness among the midgets who played the Munchkins, and before he found out what did lie at the end of a rainbow. How different it might have been if he had seen 'The Dirty Dozen', his mother had never taken him to 'The Wizard of Oz' and he had never developed a fascination for chasing rainbows.

6

Los Angeles, March 1996

An indistinct figure makes its way through a misty pine forest and looks down upon a patchwork of lights. Go back, go back, the man in the seventh row shouts silently. The little figure seems to purr in wonder, but still we do not see him. There is a roar like a lion as a vehicle grinds to a halt. Other vehicles appear all bright light and violent movement, shattering the tranquillity of the misty night. They seem to encircle the figure.

The man in the seventh row remembers how Rosebud shook her head, eyes never leaving the screen when he asked her if it was too scary. He would hold her hand and assure her everything would be alright.

On screen the little figure screams, like a cat, in alarm. The ferns dance wildly as the figure dashes through them. It seems to give off a light as it goes. Torches cut the night air like light-sabres. The men from the cars pursue the half-seen figure as it dashes towards the point where it knows its friends are waiting. Almost there.

'Quick, hurry,' Rosebud would entreat, having watched the film numerous times. She knew the figure was hurrying back to the spaceship, but she refused to accept that it would never make it. Maybe this time. Maybe this time it would get there in time. Oval like an Easter egg, lit like a Christmas tree, the craft rises above the pine trees.

And E.T. is left behind. Alone.

'Don't worry. Everything will be alright,' the man in the seventh row would assure Rosebud.

The man in the seventh row sits alone now. And he sobs too. Great, heaving, silent sobs that shake his shoulders and grip his whole body. Tears stream down his face. He rises and makes his way to the exit. He can watch no more. He can take no more.

The man from the seventh row stumbles out into the day, momentarily blinded by his tears and the shock of bright sunshine after the darkness of the cinema. He was alone in the cinema with his thoughts. Now he is a figure in a busy urban landscape. He rubs his eyes with the heel of his hand. Two young men watch him with little curiosity. Tiredness shows in his face and sunshine glints on three-day-old stubble, black in stark contrast to the hair on his head. He pulls mirrored sunglasses from the inside pocket of his crumpled black linen suit. One youth says something to the other. The man starts to make his way along the sidewalk and the youths follow him with their gaze.

He walks unevenly, as if slightly drunk or shell-shocked. Perhaps sensing a kindred spirit, an old man silently proffers a brown paper bag to the passing stranger, who ignores or does not see the outstretched arm. He keeps walking as if in a daze, leaving it for others to get out of his way, until he reaches a newspaper dispenser at the side of the road. Through the window of the contraption he stares at the headline in the Los Angeles Times - 'City gripped by new terror' - but it is unclear whether the words register. He puts several quarters into the slot, hesitates and walks on without taking his paper. A blue Ford pick-up blares its horn when he steps out onto the road, the sound quickly lost in the din of men drilling and traffic moving. The aroma of bacon and coffee drifts out into the sunshine from a diner. He climbs the steps of an old stone building and enters beneath the sign 'Police'.

His stride seems surer now. He walks with a new determination, along a white-walled corridor towards an inquiry desk. Just short of the desk he stops and asks a uniformed officer a question. The policeman glances at the newcomer and resuming his previous conversation gestures with a thumb over his right shoulder. The man follows the direction indicated, down another long corridor, at the end of which is a door marked 'Homicide Division'. He enters.

Plain-clothes officers are sitting around desks. The man asks to see someone in charge. He is shown into a room, where a middle-aged officer in a suit is sitting behind a desk considering some papers.

'I want to report a murder,' says the visitor.

'Sit down,' says the man behind the desk. There is a hard edge in his voice. He is a man who says no more than is necessary, sometimes not even that much.

'Who was murdered?' he asks.

He looks at the newcomer and the visitor pauses, like a professional actor attempting to crank up the tension and heighten the sense of expectation. The man behind the desk looks at him impassively, and waits for him to speak. Murders in Los Angeles are about as remarkable as tulips in Amsterdam. The man behind the desk has heard it all before, and seen it too.

His visitor takes a deep breath, considers the question 'Who was murdered?', and weighs up his response.

'I was,' he says.

The policeman's face shows not a flicker of reaction. He picks up another piece of paper and begins to read it, as if the topic of discussion has turned out to be too trivial to warrant any further attention.

'Do you want to hear my story or not?" asks the visitor. "I don't have much time left. A day, two days, a week at the most. And then I will be gone.'

'Where?' asks the policeman.

'The movies,' says the man.

The policeman raises a quizzical eyebrow. Now it is his turn to pause. 'You're going to the movies?' he says, his voice rising only very slightly at the end.

'I'm disappearing into the second dimension,' says the

man. Quickly reconsidering the melodrama inherent in his comment, he feels he must elaborate. 'The movies are taking me over,' he says. 'Taking over my thoughts. Taking over my body. I can walk and talk but I have no life of my own anymore, no life outside the movies.'

The policeman frowns and raises a hand to his chin; as if he does not know whether to laugh or cry for assistance. The policeman is not someone to whom laughter comes easily. And he never cries.

'Name?' says the policeman.

The visitor appears to be considering whether he should tell him. They sit looking at each other, the impassive grey-suited policeman sees his own image looking back at him from across the desk, reflected in the sunglasses the stranger is still wearing. Instinctively, the stranger reaches up to the glasses and takes them off. For the first time the policeman looks into the tired blue eyes of the other man and is struck by the beauty of the face. He reckons the man is in his mid- to late-thirties, but there are still signs of youth in the delicately chiselled features, an angelic, innocent quality in a city that was named after angels, but long ago lost the last traces of whatever innocence it may once have possessed. The policeman can appreciate beauty in a painting, in a passage of music, in a woman, in another man's face, even. He appreciates them in secret. In the eyes of this man who thinks he is being taken over by the movies the policeman sees a child.

Most people in this city are taken over by the movies. That is why they are here. Serving beers. Waiting tables. Just waiting. Waiting for the big break that will turn them into the next Tom Cruise, or the next Julia Roberts. But more likely the only movies they will ever make will involve sex with strangers filmed by other strangers. They are no more than children when they come to LA. They quickly grow old, lose their looks and mislay their innocence. Every day the policeman sees people who have been taken over by the movies. They live in trailer parks and dirty, cramped

42

apartments, and they turn tricks on Sunset Boulevard until their own suns set. He has looked on their corpses, abused by drugs and sexual perversion and sees a dream that turned into a nightmare. They were dead long before they were taken to the morgue.

He looks into the blue eyes of this stranger. And he sees something entirely different. The policeman used to go to the movies, quality films, arthouse films, that his buddies on the force would never have heard of. He went in secret. The visitor is British and he reminds the policeman of a young Terence Stamp as Billy Budd, when he has killed the dreadful Claggart. The policeman looks into the blue eyes of this stranger and says nothing.

The man from the seventh row looks at the policeman.

'The name's Batty,' he says at last. 'Roy Batty.'

The policeman turns away.

'I can't help you,' he says, shaking his head. 'There's nothing I can do.'

His voice suddenly hardens again. 'Go on, get going.'

The man turns and the policeman watches him leave.

7

On Hollywood Boulevard, among the fast-food joints and souvenir shops, stands an ancient temple, with a green sloping pagoda roof like a fancy, exotic hat, and bright red pillars and canopy. Stone dogs or lions or some hybrid of the two bare their teeth at the pilgrims who come here with bowed heads to pay homage to their gods. The pilgrims gather in small groups and pose, smiling, to record the moment for friends back home in Japan or Germany or Italy. They press their hands into marks made by Bogart in the cement before they were born. Though he is dead now he has left his gospel on celluloid and his handprints in concrete, just like Christ left his gospel in a book and his image in a shroud. But there is a lot more certainty about Bogart. He said he stuck his neck out for no one, but he always did in the end. The tourists climb back onto their bus.

Anna Fisher walks across the cement blocks bearing Bogart's hand and foot prints and the message 'Sid may you never die till I kill you'.

'The Chinese Theatre was built by Sid Grauman in 1927,' says an enthusiastic young guide in matching yellow short-sleeved shirt, shorts and baseball cap. It was built in the style of a Chinese pagoda,' he tells a huddle of Japanese, young and mainly female.

The guide came to Los Angeles to get into the movies and he has made it, for half a dozen video cameras capture his every gesture. He addresses them in turn, offering each a few words and a smile as big and white as Tom Cruise's.

'Actress Norma Talmadge visited the construction site and accidentally trod in the wet cement, Mary Pickford and Douglas Fairbanks Senior followed her example at the premiere of "King of Kings" and the greatest stars still come here to record their footprints and handprints in the sidewalk for your enjoyment.' He pauses to allow his audience to digest the enormity of what they are hearing and prepare themselves for the possibility of further dramatic revelations.

'And in that year, 1927 AD, not only did the Chinese Theatre open, but the very first talkie was released.'

'Aaah, Aaahl Jolson,' murmur the group, with much nodding of wise oriental heads.

'And things would never be the same again,' adds the guide.

It was also the year in which Stalin expelled Trotsky from the Communist Party, thinks Anna, who teaches 20th Century European history at UCLA. It was the year Hitler addressed his followers in Nuremberg, while Jolson told his to wait a minute, they ain't heard nothin' yet. The young man in the yellow outfit was right; things were never the same again. The movies lasted longer than the 1,000-year Reich and today German tourists come to measure their hands against those of Bogart and buy maps purporting to guide them to the homes of today's stars a few miles away in Beverly Hills.

'There were lots of glamorous premieres here,' says the guide. 'Thousands would turn up just to catch a glimpse of the stars. Has anyone seen the Gene Kelly musical "Singin' in the Rain"?'

There is much nodding of heads.

'That begins with a premiere at the Chinese Theatre in 1927,' says the guide. 'But in the story they decide to go off and remake the film with sound.'

Anna passes the tourists and enters the shade of the temple, as ancient as anything in these parts, old and yet not old, tangible and yet not real. It is not Grauman's Chinese Theatre anymore, but Mann's Chinese Theatre, part of a chain. They took Sid's name off the cinema, but they cannot take his name out of the concrete.

Anna makes her way to Cinema 2 and sits in the seventh row of the near-deserted auditorium. Few tourists venture inside. Their time is limited. They can see films at home. Only here can they see Bogart's handprints.

There is a roll of drums and a crash of cymbals as the film begins, an old grainy black and white print.

'Harry M. Popkin presents,' says the opening credit across the picture of a high-rise building, little squares of light in a few of its windows helping differentiate it against the black night. A figure walks into view. The audience gets only a brief glimpse of his back before the title credit 'D.O.A.' fills the entire screen. It is an old film and the picture is the shape of a television screen, only slightly wider than it is high.

Anna had never heard of 'D.O.A.', but it is part of a festival of old films. It had been recommended in the 'Times' and she did not have anything special to do. She never has anything special to do since she split up with Brad three months ago.

The figure moves towards the building and the camera follows him down a white-walled corridor towards an inquiry desk. Just short of the desk he stops and asks a uniformed officer a question. The policeman is talking to a man in a fedora. The officer glances at the stranger and, resuming his previous conversation, gestures with a thumb over his right shoulder. The man follows the direction indicated, down another long corridor, at the end of which is a door marked 'Homicide Division'. He is shown into an office, where a middle-aged man in a suit is sitting behind a desk considering some papers. 'I want to report a murder,' says the newcomer. 'Who was murdered?' asks the man behind the desk. For the first time we see the other man's face. He is a man in his thirties, unshaven, with a heaviness about his jowls and thick, dark hair greased back from his forehead. She is not sure if she would have recognised the actor as Edmond O'Brien if she had not just read the credits, though she knows she has seen him in black and white movies she has watched on television on weekend afternoons and late at night when she can't sleep.

O'Brien pauses for dramatic effect after the question 'Who was murdered?' 'I was,' he says.

Great beginning, thinks Anna. Great beginning.

The policeman turns away and looks at a sheet of paper. The man asks if he wants to hear his story or not, for he does not have much time. The policeman asks if his name is Frank Bigelow. The man's mouth drops open in surprise. He confirms he is Frank Bigelow. The policeman instructs a colleague to send a message that they have found him, and invites Bigelow to tell his story.

A misty whirl transports the viewer back in time. Bigelow is an accountant. Medical tests reveal toxin in his system and he is told he has only a few days to live. He discovers that one of his clients has unwittingly involved him in a convoluted web of deceit, betrayal and murder that will cost him his life. He can still talk, he can still walk, but he is no longer alive. He tracks down and shoots his own killer, tells the police his story and dies. The police classify him 'dead on arrival'.

8

The lounge bar of the Roosevelt Hotel is unusually busy for early afternoon. Tourists coming, going, hanging around. Anna has a choice. She can sit at the table of the loud, middle-aged people, who seem to represent a curtailed tour of the islands of the northern hemisphere in their costume of Hawaii shirts and Bermuda shorts. Or she can sit next to the young bedenimed Mexican couple, holidaying, perhaps honeymooning, absorbed in their Rough Guide itinerary and their love. Or she can choose the seat opposite the man in the plain black tee-shirt and black linen suit, who has just drained the brandy balloon and is now rubbing the rim of a cold Rolling Rock against his bottom lip. Angelic blond hair and blue eyes are offset by the dark stubble on his chin, the furrows across his brow and the downturn of his mouth. His hair is dyed blond. There is something slightly dangerous about him, as if he has just walked out of 'Reservoir Dogs', or maybe just something ever so slightly sleazy.

He has been watching her, hoping she would not sit at his table, and then hoping she would. She moves elegantly between the tourists, with her cup of coffee balanced on its saucer. Her brown eyes sweep the bar area, ascertaining there are no tables free. Her hair is cropped short and tinted with henna. As her face turns to him he notes the suggestion of a smile, not quite a smile, not nearly a smile, just a suggestion.

She is younger than him, early thirties, maybe even late twenties. The brandy wants her to sit down.

'Is this seat free?' she asks Roy.

Her voice is matter of fact. He says nothing, but nods, and gestures with his open palm towards the empty chair. She sits and sips her coffee and watches Roy sip his beer. He sips his beer and watches the Mexican couple chatter over the Rough Guide.

Roy never knew what to say to an attractive woman he had never met before. What would Bogie say? Woody Allen had written an entire play with Bogie as the ultra-cool role model for picking up babes.

Roy racks his brains, but all he can remember is Bogie telling a dame that when he slaps her she will take it and like it... Bogie's most memorable lines are not exactly small talk. He never seemed much good at opening conversations with women, or indeed relationships, just ending them. He packed Ingrid off on a plane in 'Casablanca' and buggered off down to Brazzaville with Captain Renault, for a beautiful friendship. And, offered romance with Mary Astor at the end of 'The Maltese Falcon', he turned her over to the cops to face a murder rap instead. Of all the bars in all the world she had to walk into mine.

Roy lifts the Rolling Rock to his lips. She watches him do it and still says nothing. His bottle is almost empty. He stops a passing waiter and requests a coffee.

'How would you like it?'

'Espresso, please.'

'Certainly sir,' says the waiter, as he moves off towards the bar.

It is Anna who eventually opens conversation.

'You're English,' she says.

He is about to speak, but she raises her hand to stop him, reconsidering the way he had rolled the R of espresso momentarily on his tongue before letting it go.

'No, not English . . . Scottish. Like Sean Connery.'

'We grew up in the same street,' he says. 'Same street,

different time . . .'

'I knew Scotland was small, but I didn't know it was that small,' she says.

He thinks the joke sophisticated for an American, displaying a knowledge of geography beyond that of most of her compatriots. Her lips carry the faintest trace of lipstick and the merest hint of a smile.

'Glasgow? Or was it Edinboro, that he came from?'

'Edinburgh.' He pronounces it almost as if might rhyme with 'hurrah', but not quite.

He is not unattractive, she thinks, the youthfulness of his blond hair and blue eyes offset by the stubble on his face and a world-weary air.

'I love Sean Connery's movies,' she says and quickly realises she is indulging herself in that most American habit of overstating enthusiasms.

'I love movies,' he says. 'It's almost like a compulsion for me. Bond movies, good movies, bad movies. I've always loved films, the whole experience.'

'I love it too . . . though I'm not exactly a cinephile' she says and she almost smiles. 'I've just come out of an old movie that was wonderful. I'd never heard of it ... "DOA"?'

'Yeah, yeah,' he says, his eyes lighting up in recognition and enthusiasm. 'I want to report a murder,' he says.

'Who was murdered?' she responds.

'I was,' he says.

'It must be about the best beginning to any movie ever,' she says. And they both smile at a shared enthusiasm.

'About the best,' he says, thinking of beginnings. But she beats him to it.

'"The Godfather",' she says. 'The first words when the screen is black: "I believe in America". The guest at the wedding who wants Don Corleone to avenge the assault on his daughter . . . Remember?'

Roy nods.

'But he doesn't even call Marlon "godfather".'

Roy is impressed by her memory and her enthusiasm,

51

though he has never been impressed by the common practice in Los Angeles of calling film stars by their first names as if imparting some tasty little titbit of gossip about a mutual friend before Marlon or Marilyn or Mel gets back from the washroom. 'Did you hear that Julia is going to be in . . .' or 'I see that Sean is coming to the Oscars . . .'

'Ah,' he says, 'but I think the best beginning to a Francis Ford Coppola film is . . .'

She raises a finger.

'I know what you're going to say.'

She pauses as the waiter delivers the espresso Roy ordered. Roy smiles suspecting she does know.

'This is like one of those riddles,' she says. 'Which end is a beginning?'

Roy nods in confirmation.

'The peaceful jungle . . . the sight of a helicopter . . . and the jungle explodes in flames as Jim Morrison announces, "The End." '

'Apocalypse Now.'

The words instantly transport Roy to another place. The face of the woman opposite is transformed by the mists of time into that of a young man. Roy can no longer remember his name, but he thinks of him sometimes when 'Apocalypse Now' is mentioned. They played 'charades', and the young man whose name Roy has forgotten mimed someone holding a sort of container in both hands, and shaking something into it, and lifting a small object from it. The object was hot, so he blew on it, before popping it in his mouth. He ate one, and then another, until the container was empty. He crumpled the container into a ball and tossed it away. 'A poke of chips now.' Not only did it make Roy want to see the film again, but he had a sudden hankering for chips, like he used to have, wrapped in newspaper, after he had been to the Playhouse in North Berwick with his father.

The woman opposite hardly pauses before urging him to remember 'Butch Cassidy and the Sundance Kid'.

'The wonderful, grainy, old newsreel. And the movie

begins in sepia monochrome. Paul Newman goes into the bank, with its metal bars and security guards, and asks what happened to the old bank. The guard says people kept robbing it. And Paul says that's a small price to pay for beauty.'

'And Robert Redford,' says Roy, 'is playing cards and this other man accuses him of cheating.'

Anna jumps in: 'Robert Redford doesn't say a thing. And Paul comes and encourages him to leave.'

'And the other guy,' says Roy, 'is obviously going to push it. Newman says to Redford something like 'We've got to go, Sundance'. And the other guy immediately backs off. It is the first time he has realised who his opponent is.'

Anna has pulled her chair closer to the table and is resting her arms on it.

'I remember it so-o well.' she says, 'I've seen it half a dozen times, though I haven't seen many westerns. I like European films.'

'European films?' asks Roy. 'Bertolucci?'

'Yes, yes,' she nods. "Last Tango'. 'Last Emperor'. Just stick a 'Last' in it and I'll like it.'

'Here's another great beginning,' he says. 'European film, Bertolucci film . . . and a western. Three men are waiting at this train station. Three more villainous, meaner-looking characters you wouldn't find anywhere. They wait and wait. Nothing much is said and nothing much happens, except a fly buzzes around squinty-eyed Jack Elam, and water drips on Woody Strode's bald head and the third one, whose name no one can ever remember, cracks his knuckles. But all the time the tension and the sense of expectation keep building. More and more. And when the train comes no one gets off it. But as it pulls away they hear this harmonica playing, really slowly, eerie, haunting, and there's Charles Bronson on the other side of the tracks. He asks where his horse is. And one of the men looks at their three horses and says they seem to have brought one too few. And Bronson says no, two too many, and draws first and kills them all.'

'Once Upon a Time in the West,' she says.

'You've seen more westerns than you make out.'

'I saw it on TV once,' she says, 'or read about it. But wasn't it Sergio Leone? How does Bertolucci come into it?'

'Bertolucci wrote the story with Sergio Leone and Dario Argento, who became a horror director . . . Here's a western you won't know: It rivals 'DOA' as one of the cleverest beginnings ever and is just as slow as 'Once Upon a Time in the West'. Three mean-looking villains ride into town . . .'

'I think we've done this one,' says Anna. It occurs to her she feels incredibly comfortable and confident with a man she has just met. Then she wonders if she is talking too much.

'This is another Sergio Leone storyline,' says Roy. 'The villains tie up and gag the barber and his son. They're waiting for someone. Henry Fonda arrives and one of them pretends to be the barber and begins to shave him. He is obviously thinking of cutting Henry Fonda's throat when he hears the click of Fonda's revolver and realises it is pointed straight at him. He shaves him and Fonda is looking at himself in the mirror when the other two baddies appear outside and one shoots through the window. Fonda spins around shooting all three. Fonda sprays himself with cologne and leaves $10. The barber and his son appear having managed to free themselves. The boy says he heard Fonda fire only one shot. His father says that is because he is so fast. 'Is nobody faster?' asks the kid. 'Nobody is faster', his father says.'

'What film is it?' asks Anna.

'Ah, that's the punchline,' says Roy. 'Remember the father says, 'Nobody is faster'. The film cuts away to actor Terence Hill and we finally get the title credit. Ten minutes into the film, it comes up: "My Name is Nobody".'

'Oh God,' says Anna, breaking into a broad smile, 'that is clever, that's really clever . . .'

'The unexpected play on words,' says Roy. 'It's like Shakespeare when Macbeth is told that "none of woman born" can harm him and then Macduff reveals that he was "from his mother's womb untimely ripped".'

'I'll watch out for that one,' says Anna. 'My Name is Nobody," she adds quickly. 'I didn't mean Macbeth.'

Roy sips his espresso. Anna's cup is empty, but she continues to sit there.

'"Blue Velvet" has a good beginning,' she says. 'Small town America with the friendly, waving fireman, the house with the garden and picket fence, and then the camera goes down into the grass and it's a jungle of insects killing each other; and that wonderful song . . . And "Taxi Driver": the taxi gliding through the steam and the really dramatic music . . . And, of course, "Citizen Kane" . . . In Xanadu did Kubla Khan a stately pleasure dome decree.'

She is eager to show that she can quote literature too.

'The gothic mansion all eerie and uninviting. The old man dropping that little glass hemisphere with the snowstorm scene in it. It smashes on the ground and he says that one word "Rosebud".' She imitates Orson Welles's voice, prolonging the word and letting it trail away, into nothing. 'And he dies. Great, great beginning.'

Roy nods. Anna awaits his response, while her mind flies across other openings. The ape inventing the club in '2001'. The spiders and poison arrows and then the giant boulder that almost crushes Harrison Ford to death in 'Raiders of the Lost Ark'. The banter in 'Reservoir Dogs'.

'Yes,' says Roy. '"Citizen Kane". Great beginning.' But the passion seems to have gone from his voice, as if he has suddenly tired of the game.

'It's been, eh, really nice meeting you . . . I'd better be going,' he says. And before she has the chance to say anything more he has gone.

It seems it was not such a great beginning after all. She always talks too much.

She didn't even get his name.

9

Roy looks at the grey ticket stub, with 'Mann's Theatres' printed on it in white and details of the film added electronically in black. He wonders how many stubs he has held in his hand over the last 30 years, reading their limited information time and time again, while waiting for the darkness to embrace him and the magic beam of light to transport him to another world. This stub carries the name of the cinema, the title of the film, the time of the performance, time and date of purchase and the price. Once upon a time all his stub would have said, after it had been torn in two by the usher, was 'alls' or 'Circ', to denote the part of the house in which he was entitled to sit, printed on a rough grey or purple scrap of paper smaller than a bus ticket. How many tickets had he held between that first 'alls' ticket for the Playhouse, North Berwick, and this $4.50 ticket for Mann's Chinese Theatre, Hollywood? For how many films? In how many cinemas? How many before Los Angeles, with its historic old Chinese and Egyptian picture palaces on Hollywood

Boulevard and its new multiplexes in the shopping malls, where Roy watched films from ten in the morning until one the next, sustaining himself on nachos and mega-sized, mega-priced Cokes that fitted into a hole in the armrest of the seat.

Old cinemas and new. The Playhouse in Edinburgh sat more than 3,000 and the North Star on the island of Shetland, off the north coast of Scotland, sat 200 and had only an upstairs, the seats having been removed from the stalls to facilitate dancing. He saw 'Taxi Driver' and 'Midnight Express' in a double bill there. Brad Davis, stuck in a Turkish jail for drug-smuggling, kisses the prison informer, a long deep kiss. He turns away and spits out the man's tongue. A woman in the audience screamed and fainted.

The Odeon in Edinburgh was designed to look like a Greek amphitheatre. It had statues around its walls and twinkling stars in the ceilings. Some cinemas were plain, functional rooms, a screen at one end, a projection box at the other. You might think cinemas are all the same when the lights go down: the screen at the front and the projector at the back and the audience in the middle, not like a theatre where you can put the stage in the middle and have a chandelier come crashing down just before the intermission, if you're Andrew Lloyd Webber. But cinemas are no more the same in the dark than women. They sound and feel and smell different.

Some cinemas smelled musty, of sweat and cigarette smoke and disinfectant. They smelled of darkness. Some stink of popcorn and hotdogs. In some there is an aroma of lemon cleanliness, plastic bits and newness. And they smell of light.

A mint print on a pristine white screen is not the same as an old film showing all the lines of age, projected through a nicotine cloud onto a yellow screen that remains fuzzy around the edges and has a patch in one corner where some drunk threw a bottle at a late-night screening. In today's plexes the film is one long strip that runs horizontally through a projector and may continue on its merry way to another projector farther down the projection booth, serving the auditorium next door. So the audience in Cinema 2 sees exactly the same film as patrons in Cinema 1, only a few seconds later. One reel of film serves two cinemas or more. Some small cinemas had only one projector and there would be a short intermission each time the reel needed changing. There is no longer so much scope to liven up a familiar programme by varying the order of the reels.

Red Grant is not the only one who is confused when he orders red wine with his fish - after all James Bond killed him ten minutes previously. Will he kill him again? Roy never found out, because the film ground to a halt, the groan of the slowing film matched by the human groan in the 'alls'.

'I'm sorry ladies and gentlemen,' said the manager, in his customary evening dress, 'but we appear to have a technical problem.'

Not as much of a technical problem as James Bond. You kill someone and ten minutes later they're ordering red wine with their fish.

Roy had been to cinemas with noisy audiences, he had been to cinemas where the audience treated the cinema like a library; he had been to cinemas where there was no audience at all, except him, and he wondered whether they would still have run the film if he had not turned up.

At some cinemas the slightest rustle of sweetie papers met with angry shushing noises. The audience is unique at the Dominion, in Edinburgh's Morningside area, staple for generations of local comics since the original anonymous observation about fur coats and no knickers. Children at the Dominion behave perfectly. There was hardly a whisper when Roger Moore's speedboat leapt from the bayou, flew across dry land, and dropped back into the water on the other side in 'Live and Let Die'.

But the pensioners? They chatter away throughout the programme like sports commentators.

'Oh look the boat is flying through the air,' says one senile delinquent at the top of her voice.

'Well I never,' says another.

'I think he'll get away now,' says a third.

'Of course he'll get away', says Roy. 'He always gets away. He's James Bond. It's a film. It's in the script that he gets away. It's not real'

And they all turn and glare at him like the children in 'Village of the Damned'.

'Sh-sh-sh . . .'

It was the one local neighbourhood cinema in Edinburgh that survived beyond the great cinema depression of the Seventies and early Eighties. It became first a twin cinema, with real domestic armchairs in Cinema 1 and a screen that was far too small. Eventually they turned a broom cupboard into Cinema 3 and 'Gregory's Girl' ran there for a record 63 years or something like that. 'Gregory's Girl' was one of the first British films to utilise a new technique devised by Bill Forsyth called Wimporama in which the heroes were all wimps. America gave the world John Wayne and Scotland responded with Gordon John Sinclair, a man so stupid he could not remember to put his three names in the same order from one film to the next. For once it was not Halliwell's that got it wrong but the boy himself.

When he was sixteen Roy took Alison Westwood to see 'Magnum Force', the second Dirty Harry film, at the Dominion. He paid for both their tickets and she kept wanting to kiss him. It was not her money, nothing to her if she missed the film, but he wanted to see it. He kept having to push her off.

'I'm trying to watch the fucking film,' he said finally.

'Sh-sh-sh-sh-sh,' said the Grandparents of the Damned.

Alison walked out and Roy never saw her again, but at least he could watch the film in peace and he had a lasting relationship with Clint Eastwood.

He was far too young to get in to see 'The Good, the Bad and the Ugly' when it came out, but he and his friends would play at being 'The Good, the Bad and the Ugly', a variation on the standard cowboy shoot-out which, for reasons Roy never understood until many years later when he saw the film, could only be played in the local cemetery. Bob always got to be Clint Eastwood because he was oldest and, as he pointed out, he was the only one who could whistle the tune and they needed a soundtrack. Roy was never sure whether it was better to be the bad or the ugly.

'Do ye know who's Scotland's answer to The Good, the Bad and the Ugly?' asked Fat Bob.

Roy shook his head.

'Jock Stein, Colin Stein and Frankenstein,' said Fat Bob, rocking with laughter at his own wit. Roy pointed out that Frankenstein was not Scottish. Bob stopped laughing, stared at Roy in disbelief and turned and walked away. Bob could be like that sometimes.

Roy first saw Clint Eastwood in 'Paint Your Wagon' at the Playhouse in North Berwick. It did not show him to best advantage. Not only did he sing in it, but he sang to trees in a clear tenor (or maybe just baritone and no more), while Lee Marvin was declaring a manly wanderlust in a voice that sounded as if he were gargling with gravel. But these are Roy's thoughts now. At the time he loved them both equally and found it easier to imitate Clint Eastwood's singing to the trees. When he tried to sing like Lee Marvin he ended up with a sore throat. Roy not only remembered seeing the film for the first time in North Berwick, but he remembers seeing the trailer. Lee Marvin following his wanderin' star through mud and rain and Rotten Luck Willie, a gambler who has held the riches of the world in his hand and gazed upon all her wonders, declaring the men's respect for the elements in the most powerful operatic voice in the film, and revealing that they call the wind Maria, with that memorably hard, long 'I' in Maria. Roy needed to see only the trailer to know that prospecting was a life for real men.

He saw Clint Eastwood the soldier in 'Where Eagles Dare', Clint Eastwood the cop in 'Dirty Harry', Clint Eastwood the western anti-hero in 'High Plains Drifter' and Clint Eastwood the DJ in 'Play Misty for Me'. He remained faithful to him throughout that strange period when he

60

decided he was Clint Eastwood the comedian and his perfect co-star was an orang-utan called Clyde. Given a straight choice between Clint Eastwood and Alison Westwood, it was no contest. So when she walked out, Roy stayed with Clint Eastwood. A contest between Alison Westwood and Clyde the orang-utan might have been harder to decide.

Roy had asked Alison Westwood out only to show his friend Stuart how it was done. Stuart had not seen as many films, he had never seen 'Camelot' and therefore was ignorant of even the rudiments of handling a woman. So Roy took him into the telephone box outside the Ritz Cinema, where they had just been to see Bruce Lee in 'Enter the Dragon'. It was the must-see kung fu movie, but it contained few hints on how to chat up girls. Stare hard, move your hands around in front of your naked torso and say: 'Eee-chaa-oooooooo?' It might just work with Clyde the orang-utang. It might just work with Alison, come to that.

'Hello, is that Alison? It's Roy here, we met at the school disco. Yes, I'm the one who told you I was going to be a cowboy when I grew up. Well, I wondered if you were doing anything on Friday night?'

That was the key line, and was usually met by confirmation of the girl's availability or alternatively with the information that she had to wash her hair.

'I was thinking I might go and see the new Dirty Harry film and I thought maybe you might want . . . It's a cop film, you know with Clint Eastwood? Eastwood. Yes, it is a coincidence, almost . . . You want me to come round for you? OK. Where do you live? That's Morningside, isn't it? Right . . . I'll be there at seven. See you then. Don't bother with the fur coat either. Bye, Alison.'

The Ritz had been the first cinema Roy ever attended without an adult. It was a half-hour walk from his new home in Learmonth. He went, that first time, with his friend Johnnie Grant, the red-haired, freckled boy, who lived in a top-floor tenement flat in Comely Bank Row. His parents did not have much money - his father was a joiner or something like that -

and Johnnie slept in a windowless box-room but he knew things that Roy didn't know. He knew about the balloon machine in the gents at the Ritz and he knew about poetry. He taught Roy a poem on the way to the cinema, reciting it with all the meaning he could muster, as he strode along, his pace dictating the delivery of the lines

'Skinny' Malinky Long-legs, Um-bi-rella feet,
Went to the pictures and couldnae find a seat.
When the picture started,
Skinny Malinky farted.
Skinny Malinky Long-legs, Um-bi-rella Feet.'

It was terribly rude, but Johnnie urged Roy to join in. Before they reached the cinema they were marching, stride for stride, arm in arm, as they recited the poem together.

They were expensive balloons from the machine in the gents' toilet at the Ritz and they felt slimey, like snails. Johnnie blew one up and released it when John Wayne told Robert Duvall to fill his hands, the sonofabitch. It flew around the cinema with a farting noise and landed somewhere in the front stalls. An usherette shone a torch along their row.

'It was them,' said a girl in pigtails a few rows behind, pointing an accusing finger.

Roy and Johnnie stared intently at the screen and the usherette said nothing, but Johnnie did not dare blow up the other two. After the film Johnnie chased the pig-tailed clipe out of the auditorium. He followed her no farther, but retreated to the toilet where he attached the remaining condoms to the taps. They gradually swelled with water and Johnnie and Roy carried one each, beneath their jackets, out of the cinema.

They climbed a nearby tenement, right to the top, four, five storeys up, and held the water balloons over the banister. Johnnie held his balloon out as far as he could reach and when he was finally satisfied that it was lined up over the desired spot he released it with a shout of 'Bombs away'. A split second later Roy's balloon followed it. Johnnie let out a yelp of delight as they hit the hard stone floor, one after the other, in quick succession, and water exploded everywhere. He climbed over the banister, so he was standing in the stair well, as if he might follow the balloons to the concrete below. The front half of his foot was on the very edge of the step, on the wrong side of the railings, the dangerous side, the heel supported by nothing other than forty feet of air. Holding onto the railings, he climbed down one stair at a time, moving with the assurance and speed that comes with regular practice. He jumped the last three or four feet and inspected the wreckage of the Durex water bombs. They galloped home through Stockbridge and Johnnie went round saying 'Fill your hands, you sonofabitch' for days. He even acquired a black, plastic eye patch like the one John Wayne wore in the film, though Roy thought John Wayne's probably wasn't plastic.

Johnnie and the Ritz are both gone now. Johnnie was killed within the month when he fell from the top floor landing of his own tenement, so Roy always remembered him as a ten-year-old with an eye patch going around saying 'Fill your hands you sonofabitch' and letting off slimey balloons into the darkness. John Wayne won an Oscar. Clint Eastwood survived his comedy period, returned to westerns and he too won an Oscar. Stuart asked Alison Westwood out and they got married. Sometimes Roy remembers Alison on those rare occasions he goes to the Dominion. He always remembers Johnnie and the balloons when he passes the site of the Ritz cinema in Rodney Street.

How many of the cinemas he'd visited have gone now? Old cinemas, in which the red crushed velour seats had been blackened and matted by thousands of overweight arses. Fleapits they called them. Roy did not know if they really had fleas. He had never seen a flea, but the ABC in Edinburgh had a cat which often came and sat on his lap. Cats always seemed to seek him out, despite or maybe because of his allergy. The purpose of the ABC cat, he reckoned, was to keep mice away. And in an open-air cinema in Africa he saw a lizard during

'Chariots of Fire'. It ran across the screen and finished ahead of Eric Liddell, which pleased him - Liddell was such a sanctimonious character.

How many cinemas had he been to before he visited Mann's Chinese Theatre for the first time a few days ago to see Spike Lee's 'Girl 6'? It's not exactly vintage Spike Lee, not a patch on 'Do the Right Thing', with its freshness, rich characters and violent energy. The central character in the new one is an aspiring actress, reduced to working for a company offering 'phone sex'. She is 'Girl 6'. The aspiring actress finally makes it into the movies and the film closes with her walking down Hollywood Boulevard, along the Walk of Fame, where celebrities' names are inscribed on bronze stars on the sidewalk. She is seen making her way towards the Chinese Theatre, where the words 'Girl 6' are displayed on the marquee.

That was weird. He was sitting in the cinema watching a film and the character in the film is shown approaching the very cinema in which he is sitting. It was as if she might suddenly appear alongside him and watch herself on the screen.

It never happened at the Warner Village at Leicester or the Point at Milton Keynes. In all the hundreds of times he had been out to the multiplex at Newcraighall, near the old coal workings on the edge of Edinburgh, never once had he seen a film in which the star was seen getting off the 14 bus on the main road, walking past the pet superstore and Toys R Us, and crossing the car park towards the multiplex.

Roy went back to see 'Girl 6' again. He did not care too much for the film, but he loved that ending, and felt he was a part of it. And he loved the Chinese Theatre. He saw Woody Allen's 'Purple Rose of Cairo' there, in which Mia Farrow escapes the drudgery and pain of real life through regular visits to the cinema. And as she watches a favourite movie the main character steps out of the screen and they run off together.

He had not seen 'The Purple Rose of Cairo' before. He

64

had seen 'The Graduate' before, so he knew what to expect from it, just classic, uncomplicated, pre-post-modernist comedy. He knew the stars would not come walking down the street towards the cinema and the characters would stay firmly rooted in their own world, up there on the screen. That was yesterday and a lot had changed since then.

At last the lights dim and the film plays. Three men ride into town, they gag the barber and his son, they wait for Henry Fonda and in the blink of an eye he shoots them. The barber's son asks if nobody is faster. And the barber says that nobody is faster. But Roy thinks he hears him add the word 'except . . .' under his breath. Roy shudders as he sees the title 'My Name is Roy Batty' appear on screen.

10

A voice catches Roy unawares.

'You've been a long way away.'

He focuses for a moment on the 'Snow White' pictures, turns and sees the young woman from the Roosevelt Hotel and smiles. 'My Name is Nobody?' he asks.

She nods. 'My name is Anna Fisher,' she says.

'Batty . . . Roy Batty'.

* * *

'What's the difference,' says Roy as they step into the Hollywood sunshine, 'between Bing Crosby and Walt Disney?'

They sit at the same table in the lobby of the Roosevelt Hotel, with its potted palms, whitewashed walls and ornate, painted ceiling. The Spanish revivalist building hosted the first Academy Awards in 1929 when 'Wings' became the only silent movie to win best picture. The hotel's owners included Louis B. Mayer, Douglas Fairbanks and Mary Pickford and for a long time it was a regular meeting place for producers, stars and directors, including Uncle Walt himself. He made it his command headquarters in 1941 when his animators began a long and bitter strike over low pay and long hours. More recently the producers, stars and directors had retreated to their strongholds in Beverly Hills and Burbank, Bel Air and Malibu and left Hollywood to the pushers, the whores and the Japanese video-makers. But for Roy this is still the heart of the film business, a bruised and broken heart perhaps, but still pumping the stuff of dreams. Roy sits not just with Anna Fisher, but with Gable and Lombard, Errol Flynn and debonair David Niven, surrounded by imaginary happy crowds, like Jack Nicholson in 'The Shining'. He sips not just a Budweiser but Hollywood itself.

Roy explains 'disnae' is Scottish vernacular for 'does not'.

'Oh, I get it,' says Anna. 'Bing sings and Walt dizznay. Neat.'

A smile curls around her lips. She looks down momentarily, a thought flits through her mind, and the smile is still there when she looks up again. 'Have you ever met Sean Connery?' she asks.

'No,' he says. 'We lived at the other end of the street, Fountainbridge. Our paths crossed, but at different times.'

'Fountainbridge? That was the name of the street? Was there a fountain? Or a bridge? A bridge over a fountain?'

Roy laughed. 'There was no fountain when I lived there. Just a brewery. It's a big long street, stretching out from the edge of the city centre - that's where we lived - past the brewery, which is where Connery stayed. Not in the brewery exactly, but in a tiny old tenement flat. I think it was different when he was there. The area was different. His family had come from Ireland, his mother was a cleaner and they lived in a two-room flat without its own toilet, beside the brewery, the smelly part of Fountainbridge. It was much rougher then.'

'And the Battys?'

'The Battys lived in a two-bedroom flat, with its own toilet, above their own butcher's shop, at the city centre end of the street.'

Quick as a flash Anna chips in: 'That must have been offal too.'

His mother thought it was awful. Her father had worked in a bank, but both her parents died before Roy was born. She always said Fountainbridge was temporary, as if she expected to wake up one morning and find the whole neighbourhood gone. Doreen would have been happier if home had been in Marchmont or Comely Bank, and if business had not been such an offal business, but her main complaint was the neighbours and the neighbours' children.

'You can take the man out the bog,' her husband said, 'but you can't take the bog out the man.'

Roy tried to translate this into words he understood: 'You can take the man out the toilet, but you can't take the toilet out the man.' Yes, it seemed to make sense.

'What does cunt mean Mummy?' Stephen asked. 'Mary wants to show me her cunt for thruppence.'

His mother shrieked and said they must leave, leave, leave. Three times. Just like that. And she cried when Roy came home with a bloody nose given to him by two boys who claimed to be 'the Brewery Boys'. Somehow it became four boys when Roy tearfully related the details. It was no ordinary bloody nose. There was blood everywhere, a trail that led from the flat, down the stairs, back to the scene of the crime. But it was not simply the amount of blood that qualified the bloody nose as extraordinary, but the way in which it was sustained. One of Roy's assailants had stuck a pen knife up Roy's nose and pulled it right through the flesh.

'I hate this place,' Doreen Batty said. 'Sometimes I just want to . . .' She held her head in her hands.

'Kill yourself?' suggested Roy innocently.

'It would be worse if you weren't here, Mummy,' he continued, as the blood dripped from his wound. 'I saw it on television with Grandad and he explained it.'

His mother looked up.

'The man thought he couldn't look after his family and he wanted to kill himself. But the angel showed him how much worse they would be if he wasn't there. The angel showed him that it is a wonderful life.'

Roy's mother pulled him to her and cried even more. Her tears diluted his blood.

He smiled to cheer her up, though, in truth, he had not liked the film much. Neither had his grandfather, who said it was a load of bunk, which sounded like swearing to Roy. He considered it best not to repeat his grandfather's word.

Roy and his grandfather preferred westerns and war films. Or silent comedies, with Buster Keaton and Harold Lloyd. His grandfather had first seen them when he was Roy's age and now they were repackaged in segments for television, wild, surreal slapstick that ended with the most poignant, haunting music Roy had ever heard, an elegy for a departed era. Departed eras. Departed eras provided films like 'The Adventures of Marco Polo', 'The Adventures of Robin Hood' and 'The Last of the Mohicans'. Adventures on the high seas with titles like 'Captain Blood' and 'The Buccaneer' that told you all you needed to know about what you were about to see. Adventures in far-off lands with titles like 'Gunga Din' and 'Beau Geste' that were full of exotic promise and mystery.

'Beau Geste', his grandfather sighed, 'they don't make them like that any more.'

'Is it a true story?' Roy would always ask. 'Is it a true story?'

And, more often than not, it would be, no matter how incredible it seemed. Robin Hood really did steal from the rich and give to the poor, Marco Polo really did discover China and bring back silk and mints with holes in the middle, and John Wayne really did defeat the Japs at Iwo Jima.

It was his grandmother who had wanted to watch 'It's a Wonderful Life'. It did not sound like there would be much adventure in it, little chance of an Indian attack, a fencing duel or a showdown in the main street at high noon. Roy's doubts were well founded. There is no fencing, no shooting, no fighting and hardly anyone dies at all.

'Is it a true story?' asked Roy very doubtfully.

'It is a true story,' his grandmother told him, 'in spirit.'

'I don't believe in angels,' said Roy.

'Oh, but there is such a thing as angels,' said his grandmother. 'Maybe they don't have wings, but that doesn't mean they're not angels. You're my little angel.'

Roy put his arms around his mother.

'I'll be your angel, Mummy,' he said sweetly. She was

not entirely certain that he was not poking fun at her. The cut looked more dramatic than it was. It needed only three stitches, though it left a tiny scar. Roy's father reported the matter to the police, but they never caught his assailants.

Roy had bled at the hands of the Brewery Boys, but he had seen enough films, from 'Oliver Twist' to 'Lady and the Tramp' to know that just because someone (or some dog) was dirty it did not necessarily mean they were dirt. This was before 'The Dirty Dozen' of course, when dirt took on the attributes of positive virtue. 'The Clean Dozen', 'The Washed-behind-their-ears Dozen', even 'The Always-wash-their-hands-at-mealtimes Hundred' were never going to strike fear into the hearts of Jerry. It was the dirt that did it, the threat that it might come off on the tablecloth and contaminate polite Aryan society.

After seeing 'Dr No' Roy went to look for Connery's house at the other end of the street. Finding James Bond's house was his secret mission. Maybe Roy expected a plaque on the wall, or graffiti to proclaim 'James Bond wiz here', or a little cluster of fans and tourists on the pavement outside. Something. Something to mark it out as James Bond's house. But there was nothing.

He met Alan Robertson, a boy he knew from school, and asked him. He did not know where James Bond lived, but invited Roy to play football with him. Alan was a dirty boy with skinned knees and a hole in the elbow of his jumper, a grey school jumper, despite this being the holidays. They played football on Bruntsfield Links where Tommy Connery played, long before he became Sean, little boys in short grey trousers, with shirt tails flapping, both dreaming of scoring winning goals for Scotland, 30 years apart. Tommy left school at 14 and joined the Navy. He never fulfilled the dream of playing for Scotland, he became James Bond instead. Roy spent a summer in that park and he would follow Tommy's route back to Fountainbridge, wandering downhill from Bruntsfield, allowing himself to be enveloped in the rich, sour smell that permeated the air around the brewery.

The local cinema was the ABC Regal, just down the road from Roy's flat. It was not really a local, but an enormous city centre establishment, with seating for almost 3,000, the flagship of Associated British Cinemas. It seemed just as likely to Roy that he might see Sean Connery there as it did that he would see him in Fountainbridge. It seemed logical that he would need to check how his films were doing or that he would have some business to transact with the manager, collect his share of the ticket money maybe. Not that Roy can remember a James Bond film ever playing at the Regal. Nor did he remember ever going to the Regal, despite it being the nearest to home. It may or may not have had an ABC Minors Club, the legendary Saturday morning programmes of cartoons and serials that introduced many of Roy's generation to cinema, but Roy never went. Roy's formative cinema experiences, and subsequently his formative sexual experiences, took place down the coast, not round the corner.

Roy did go to the pictures sometimes in Edinburgh. He went to 'True Grit' at the Ritz with Davie, a boy in his class. The other children made fun of him because he was poor and not too bright. It was a rare treat for Davie to have money to go to the cinema. He was not a particular friend. It was the only time Roy had gone to the cinema with him and they had lost touch long ago. Roy saw 'Thunderbird Six' at the Regent and 'Born Free' at the Playhouse, where his grandfather dropped him and Stephen off and had to wait outside for half an hour when he came to collect them because they had stayed to see the beginning of the film again. But Roy could not remember ever going to the Regal. What he could remember were the teenagers who queued outside for a week for tickets. After school he would walk down past the Regal to see if they were still there. Every time he went, there were more of them. He asked his mother which film they were waiting to see. She told him they were not waiting for tickets for a film, but tickets to see a pop group called The Beatles.

Roy started a scrapbook, cutting pictures of John, Paul,

George and Ringo from his father's newspaper. Pictures of them jumping up and down, having pillow fights, having fun. He saved up his pocket money and his mother took him to buy 'Help!' his first ever record. The family did not have a record player, but he took it with him every time he went to visit his grandparents and played it the whole time he was there, again and again and again. His father told him he should listen to Bing Crosby. His grandfather told him he should listen to Beethoven, though Roy never once heard his grandfather listen to Beethoven. Father and grandfather both agreed the Beatles would be forgotten within a few weeks, ignoring the fact that they had already been around for a couple of years. A fad, his father said. A phase, his grandfather added. A craze, his mother said. John Lennon could have drawn inspiration from the Batty family for his word play.

Roy collected Beatles bubble gum cards, kept the cards, smelled the curious, thin, pink wafer of bubble gum and threw it away. Children would gather in the school playground in twos and threes at playtime, flicking through their decks of cards like Mississippi gamblers, transferring each card from the top to the bottom after a split-second on display.

'Got, got, got. Not got,' said Roy, when the dealer reached an elusive picture of George. Roy had a list of the cards he did not have, which he kept updated in his pocket, though of course he had memorised every one.

'This is really difficult to get,' said the dealer. 'Let's see your doublers. I want three for it. Or four.'

And the deal would move to Roy, quite prepared to give up as many doublers as it took to complete his set. Completion was everything.

He collected other bubble gum cards too. 'The Man from UNCLE', with Robert Vaughn from 'The Magnificent Seven' as Napoleon Solo and David McCallum from Glasgow as Illyia Kuryakin. The Rolling Stones. The American Civil War. World War Two. And of course James Bond. There is material for a thesis in the thinking behind such a selection of subjects for bubble gum cards. Film, pop, television and war: discuss. Roy never did complete his 'Thunderball' set. The story was that the manufacturers had withdrawn Card No 24, because it was a picture in which James Bond appeared to hit a lady and they could not allow that, even though it was really a SPECTRE agent disguised as a lady. Where would James Bond be if he had shared their scruples? Dead, that's where.

'Their hair's a bit long,' his grandfather said when he saw the Beatles cards.

'Do they get paid for that?' his grandfather said when he heard them on the radiogram.

But eventually it was his grandfather who took Roy to see the film 'Help!'. Not only did it have really fab songs, but wonderful, dry, surreal, silly humour way ahead of its time and beyond the appreciation of many critics - John, Paul, George and Ringo go through the doors of four neighbouring terraced houses, and it turns out they all lead into one big, long house, and, on the pavement outside, Dandy Nichols declares they haven't changed at all. 'Still the same as they was before they was.'

But people weren't going to the cinema anymore, not to see films, not in the numbers that they used to, before TV. Rather than closing the Regal, Associated British Cinemas took the imaginative step of turning it into Britain's first multiplex, or at least Britain's first triple cinema. All the seats in Cinema One were red, those in Two were blue and those in Three were yellow. By this time Doreen Batty had fulfilled her dream of moving away from Fountainbridge and the family were installed in the leafier surroundings of Learmonth, close to Fettes College. James Bond completed his schooling at Fettes after being expelled from Eton and Tommy Connery delivered milk for the Co-op there before he became James Bond. So the Regal, or ABC Film Centre as it became, was no longer Roy's local cinema. It was not long after it stopped being his local cinema that he started going to it.

It was round about this time too that he caught up with

the early Bond films. He saw 'From Russia with Love' and 'Goldfinger' among the chattering classes at the Dominion. You might think that there was no such thing as the chattering classes in the Seventies, but the Dominion was long in the grip of the chattering classes. He saw 'You Only Live Twice' at the Tivoli, near Hearts' football ground in Gorgie, and 'Thunderball' in a double bill with 'Dr No' at the Playhouse, though he was familiar with the villains and the gadgets and some of the action sequences from his bubble gum collection and the James Bond annual he got one Christmas. He had a James Bond pistol and a toy Aston Martin with various buttons. One resulted in the appearance of machine guns from the front bumper, another produced a bullet-proof shield at the back, and a third resulted in the operation of the ejector seat and Bond's passenger flew out of the car, off towards the fireplace. Roy kept the car in its box to ensure it remained in mint condition and got into a terrible state once when he found Stephen and his friends playing with it in the back green. There it was in a line of traffic with a taxi and a red double-decker bus, all stopped at little traffic lights. As if James Bond would wait behind a red double-decker bus at traffic lights!

'That's not what it's for,' screamed Roy, snatching it from the queue.

Roy kept his bubble gum cards, his annual, his pistol, his Aston Martin and the record of Shirley Bassey singing 'Gold . . . finger' on a shelf in the cupboard of their room, which Stephen was unable to reach without the help of a chair. He kept them all in perfect condition, but he gave away his Aston Martin to Alan Robertson when the family moved to Learmonth. All he had left now was the souvenir book he bought for 'Diamonds Are Forever' at the Odeon and the poster for 'Dr No' and 'Thunderball' - 'Double Big! Double Brilliant!! Double Bond' - which he got from one of his Sunday cycles around the cinemas to see if they had any posters they were finished with. The Playhouse almost always had a poster or two for him to tuck into his leather saddlebag. Sometimes he gave them to friends and once he sold a poster from 'Diamonds are Forever' to a shop in London for fifty quid. It had been printed with the certificate 'AA', prohibiting its exhibition to anyone under 14. At the last minute the film company must have made the cuts required to have it recertified as an 'A' and a small square of white paper had been stuck over one of the As. It would have been worth much more, Roy guessed, but it had been up and down off his wall for over 20 years and somewhere along the line a skylight had leaked and it was badly water stained.

Roy finally found out that it was No 176 Fountainbridge where Connery had lived. He went to look for it again. But it was no longer there. There was a small section of distinctive old stone tenements near to where it must have stood, but No 176 had been swallowed up by the brewery or something like that. It was gone, just like Roy's Aston Martin and his bubble gum cards. There was nothing there to prove that No 176 Fountainbridge ever existed or that Sean Connery had once lived there, a little boy who went off to play football in the park like all the other kids. There was no evidence to suggest that Sean Connery was anything more than a character in the movies.

11

'Why?' asks Anna.

'Because,' says Roy, 'of the way they looked. Because of the way they spoke, the poetry of a mythical west. Because of Elmer Bernstein's music that made you think you were up there riding over the Mexican border with them. Because it was my first time . . . And because of Yul Brynner's hair.'

'He didn't have any hair,' says Anna.

'I know,' says Roy. 'What's your favourite?'

'I don't like lists. It's so artificial choosing one movie over another. And I always feel my favourite movie will be the next one I see. I haven't seen enough movies.'

'I told you mine, now you have to tell me yours,' says Roy.

Without further hesitation Anna nominates 'Brief Encounter'.

'Why?'

'Because you forced me to choose one and it came into my head . . . And because I like old black and white movies.

And I like English movies. And I like Celia Johnson's hat. It reminds me of England.'

Roy says nothing, his silence itself a question.

'I did a year at university there. A long time ago . . . I like Ealing comedies and costume dramas and stiff upper lips and Beatles movies and James Bond.'

'What were you studying?'

'History. I teach European history at UCLA. What do you do?'

'These days I'm in the movies.'

'What . . .'

'Do you like "The Third Man"?' interrupted Roy. 'It's my favourite British movie, even if it is set in Austria and has American stars.'

'Yes, yes,' she says. 'It would be near the top of my list.'

'I thought you didn't make lists.'

'I said "would". If I had a list, it would be near the top.'

'It has my single most favourite scene in any movie,' says Roy. 'Remember Joseph Cotten goes to Vienna and discovers his old friend, Harry Lime, is dead – the Orson Welles character. He visits his bereaved girlfriend. Her cat runs away from him and she explains it only liked Harry. The camera follows the cat into the street, where it rubs against the legs of a man in a darkened doorway. A light goes on. And Harry Lime smiles, and then he disappears in a burst of zither music. Well, he would smile, he's supposed to be dead.'

'It wouldn't have worked with my cat. She won't go near any men. Tiffany. Her name is Tiffany.'

'After "Breakfast"?'

'After breakfast, before breakfast, all the time . . . Yeah, she's named after the film.'

'And your favourite scene is the one where Audrey Hepburn has rejected George Peppard's declaration of love, thrown her cat out of the cab, but they all end up reunited in the rain together, having a three-way cuddle, "Moon River" playing on the soundtrack?'

Anna seems to be considering whether it is her

favourite scene.

'It always makes me cry,' she says. 'Doesn't it make you cry?'

'No.'

'Do you never cry at movies?'

'No.'

'Not when Bogart says goodbye to Ingrid Bergman at the end of "Casablanca"?'

'He still has Captain Renault.'

'Not when Anthony Hopkins finally works up the courage to tell Emma Thompson how he feels about her in "The Remains of the Day", and it's too late, she loved him, but now she has married someone else?'

'That's the English for you. Why didn't he tell her he loved her earlier? And on the subject of English country houses, why didn't Joan Fontaine just give Mrs Danvers the sack in "Rebecca" instead of moping around thinking about killing herself?'

'Don't you cry when Ali MacGraw dies in "Love Story"?'

'I never could empathise with someone whose taste was so catholic that it could include the Beatles, Beethoven and Ryan O'Neal.'

'Not when Winona Ryder asks Johnny Depp to hold her in "Edward Scissorhands" and he can't because he has no hands? Or are you like the guys in "Sleepless in Seattle" who cry only at men's movies, like when whoever it was got killed in "The Dirty Dozen"?'

'I've never seen "The Dirty Dozen".'

'Didn't you cry when the black soldiers marched into battle at the end of "Glory", with their heads held high, knowing they are going to die, but that they will die free men?'

'Nope,' says Roy, 'not even when the priests of Sikandergul kill Sean Connery in "The Man Who Would Be King" and he sings "The minstrel boy to the war has gone" as his executioners hack at the ropes that support the bridge on which he is standing, and his buddy Michael Caine is left to finish the verse alone. Not even when Tom Berenger shoots Willem Dafoe in "Platoon" and the helicopter takes off without him, and the troops on the chopper see Dafoe running out into the clearing, with the Vietcong closing in around him, and there is nothing they can do. And Samuel Barber's "Adagio for Strings" plays as Dafoe falls to his knees, his arms outstretched in a crucifix for a moment, before he falls forward, dead. Mind you someone once said "Adagio for Strings" could make changing a light bulb seem meaningful... How many Californians does it take to change a light bulb?'

'Or,' says Anna, ignoring the question of light bulbs, 'when Schindler's Jews gather at his graveside and you know that they are the real people who would have died in the concentration camps without him?'

'One to change the bulb,' says Roy, 'and all their friends to share the experience.'

'Or when Kevin Costner's dead father comes back in "Field of Dreams" to play the game of ball he never played with his son when he was alive?' says Anna. 'Or even when ET comes back to life? ET, the child in all of us?'

Roy stops smiling. He's silent for a moment, before he begins again.

'That's a hell of a list for someone who doesn't make lists,' he says. 'Do they all make you cry?'

'Some of them. I don't mind admitting it. I get caught up in good movies. It's a way to escape.'

'From what?'

'History.'

'Your history?'

'I mean History. History the subject. The Cold War. The Second World War.'

'Are you married?' asks Roy.

Anna averts her eyes at the directness of the question.

'Divorced.' She looks at him again. He has not taken his eyes off her. 'You?'

'I used to be married,' he says. 'Not anymore.'

'Divorced?' He nods. 'Oh right, I thought for a minute,

maybe she died, like in "Love Story" and you found the film so false that you couldn't cry at it.'

'No,' laughs Roy, 'nothing like that. Nothing so dramatic. Jo and I just grew apart and went our separate ways. Actually I quite like the film, 'Love Story'. Or I did when I saw it. It was a long time ago.'

'It makes me cry.'

'And did you cry at the end of "Braveheart" when . . .'

'No, no, don't go on,' she says. 'I haven't seen it yet.'

'But you teach European history. You must know the story. It's up for an Oscar. Everyone knows the story.'

'Not me. It's modern European history I teach.'

'How come you haven't seen it?'

'I don't know. I want to see it. I just never have.' She had been planning to see it with Brad, but they chose that night to split up instead. 'I don't know if it's on anywhere now.'

'It's on at the Fairfax on Beverly Boulevard in 20 minutes. Two dollars any seat.'

'I have a car.'

'And I have four dollars.'

'You look like a blond Mel Gibson, you know,' she says, as they rise.

'Really? I always wanted to look like Kirk Douglas. Look at the dimple in my chin.'

12

It is the beginning. Everything is misty as Roy and Anna take their seats. And out of the mist comes the title. 'Braveheart'. Across a loch the audience fly, and up over mountains that still harbour spring pockets of snow.

'I never made it to Scotland,' says Anna. 'I wish I had.'

The audience is deposited in a glen where Scottish nobles are strung out like Apache warriors on their ponies. Roy can taste the slightly sweet smell of Anna's breath as she leans towards him and asks if he has been there.

'Yes,' he says, 'I was there.'

The narrator tells of death and civil war in Scotland and war with King Edward of England. Edward invites the Scots nobles to peace talks. William Wallace is a boy of seven or eight, with a face full of sweet mischief. His father and elder brother go to the talks, but arrive too late. All they find is a place full of treachery and hanged countrymen. They are alarmed when they hear someone else arrive. It is William. He has followed them. He looks on, wide-eyed in horror.

Roy grew up with stories of William Wallace, Robert the Bruce and Rob Roy, tales from his grandfather, whom he once imagined as a near-contemporary of these ancient Scottish heroes. When Disney filmed the story of Rob Roy, Roy thought he might call himself Rob Roy Batty, rather than just Roy Batty. He wondered why Disney never filmed the story of Wallace and Bruce and drew imaginary lobby stills illustrating the great Scottish victories at Stirling Bridge and Bannockburn. The story goes that in his darkest hour Bruce watched a spider trying to pull itself up on a thread and falling back down and starting all over again, never giving up. Disney could have made that spider a star. But it was Mel Gibson, not Walt Disney, who lifted the Scottish standard and held it triumphantly over Hollywood.

Anna knew nothing of Wallace or Bruce or Rob Roy or any spiders. Her parents told her stories of Abraham Lincoln and General Grant, and JFK and Martin Luther King. Her history was a different history, and although she was fascinated by England and Europe, Scotland was little more than a mountainous blur on the edge of her perceptions. For her William Wallace and Scotland and Roy Batty truly do emerge out of the mist, a land and people as exotic as the Apache had been to Roy as a child.

Roy lays his jacket next to him and puts his arm on the rest between the seats, where it touches Anna's bare flesh, cool after the heat of the Hollywood afternoon. Instinctively he pulls away.

'It's OK, we can share it,' she whispers, without looking away from the scene in which Wallace's father and brother are returned from the wars, dead. His uncle takes him away from the violence and unrest to Europe. He grows up to become

Mel Gibson, insisting he wants no part of the hostilities with England. He is more interested in wooing Murron, the girl who gave him a flower at his father's graveside when he was a boy. They marry in secret to avoid the local English nobleman coming to claim his right of deflowering new brides. When a soldier tries to rape Murron, Wallace helps her escape and they arrange to meet. She never gets there. She is captured and the local magistrate determines to make an example of her. She is tied to a stake and, with hardly a glance in her direction, he cuts her throat. Wallace exacts a terrible revenge and only then does he become a focus of resistance against the English.

Roy and Anna do not talk. She is enthralled by the film. He watches familiar scene follow familiar scene, each line of dialogue suggesting itself to him before it is delivered by the actor on screen. More and more men join Wallace as he makes his way to Stirling and a rendezvous with history. No bridge in the film. Just Stirling. Audiences in Beverly Boulevard care nothing for an absent bridge. What they will remember is the scale of the thing, the thousands of men, the horses, the colour, the spectacle, the passion, and Wallace's men with their staves, twice the length of a man, with sharpened points, laid out in front of them. The English knights charge, their horses thundering across the plain, towards the line of Scottish infantry.

Wallace urges his men to wait. His hair is braided, his face masked by blue woad right down one side, like a Swedish football fan. The horses speed towards the Scots.

'Hold . . .' cries Wallace.

The faces of the men around him are set with determination beneath their war paint.

'Hold . . .'

The horses get nearer and nearer, bringing with them the prospect of death. At the last minute the Scots grab the staves to form a lethal barricade over which English knights and horses are fatally thrown by their own momentum.

Each face around Wallace seems frozen for a split-second. The big, burly, bearded friend from Wallace's childhood. A curly haired man with a brow furrowed by too much hope and too much loss. A dark-haired young man with his teeth bared. And another, whose features are partially hidden beneath the flash of blue lightning painted on his face. The audience is thrown into the midst of the bloody battle. Swords swing through flesh. And there, in one corner of the screen, in one little private part of the mayhem, is the man with the blue flash of lightning on his face. His blue eyes twinkle in the sunshine and look, for just a moment, straight at Roy and Anna. Then he is gone. Roy saw him. Anna probably did not.

The camera follows Wallace through the gore. The clash of steel against steel, then a scream as steel meets flesh. Bodies tumble and in an opening, suddenly . . . the man with the lightning on his face. He grits his teeth as he raises his sword, two-handed over his shoulder. With a terrible shout, heard above the clamour of the combat, he swings it across the body of his adversary in one single motion. The viewer sees only the victim's back but can imagine the blow must have cut the man almost in half. Blood splashes the camera.

Anna's fingers grip Roy's arm for a second. The swordsman is momentarily hidden from view behind the English soldier. When he falls, for a moment the viewer's gaze is square upon his slayer's face, perspiration gathering on his brow and running down his cheeks into the dimple on his chin. And then he is gone.

Roy is unsure what Anna may have seen. The battle moves on. The camera follows Wallace. The man with the lightning on his face is lost in the fight. Anna leans towards Roy. He can smell the sweet, enticing bouquet of her breath again.

'I see what you mean,' she says. 'You do look like Kirk Douglas.'

Every morning at four o'clock Seamus shook Roy awake and in military formation they would proceed through a series of tents that would transform them from middle-aged

Scottish civilians into medieval Scottish soldiers. Long queues waited sleepily at the mouth of each tent. The first issued plaids to the Scots, Italian chain-mail and armour to the English. No one wanted to be English. In the second tent their faces were painted. Roy suggested the lightning design himself. The make-up girl looked dubious, but someone muttered something about 'primal forces of nature' and his face was duly daubed with lightning. The third tent handed out hair and wigs, but Roy's hair was long anyway at that time and it had been dark brown. Some of the Irish soldiers who were there as extras had very short hair and Roy always thought you could spot in the film, crew cuts with the odd long braid dropping curiously over one red ear.

The Irish soldiers were there only for the big battle scenes, Roy and Seamus had been with the film since the start in Scotland. Seamus Wallace knew the people in the Wallace Clan Trust and he was a professional historian. He was there through the trust, both as a historical advisor and an extra. And Roy was there because he was a historian too, so Seamus had told the trust, which was not exactly true but not entirely false.

'You're a sort of historian,' Seamus insisted, "You're an archaeologist."

Roy looked doubtful.

'Well, you are the biggest film fan I know and you'd like to see a film getting made, wouldn't you.'

They stood on the Curragh plain with their faces painted blue and 150 English cavalry charging towards them. Day after day for a fortnight they fought and re-fought the Battle of Stirling, till Roy felt it had been going on about as long as the Vietnam War. In between takes they played cards, talked to some of the supporting actors about other films on which they had worked, and they waited. There was a lot of standing around and waiting.

'Hold, hold, hold . . . and cut.'

Hundreds of men exhaled in relief and walked away in all directions, just to enjoy the freedom of being able to do so, because their bodies were their own again for a while, until the film would claim them once more.

Roy liked to watch Mel Gibson directing other, smaller scenes. Each scene was laboriously set up, cameras arranged and Gibson looked through the viewfinder at actors who would never appear on film. When he was satisfied, the real actors would arrive and the stand-ins would step aside, their moment in the spotlight over until the next set-up. They would film and film and film again. Roy wondered what Wallace would have thought. Wallace was finally going to be an international star 700 years after his death, like Ben-Hur and Robin Hood and Spartacus. Children might play at being Wallace when they tired of Power Rangers.

Roy watched mechanical horses accelerate from zero to 30 miles an hour on a 20-foot track and finish off with a somersault. He watched Gibson sitting alone, thinking about his next scene. Gibson nodded distractedly to him once as he passed, but they never spoke. Gibson ate with his men, stood in line for his meals with his men and his children played football with his men. Once or twice he joined a knot of actors as if keen to hear the story unfolding, but the storyteller would fall silent. It was the loneliness of command, for they did not know if he was coming to listen or to issue his orders. Or maybe it was the loneliness of being, not an actor, but a film star.

Gibson worked and worried. Roy watched and waited. Each day the army rose at four, dressed in plaid or armour, donned their war paint, brushed and ruffled their hair, collected their weapons and waited. Roy concluded there was a lot of waiting in both movies and war. And, as in a war, nobody seemed very sure what was going on. Except maybe Gibson the general. Lieutenants assembled their own little bodies of men. The army was assembled for a charge and they whispered to each other 'Shouldn't Mel be in this scene?'

'Mel's no' here,' piped up one Scots voice. They had to send for him.

'Mel, Mel, the battle's about to start without you. Come

86

quick or you'll miss it.'

The novelty of being in a film quickly wore off for the Irish soldiers. They had never been to war, so they did not appreciate the need for so much waiting nor were they good at it. They drank heavily at night. One passed out in the heat of the next day. The can of beer, which constituted his hair of the dog, leapt in the air, hit another soldier and knocked him cold too, with blood spouting from his head, at the sight of which a third soldier fainted. That was an unusually exciting day.

It was rumoured the film was running out of money. Men in suits and dark glasses arrived. Like FBI agents or people who might investigate UFOs, they looked more deadly than anyone on the battlefield, and the army speculated on what might happen. Some crew were paid off and toilet rolls became more difficult to get. But still they filmed the same scenes over and over again. Roy wanted to go home now. He had been in a film. He had done his tour of duty.

Five months earlier Roy had stood on a hillock in the rain, overlooking the glen beneath Ben Nevis, a surprisingly flat river valley, with alder, rowan and birch dotted along its length, and watching the cast and crew below. The cast in rough medieval plaid and sackcloth, the crew in baseball caps and jeans and thick waterproof jackets. Roy pointed through the rain at a figure in a bush hat with a megaphone, an assistant with an umbrella failing to keep up with him.

'That's the director Mel Gibson,' he said. 'He's in charge. He tells everyone what to do. He's the man that's actually making the film.'

'Like Walt Disney?' said the little girl who stood beside him on the hillock, holding his hand.

He looked down at her face, the colour of coffee, her lively blue eyes and he smiled.

'Yes, a bit like Walt Disney.'

A voice shouted 'action' and the glen fell silent, but for the indistinct whisper of actors' voices carried on the wind, muffled by the rain. Roy and the little girl stood and watched the strange, unreal characters in the field of dreams that was a film in the making. Her hand was small and cold and wet in his. The rain eased suddenly, the last few drops fell and the sky lightened as the voice cried 'Cut'.

'Look a rainbow,' said the little girl, pointing to the ethereal arc some way up the glen.

* * *

Los Angeles, March 1996

All Wallace had to do was say 'Mercy' and his ordeal would be over. A swift deliverance was promised, no more torture. The crowd had wanted to see the Scottish murderer suffer. But even they had had enough. They had seen him hung, drawn and quartered - cut open like butcher meat - but still alive. They wanted no more. It could end with a single word 'Mercy' that would signify Wallace's allegiance to the king.

The film cross-cuts between Edward on his deathbed, Bruce, the nobleman who cannot decide where his allegiance lies, Wallace's men in the crowd and the vision of Murron. Wallace summons up a hidden reserve of courage and energy and yells out the single, final word 'Freedom'.

Roy can hear Anna choke back a sob. He feels her hand on his arm.

The film reopens at the field of Bannockburn where it seems Bruce is about to pay homage to the English army. The English expect it, the Scots expect it, perhaps even Bruce expects it. Bruce addresses his troops dispassionately.

'You have bled with Wallace,' he says, 'now bleed with me.'

And the film ends with the Scots charging the English. Wallace is dead, but the man with the lightning in his face charges forward towards the viewer.

Tears run down Anna's cheeks and one drops heavily on Roy's arm. They watch the credits roll, each thinking their separate thoughts. They rise and silently make their way to the exit. Roy wants to reach out for her hand, but does not.

13

They stand on the sidewalk of Beverly Boulevard outside the Fairfax cinema, neither one of them wanting to say goodbye.

'What are you going to do now?' asks Roy.

'I'd kinda thought I would just spend the day at the festival of old movies,' says Anna. She smiles at the craziness of the notion.

'Maybe it's a bit silly - spending all that time in cinemas watching movies you can see any time on TV for free. But I've nothing else to do.'

They stand a moment without saying anything. Anna thinks he must be about to go. It had been a brief encounter, a moment in time when their lives touched and separated. If he walks away, she cannot expect to meet him again by chance in Mann's or the Roosevelt, can she? No, almost certainly not.

It is not impossible. Fate might throw them together again. But she does not believe in Fate. They will not meet again. She will know no more about the man from Sean Connery's street who had a part in 'Braveheart'. Roy Batty. Soon he will be the Man With No Name in her memory. Just a fading picture of a blue-eyed, blond-haired man whom she might have liked to know a little better. He is divorced. Does he have children? What does he do? Who is he? She knows almost nothing about him. She knows where he came from, but where is he going? And when next she sees 'Braveheart' on television, there may be a pang of regret when she sees the warrior with a lightning flash of woad on his face.

'Where are you going?' she asks.

'The movies,' he says.

'Let's go together,' she says.

They sit in her old red Buick poring over the extensive cinema listings in the Calendar pages of the LA Times. Anna suggests 'The Searchers'. She has heard about it, but never seen it. John Wayne as a Civil War veteran who spends seven years on the trail of Comanches who have kidnapped his niece. Brad was not really a western fan, not really a film fan actually. He preferred books and chess and politics.

'Have you seen "The Searchers"?' she asks Roy.

'About a dozen times,' he says. His mind flashes back to the very first time, more than 20 years ago. He can still remember Debbie's tears. He can still remember her walking off towards Princes Street and out of his life after all they had been through together. And why did they split up? Because of John Wayne and 'The Searchers'. It is a dangerous movie. She had loved him and he thought he loved her until they went to see 'The Searchers'. It turned out they were completely incompatible and he never saw Debbie again.

'We'll go to something else,' says Anna.

'No,' says Roy, 'They say you see something different every time.' And Roy is sure he will.

'I don't see why we have to see another western,' said

Debbie as they walked past the Playhouse towards the little Salon cinema 50 yards or so farther down the road. If the Playhouse was the father of Edinburgh cinemas, the Salon was the baby, and a rather dirty, unattractive runt at that. The Playhouse's elegant dark stone facade dominated Greenside, while the Salon hid in its shadow, a narrow entrance, squeezed between shop fronts, and disappearing under the Georgian houses behind it. Other second-run cinemas showed films that were a few months or maybe even a few years old but the Salon showed films that were a few decades old, some of which no one had wanted to see even when they were new. 'The Searchers' was different. Roy had already read up on it in his 'Pictorial History of Westerns', which promised one of John Ford's most haunting films and a superb performance from John Wayne.

Roy handed over his pound note and took his change before they made their way downstairs to the dingy stalls. There was no balcony.

'What a fucking dump,' said Debbie. 'It stinks.'

'You get used to it,' said Roy.

'What is that smell?'

'It's the smell of history,' said Roy as he settled in the seventh row.

'It's the smell of dust and piss,' said Debbie as she inspected the blackened seat next to him. The cinema was empty, but for a woman offering Eldorardo ice cream from a tray.

'I don't know why I agreed to come. It's not even a new film. You could watch it on TV.'

'Not on a big screen.'

Debbie sat down huffily and they both sat in silence. Soon the faded red curtains would draw back in a strange striptease, to reveal a naked off-white screen, stained by the cigarette smoke of past audiences. The house lights would dim and John Wayne would once more appear to take Roy away from cold, rainy Edinburgh to ride the ranges of that place they called the Wild West.

'I hate John Wayne,' said Debbie, as the Warner Brothers logo appeared on a brick wall. Roy could not remember seeing this opening card before and thought a brick wall a curiously inappropriate motif to introduce a western.

'He's a man's actor,' said Roy.

'Shite,' said Debbie. 'He's a crap actor . . . and a fascist.'

The film opens with a plaintive ballad that asks what makes a man to wander and to roam, what makes a man turn his back on home.

'What a naff song,' said Debbie. 'Is this a comedy?'

'Give it a chance,' said Roy.

John Wayne plays Ethan Edwards, who returns to the family homestead in Texas after fighting for the Confederacy in the Civil War. It has taken him three years to get home. He returns with a medal and two bags of freshly minted Yankee dollars, but little in the way of explanation for his prolonged absence. There is something about the way John Wayne looks at his brother's wife that suggests more than brotherly affection, which Roy did not really appreciate that first time round. Ethan gives the medal to his ten-year-old niece Debbie.

'Oh, she's called Debbie too,' said the other Debbie and Roy interpreted her subsequent silence as evidence that she was beginning to enjoy the film.

Ethan rides off with a posse in pursuit of rustlers. They find the cattle dead and realise the cattle raid was a diversionary tactic. Ethan looks off across the desert, his eyes full of pain and impotent rage. He knows what is happening. Big John always knows what is happening. But there is nothing he can do. Not this time.

Ethan's brother Aaron watches birds take off in alarm and spots something flashing off in the distance. His wife tells Debbie to go and hide where her grandmother is buried. She settles down beside the tombstone.

Roy felt Debbie jump as a shadow fell across her little namesake. She reached for his hand and squeezed it.

It was the shadow of the Indian chief, his face painted

in red and yellow.

Roy and Debbie had been going out together for six months. The longest he had ever gone out with anyone before was three weeks. His friends called her Mrs Batty and though he was not sure how he felt, he could tell she liked it. He was not sure he was the type who would stay at the homestead with the little lady. He saw himself more as the one who would turn his back on home, coming back only occasionally with his pockets full of Yankee dollars, no questions asked, no explanations proffered.

It took Roy about three months to get Debbie to go on the pill and sleep with him. They progressed fairly quickly from snogging to fondling to petting and he could unhook and remove her bra down her sleeve without her having to remove her top. Her bedroom was the only upstairs room in her house. Her parents never went up there, communicating by shouting from the foot of the stairs. Roy and Debbie spent most of their time smoking cannabis, listening to the Eagles and exploring each other's bodies, with their eyes and their fingers and their tongues, until he was sufficiently familiar with her every nook and cranny to draw the shape of the portwine birthmark on her left buttock from memory. Lately they had not had sex quite so often.

By the time John Wayne gets back to the homestead his brother, sister-in-law and nephew are dead. Debbie and her older sister Lucy are gone. Big John does not cry. Not on the outside. He does his crying on the inside and sets off with the posse after the Comanche who have taken his nieces. He follows their tracks, he reads their signs, he understands their ways, and he hates them. He shoots out the eyes of a dead Comanche, because the Comanche believe that without eyes a dead man cannot enter the spirit world and must wander forever between the winds. Big John always knows what is going to happen and he knows when the Indians will attack. He is, as always, the man you would want to be next to when they came - a leader, a hero, a real man, John Wayne. But

94

inside . . . inside. . . . he lost his war, he lost his country, he lost his woman and now the Comanche have taken the last of his family. He finds Lucy's body, horribly mutilated, only telling his young companions much later. Ethan can stand the sight of it, but lesser mortals must be shielded from such truths.

Ethan continues the search for the band of Comanche led by Scar. He is accompanied latterly only by Martin Pawley, a part-Cherokee, part-English, part-Welsh orphan, raised as one of Ethan's brother's family. He was played by Jeffrey Hunter, in the original.

In the version Roy watches with Anna, Marty is played by Roy. He sticks faithfully to the script, or at least fairly faithfully, though he cannot help but appropriate Ethan's catchphrase of 'That'll be the day', once or twice, and the looks exchanged between the two searchers take on an extra depth.

For seven years they search for Debbie who has grown to be a young woman. She will, to be precise, have grown up to be Natalie Wood. Slowly it becomes clear that Ethan continues the search, not to rescue Debbie, but to kill her, because she will have been polluted by the Comanche. It will be like putting a dog or a horse 'out of its misery'.

A Mexican arranges a meeting between Ethan and Scar. When Ethan tells Marty he cannot come to the meeting, Marty looks him full in the eye and says 'That'll be the day.' Scar tells Ethan how he lost two sons, killed by white men. He asks one of his wives to bring the scalps he took in retribution. It is Debbie who brings them.

'Do you know where the toilets are?' asked Debbie.

'Toilets,' said Roy, 'Toilets? They've been looking for her for seven years, and just when they find her you have to go for a piss.'

'Don't be stupid. I'm bursting.'

Debbie Edwards tells Ethan and Marty the Comanche are her people now and tells them to go. Ethan tries to kill her, but Marty stands in the way. Finally by chance Ethan and

Marty discover the whereabouts of Scar's encampment, which is about to be attacked by the Cavalry. Before they attack, Marty rescues Debbie and kills Scar. Ethan subsequently scalps the corpse. Debbie runs away but he catches her, lifts her as he did when she was a child and declares that it is time to go home. They return to one of the homesteads, and in one of the most famous final sequences of any film, they all enter - a mish-mash of different nationalities and cultures, all except Ethan, who takes one step towards the door and turns away. The door closes on him. The film ends.

'Brilliant,' said Roy to Debbie.

'Brilliant,' says Anna to Roy. 'He's really a tragic character. Isn't he?'

'I said that too,' says Roy.

Anna looks quizzically at him.

'I once split up with someone because she disagreed. I told her it was the best film ever made. And she said it was . . .'

He can see the curiosity in Anna's eyes. She said it was what? Crap? Too violent? Boring?

'She said it was "only a western".'

She said it was only a western and that John Wayne was a racist and a fascist and she was not going to see any more of his films "on principle".

"You're missing the point," Roy said. "John Wayne's character is a racist, but the film doesn't condone or excuse it, it explains it, explains the rottenness that has eaten into his heart. A hero gone bad. He looks like he is in total control, living life on his terms, but really he's a loser. He lost his war, he lost his country, he lost his woman and he lost all the family he ever had. And in the end there is no place for Ethan in civilised society. In the end he loses everything. That is the tragedy.'"

'His tragedy is pretty tragic for the Indians too,' said Debbie.

'The fact you think it's only a western, that is the real tragedy,' said Roy.

'It's a film about John Wayne the racist killing Indians, pretending to be a film about John Wayne the hero killing the savage who murdered his family.'

'You're right about one thing, that Ethan's tragedy is the Indians' tragedy too. Scar is Ethan's alter ego. He sees himself in Scar. It is a mirror image, a distorted mirror image. Even the name "Scar". He sees himself in the mirror and wants to kill himself, because despite the dignified exterior he loathes himself. He is the past, not the future. There is no place for Ethan or Scar in the future.'

His voice rose aggressively as he forced home his point, striding ahead of Debbie up the road towards the East End.

'I'm entitled to my opinion,' she said, falling behind. 'I think it's only a western, an old, racist western.'

'Well, if that's your opinion, you might be best to keep it to yourself. You just didn't understand the film.'

Debbie started to cry.

'And how could you, you went to the toilet at the most important part? What's the point in going to the cinema at all if you don't see the whole film? There's no point in talking about it.'

'Is there any point in talking about anything?' she said.

'No,' said Roy, though only because it was the answer the question had invited. He stopped. She walked past him, crying, and continued to walk. He waited for her to turn back and they would kiss and make up. But she kept on walking. He watched her figure get smaller and smaller and disappear among the Saturday afternoon shoppers. He caught one final glimpse of her red jacket through the crowd. And then she was gone.

'I wanted her to phone, but she never did,' Roy tells Anna. 'And I never phoned her.'

'You must have been unbearable,' says Anna.

Roy smiles sheepishly. They look into each other's eyes.

Anna leans forward and their lips brush against each other.

14

Roy had always been tall for his age and he had dark, downy fuzz on his upper lip by the time he was 12. This was in the days before designer stubble, certainly the days before designer stubble was acceptable as part of the uniform of one of Edinburgh's selective schools. Shaving was a hassle at first. But Roy quickly learned that his five o'clock shadow was a virtue when it came to girls and movies, both of which operated a system of prohibiting entry to certain events deemed unsuitable for those under a certain age.

When he was at primary school they filmed 'The Prime of Miss Jean Brodie' in Edinburgh and one of the girls in his class was in it. It was not a big part: she was on the bus that passes the school at the end. Roy's father took him to see the film being made in Stockbridge, and they watched girls pouring out of Donaldson's School for the Deaf in 1930s uniform. Roy waited months and months and months for the film to appear in local cinemas and when it did it was an 'X' - no one under 16.

'But why is it an X?' he asked his mother.

'Because one of the actresses has no clothes on,' his mother said.

'She goes right through the film without wearing any clothes?' asked Roy incredulously. All the girls he had seen at Stockbridge had clothes on.

'No, she just takes her clothes off once or twice,' his mother told him.

Roy thought about whether it was a shame that he could not see the film because of this naked actress, or whether the promise of a naked actress was something to look forward to in the future. His pal Johnnie had shown him a magazine called 'Parade' that contained pictures of women without clothes, the sight of which had produced a pleasurable swelling in his shorts. And one of his 'Animal Life' magazines contained a picture of a bare-breasted native woman wearing bird of paradise plumage in her hair. He often consulted that issue. But films held out the promise not just of naked women, but of moving naked women.

For reasons he never quite understood, the film 'Little Big Man' marked the beginning of his adult passion for movies. He had not been to the cinema for a while when he went to see 'Little Big Man' at the ABC 3 with his father in the autumn of '71. The ABC Film Centre had been open for almost two years, but with his move from Fountainbridge to Learmonth, it was no longer the local cinema and he had never been. It seemed new, different and luxurious. Just 300 gold-coloured seats, smaller than any of the local cinemas he had visited. He went with his father, just the two of them, on a school night, to the last performance. His father had been working late and they met at the shop, walked round to the cinema together and sat seven rows back.

'Little Big Man' had an AA certificate, which meant no one under 14 should be admitted, and Roy was one month short of his 14th birthday, which gave the film the taste of forbidden fruit. It was a western of course. Dustin Hoffman played 121-year-old Jack Crabb, whose memories seem to embrace the entire history and mythology of the west, from Wild Bill Hickok to Custer's Last Stand. But it was a different history, a different mythology. For Hoffman's character was not a barrel-chested Indian-killer. He was raised by the Cheyenne and in this film it is the white men who are the savages. It was at times gentle and humorous, like the Cheyenne, at other times bitter and disillusioned, like the white man. Roy loved it.

While other kids played rugby or records after school, Roy went to the cinema. He saw Dustin Hoffman in 'The Graduate' at the Dominion in a double bill with 'The Thomas Crown Affair', with Steve McQueen, who was of course one of the seminal North Berwick seven, playing a really cool bank robber. He saw 'Deliverance', the story of four city men fighting for survival against rapids and hillbillies, at the ABC, in a double bill with 'Bullitt', with Steve McQueen playing a really cool cop, with a jazzy soundtrack, a jazzy blue polo neck and a jazzy Ford Mustang.

At the Ritz, Roy saw 'A Gunfight' with Kirk Douglas, the original man with the dimple, and Johnny Cash, the 'other' man in black, as two old gunslingers. Roy was listening to Cash's 'A Thing Called Love' while other kids were getting into T. Rex and Deep Purple. Down on their luck, Cash and Douglas agree to one last gunfight in a bullring, charging spectators to get in, winner takes all, loser dies. Cash shoots Douglas, but then there seems to be an alternative ending where Douglas shoots Cash. Or was Cash just imagining that?

Roy wished his father was there, so he could ask him, like he used to ask him 'What happened next?' when the ending of some film they would be watching on telly was not entirely clear, like 'The Day the Earth Caught Fire'. Atomic bomb tests have knocked the Earth out of its orbit and it is headed towards the sun. So what do they do? In one last desperate throw of the dice the powers-that-be decide they had better explode four more bombs, simultaneously in different parts of the world, to knock it back on course. At the end there are two newspaper headlines prepared reading

'World saved' and 'World doomed'. And that is it. But which is it?

'What happened next?' said Roy.

'It's up to everybody to make their own mind up,' said his father.

'What do you think happened next?' said Roy.

'I don't know.'

'But it's like stopping the film half way through . . . or the end of an episode of Dr Who,' Roy complained. 'But then we find out what happened to Dr Who next week . . . The writer must know whether Earth was saved or doomed.'

'I'm inclined to agree with you,' said his father. 'I don't like films like that.'

Roy and his father agreed they liked a definite, unambiguous ending. Roy was not even entirely convinced that Butch and Sundance might not have got away after they came charging out of their hideout.

Films were still shown in double bills then and while it might seem logical to put 'A Gunfight' on with another western, or at least some sort of action film it was paired with 'Carry on Teacher', a mediocre, 11-year-old episode of the British comedy series. 'The Hunting Party', one of the new crop of very violent westerns, was on a double bill with the Beatles film 'Let It Be' at the Caley. The Caley regularly screened an old western on Saturday afternoons. Roy arrived so early for 'The Hunting Party' and 'Let It Be' that he saw virtually the whole of '3:10 to Yuma' as well, with nervy Van Heflin assigned to look after outlaw Glenn Ford until the eponymous train arrives. Roy's enjoyment of it was marred only slightly by the nagging worry that some usher might come along at the end and ask him to pay again if he intended to stay for the other films. Roy rehearsed the arguments in his mind, while Heflin and Ford psyched each other out on screen. Would Ford's men come for him? Would an usher come for Roy? Heflin got Ford onto the train and Roy stayed put when the rest of the audience got up. No one queried his right to stay, so he saw a triple bill that day. '3:10 to Yuma' was the best.

In the empty expanses of the Playhouse Roy saw Burt Lancaster in the western 'Valdez is Coming', memorable for the repetition of the title 'Valdez is Coming', as promise or threat. It was on with Kirk Douglas in the war film 'Cast a Giant Shadow'. The programme ran for more than four hours once you included the trailers and the adverts.

You might think that James Bond was with British intelligence, but really he worked for United Artists. The man with the gong would precede the Carry Ons, Paramount had their mountain, Columbia had the lady with the lamp, MGM the lion and Universal the world. But one company dominated cinema programmes more than any other.

'Pa-pah, Pa-pah, Pa-pah, Pa-pah, Pa-pah Pa, Pa, Pa, Pa.'. Pearl and Dean heralding the adverts.

'Experience the authentic taste of India at...', and a card would appear on screen and a different voice would read,

'The Taj Mahal, Corstorphine,' or 'The Maharajah's Palace', a dingy wee diner near the Hearts ground in Dalry Road, which would be pronounced wrongly.

Everyone said Roy looked much older than his 14 years, especially the bus conductors who only reluctantly gave him half-fares. It was not long after his 14th birthday that he decided to try and get into an X film, for which the age limit was now 18. This was the time of 'The Devils' and 'Soldier Blue', but Roy decided not to be too ambitious at first. He liked to see every western that came to Edinburgh and 'Captain Apache', an AA film starring Lee Van Cleef, was playing at the Playhouse in a double bill with 'Cotton Comes to Harlem', a film about two black cops, that carried an X certificate. He practised sucking in his cheeks to emphasise his cheek bones, which he thought gave him a harder, meaner look, though it made talking slightly more difficult. He wondered if maybe he should half-close his eyes as well: snake eyes like Lee Van Cleef. He deducted four years from his date of birth and memorised '31.10.53' just in case the cashier tried to catch him out by asking him his birthday rather than his age.

'Shtalls,' he mumbled through teeth that were clamping his cheeks in place.

The cashier was so old that she could no longer remember the difference between 14-year-olds and 18-year-olds and gave him his ticket without asking either his age or his birthday. All she said, in a rather concerned voice, was

'Is there something wrong with your eyes, sonny?'

'No, no,' said Roy, hurrying through the door.

He didn't attempt to do snake eyes anymore and his eyes were wide open when Judy Pace showed off her backside in 'Cotton Comes to Harlem'.

The only time he ever got asked his age was at the Jacey in Princes Street, which specialised in 'kinky' movies, not somewhere he would usually go. But he wanted to see the documentary 'Danish Blue' because of the controversy that surrounded it.

'The controversial film passed by city magistrates,' said the advert. 'Banned in many major cities including Glasgow. Only for the broad-minded.'

Roy was not shocked, though he might have been if he had understood it. There were some queer references to what might go where in some films, but that did not stop him appreciating the visual qualities on display.

The only other problem Roy had with an X film was when he decided to go with his friend Gordon Ramm to see the western 'The Revengers' at the Playhouse. It was an AA, but it was showing with an old Frank Sinatra film 'The Detective', which was an X. He was 15 by this time, Gordon a few weeks older, but he was an inch or two shorter. It might have been alright even then, if Gordon had not decided to bring along his next-door neighbour Michael McStay, who was 14 and looked 13. They did not even get to the box office.

The commissionaire, a young man in a heavy dark green coat with polished buttons and gold epaulettes, took Roy aside and explained to him that he could not take 'kids' in with him. A middle-aged couple interrupted to say that all three were with them, but the commissionaire said the law was that nobody under 18 could see the film.

Roy, Gordon and Michael dithered about what to do. Michael went home, but Roy and Gordon walked across the city centre, through Princes Street Gardens, beneath Edinburgh Castle on its volcanic rock, and past the ABC, to the Cameo which was showing 'Walkabout', some sort of drama in the Australian outback with Jenny Agutter from 'The Railway Children', which they did not know much about other than the fact it had an AA certificate.

'Fucking hell,' said Gordon when Jenny Agutter took all her clothes off and swam, full-frontally naked, her nudity all the more delicious for its unexpectedness in an AA film.

'Fuck,' said Gordon when she took all her clothes off and swam full-frontally naked again, turning every which way, in a flashback at the end for everyone who missed it first time round.

'Michael will be really pissed he missed that,' said Gordon when the film was over.

'Yeah, it was really good,' said Roy.

'I meant the nude scenes,' said Gordon.

'Yeah, great,' said Roy, 'but it was a really good film as well.'

'Aye, but do you think it would have been such a good film if she had gone swimming in her undies?'

'It wouldn't have been as good,' conceded Roy. 'But, Jenny Agutter's pubic hair was just one factor in making it a really good film. It was really poignant at the end when she's living in some concrete jungle somewhere and she remembers a more innocent time when she swam naked with nature all around her. And there's that poem "Into my heart an air that kills . . ." And the chill air comes from her past.'

'Yeah, but even without the poetry, the nude scene would have made it a great film.'

His father and Gordon were the two people that most often accompanied Roy to the cinema. Wednesday afternoons

105

were his father's half-day and sometimes Roy would meet him straight from school. If they were going to an X film, Roy would stick his stripey school tie in his pocket and fasten up his duffle coat so the cashier could not see his blazer. They never arrived in the middle of films now. Roy wanted to be comfortably established in his seat when the lights dimmed, so he could enjoy the thrill of anticipation at the silent appearance of the opening credit, the one that confirmed that it had an X certificate, which it displayed as proudly as any school kid with his certificates.

Gordon subsequently helped Roy set up a school film club, or rather 'cinematic society', which Roy thought sounded classier. Just a dozen or so turned up for 'Carry on Teacher', 40 for James Dean in 'East of Eden', but they had three times that many and had to turn people away from 'Blow-up' and 'If . . .', which were among the first films to get a few flashes of pubic hair past the censors without having them snipped off.

The kids in 'Carry on Teacher' might seem delinquent, but it is only because they love their teachers. The kids in 'If . . .' might seem delinquent too. They do not use itching powder, they use machine-guns and massacre the staff and prefects.

'It's a serious artistic film,' said Mr Moon, the English teacher who had to approve their bookings, 'the boys should have the chance to see it.'

And so, in a liberal decision that should have shamed the national censor, the august Royal High School of Edinburgh ruled that 'If . . .' complete with pubic hairs and dead teachers, was suitable for everyone from Second Year upwards.

The announcement came up on screen: 'British Board of Film Censors, 3 Soho Square, London Wl. This film has been passed . . .' And in suddenly enormous writing 'X.' The silence was broken by the sound of young cinephiles whooping and thumping their feet on the wooden floor in appreciation.

The likelihood of a nude scene or nude scenes plural,

was becoming a factor in determining which films Roy went to see, maybe even the main factor, but it was certainly not the only one. If he was going with Gordon or his father, they would also have a say in which film to see. Whatever they suggested would invariably be fine with Roy, who wanted to see every new film that came out. More often than not however they would let him decide, for he was the one who bought the 'ABC Film Review', which could usually be relied upon for a few nude scenes of its own.

Both Gordon and Roy's father liked westerns. In the Forties and Fifties westerns constituted between a quarter and a third of all American feature films. Although the number of films and the proportion of westerns declined in the Sixties, the genre was enjoying a minor revival by the early Seventies. Not only did the period produce some belated classics, like 'Little Big Man', but also dozens of westerns that would turn up at the Playhouse or Tivoli for a week and then disappear. Films like 'Lawman', starring Burt Lancaster, and 'Chato's Land', with Charles Bronson as an Apache, which together represented the western chapter in the career of an unlikely young English film-maker-turned-restaurant critic, Michael Winner. It did not matter to Roy that they were not all classics, they all represented a classic genre, another fascinating world.

Many westerns of the period presented a revisionist view of the west with the Indians as goodies and cowboys as baddies. Gordon rated 'Soldier Blue', with its brutal cavalry massacre, as the best film he had ever seen. Roy was rivetted by 'A Man Called Horse'. The poster showed Richard Harris dangling from ropes which seemed to emanate from his chest.

'A man called "Horse" becomes an Indian warrior in the most electrifying ritual ever seen,' said the poster.

Richard Harris is captured by Sioux but becomes a warrior by enduring a terrifying ritual in which pegs are inserted through the flesh of his chest, ropes are looped round the pegs and he is then hauled up to the roof of the lodge and suspended there until he experiences a sacred vision of the white buffalo. Roy devoured 'Bury My Heart at Wounded Knee' and writings on Native American culture. He took to wearing Indian beads around his neck in solidarity with the Indians and had the poster for 'A Man Called Horse' on his wall until he left home.

'It was a bit far-fetched,' Roy's father said. A regular complaint.

The nation waited with bated breath for 'A Clockwork Orange', starring Malcolm McDowell from 'If . . .' According to the poster it was 'the adventures of a young man whose principal interests are rape, ultra-violence and Beethoven'. In a futuristic Britain, Malcolm McDowell and his gang of bowler hat wearing 'droogs', get high on milk-plus, beat up a tramp to the soundtrack of Gene Kelly singing in the rain, gang-bang one woman and beat a second to death with a giant phallic sculpture. McDowell's eyes are clamped open and he is forced to watch scenes of appalling violence as part of his aversion therapy, while Beethoven plays on the soundtrack.

All Roy's father had to say was: 'It was a bit far-fetched.'

Although Roy's father was a member of the film guild, he preferred action to arthouse. His other regular complaint was 'It's a bit slow.' He had broad tastes in cinema, which could include a bloody, controversial, anti-war comedy like 'MASH' and Pasolini's sexually explicit adaptation of 'The Decameron'. It was only much later that Roy wondered if he, or indeed his father, should not perhaps have felt some embarrassment at going to see 'The Decameron' or 'A Clockwork Orange' together, when other teenagers went with their peers and lied to their parents that they were at some Bible Class social. It never entered Roy's head that either of them should be embarrassed by the sex and nudity, though he certainly never discussed them with his father in the way he would with Gordon. He dismissed the whole idea of censorship as absurd and never for a second considered that the violence of 'A Clockwork Orange' or 'Soldier Blue' could in any way corrupt him. People had fainted at the sight of blood spurting all over the place in the field hospital in

'MASH' but Roy's father was a butcher and Roy saw blood and butcher meat every day.

When the family moved to Merchiston, Roy and his father went to films together at the Tivoli in Gorgie. Oliver Reed being burned at the stake in 17th Century France for jiggery-pokery with nuns in Ken Russell's scandalous 'The Devils'. And films no one would remember, like the Van Cleef western 'Sabata' and Hammer's 'Twins of Evil', starring Madeleine and Mary Collinson as sisters with a tendency to drink blood and take their clothes off.

Roy and his father would buy chips and eat them as they walked home.

'What did you think of it?' his father would ask as they made their way home from some neglected gem like 'Frogs', a film that did for swamp life what Hitchcock did for birds.

'I really liked it,' Roy would say.

They would walk a little farther.

'What did you think?' Roy would ask.

'A bit far-fetched,' his father would say.

Roy would cycle into the West End on Saturdays to buy the 'Evening News' as soon as it printed so he could see what was on the following week, read John Gibson's reviews and plan his cinema visits. One Saturday his eye fell immediately on 'The Dirty Dozen', but there were so many films he wanted to see, and it was old now and would be on television sometime.

''The Dirty Dozen' is on at the Astoria,' he told his father.

'I'm sure I've seen it,' his father said.

'You have; you saw it in Millport.'

'There's no point in seeing it again then. What else is on?'

'Peter Sellers and Goldie Hawn in "There's a Girl in My Soup" at the Cameo.'

'I like Peter Sellers,' said his father. 'I remember when 'The Ladykillers' came out.'

So they went to see 'There's a Girl in My Soup' in a

double bill with 'Summer of '42', in which a man recalls his first sexual relationship a long time ago in the summer of '42. Gary Grimes plays 15-year-old Hermie, who spends his summer holidays reading about sex and going to the movies and idolises Dorothy, an older woman played by Jennifer O'Neill. Her husband is away. Eventually Hermie and Dorothy make love.

'It was a bit slow,' said Roy's father and despite the promising storyline Roy didn't get to see Jennifer O'Neill's bits.

In some ways it was a distraction to be waiting for a nude scene that never comes, willing a character to take her clothes off or be sitting silently urging her: 'Get out of bed, go on, and don't wrap a sheet round you, people don't wrap sheets round themselves in real life, it would undermine the movie's integrity if you did it. Go on, get up.' Ann-Margret got out of bed and left the sheets where they should be and 'Carnal Knowledge's rating rose by one star in the little book in which Roy recorded every film he saw. Every naked actress was recorded on a mental list: Jane Fonda stripping in 'Klute', Angie Dickinson's bum in 'Pretty Maids All in a Row', Susan George's breasts in 'Straw Dogs' and the Mohican haircut below Glenda Jackson's navel in 'The Music Lovers'.

Roy's first Edinburgh Film Festival, in the summer of '72, proved a positive skinfest, providing a rare chance to see a naked Susannah York in 'Images' and Jaqueline Bisset, sans culottes, in 'Secrets', two films that even dedicated cineastes may never have heard of. But Roy retained a soft spot for Jenny Agutter. She was Naughty Naked Nude Number One on his list for a long time, until Mrs Roberts came along and he returned to real life for a while.

15

Roy's father was much older than his mother. He had been in his forties when Roy was born. Lately he had not been keeping well and increasingly he was too tired after work to go to the cinema. The family went to North Berwick for their last summer holidays together in 1973 and didn't go to the pictures at all.

That summer Roy walked along the beaches by himself and spent a lot of time reading, Steinbeck and books about American Indians. He did not have a watch or clock, but he knew it was still very early morning as he climbed the Law, the massive hill that rose suddenly from the town's southern edge. He had woken with a start and for a minute or two watched the dust dancing in the stream of sunshine that poured through the window, before deciding he wanted to be outside in the sun.

The house was silent but for the ponderous ticking of a grandfather clock on the landing. Dew had soaked the lawn and made it a rich, wet, early-morning green. Birds sang and the gate squeaked as Roy pushed it open and stepped into a deserted street. The sky was a gorgeous, cloudless blue. Like Charlton Heston in The Omega Man, Roy walked alone down the High Street, past the Playhouse, as the clock on St Andrew's Church struck five. He could hear himself breathing as he walked up Law Road. Cows in a field stopped to watch him go by before returning to the business of silently chewing their lives away.

The Law rose before Roy. He had often climbed it with his parents meandering along the path that led around the back and gradually wound its way to the summit. The dew seeped through his training shoes, chilled his feet and turned the bottom of his jeans a darker shade of blue. It was at that moment he decided that he was not going to follow the path around the back of it. He would climb the north side, despite the warning signs that is was not safe.

His breathing became more laboured as the slope became steeper and the grass thinner. The occasional gorse bush clung to the shallow soil that covered most of the rock. The bushes had been burnt, leaving only thick roots poking out from scorched earth and Roy had to occasionally grab hold of some protruding root to pull himself up. He had been able to walk up the lower slopes, but now had to climb. He had to plot his path, considering each rock and stone, each clump of root and tuft of grass that might afford a grip or toehold. He worked his feet into little crevices while overhead his hand stretched out to bared rock.

He felt a moment of dizziness as he looked down at the town far below. He thought of James Stewart in 'Vertigo' and he also thought of Richard Harris in 'A Man Called Horse'. 'A man becomes an Indian warrior in the most electrifying ritual ever seen.' The words kept playing in his head. An invisible rope must, surely, pull him to his summit. No, no, not 'A Man Called Horse'. He was not Richard Harris, he was Jon Voight in 'Deliverance', after the mountain man has shot his pal Ronny Cox, who did the duet with the banjo-playing handicapped kid. Voight and Burt Reynolds and Ned Beatty were on the rocks at the foot of the cliff, and the mountain man was waiting at the top to shoot them too when they got back into their canoe to paddle down the river. But instead Voight decides to climb the cliff, with his bow and arrows, and face the mountain man on top of his mountain.

The toe of Roy's trainer kicked and worked at the dirt of the hill, frantically enlarging a slight depression. Here was the boy forced to become a warrior to survive. They thought he was just another sap from the city, but he would show them how wrong they were. The Law was covered in a film of loose dust, but underneath the earth was hard, hard as brick. Sometimes he dug his fingers right into the caked earth beneath the grass tufts. Sometimes the grass came away in his hand along with roots and earth, if he did not dig his fingers in deep enough. More than once Roy had to move slowly sideways across what now seemed more like a wall than a hill in order to find a route upward, and once or twice he even had to move downwards to avoid a patch of uninterrupted bare earth with no rocks or roots or grass tufts to accommodate foot or hand.

Moving down was awkward, as Roy's feet scrabbled blindly and clumsily beneath him. Muscles ached, fingers found another half-inch from somewhere to reach another embedded root that would enable him to pull himself fractionally nearer his goal. His foot searched for the slight indent of dirt he knew would carry him another few inches towards the top. A few small stones came loose and fell. Slowly he moved upwards, resting more often now, fuelled by the dangerous thrill of it all and Jon Voight's determination and the knowledge that he really had no choice anyway, just like Voight had no choice. No longer could he shout for his dad to come and get him down. He was on his own.

Again he had to work his way sideways along a ledge in search of his next hold. He stretched his arm high overhead, perched on the toes of one foot. His fingernails were broken, the tips of his fingers dirty and bleeding. All that separated

113

him from the road hundreds of feet below was a little blackened dust and a lot of willpower. His hand reached for a ledge with solid roots, beautiful solid roots that would afford a safe hold. His chest and knees held to the dirt, the dirt that coated his lips and clogged his nostrils. He stretched as far as he could, but the ledge remained an inch beyond his finger tips, just an inch too faraway. His hand returned to its earlier hold and he stood helplessly on his narrow ledge, breathing heavily. He could not move up. He could see no way back. He could not move down. He was stuck.

The clock struck again. One. It seemed many miles away, down there in the little toytown in the sunshine. Was anyone in that smug little world watching the tiny figure on the hillside? Two. They would not be able to see him from the town. Too small. Three. For whom does the bell toll? Robert Jordan? Gary Cooper? Four. Roy Batty? 'Young man falls to death on early morning climb,' the papers would say. Or 'Young man falls to death in most electrifying ritual ever seen in North Berwick'. What would his parents say? Five. What would Mrs Roberts say? She had passed him a cup of tea last night. He hated tea. But he drank it for her. She was quite old. Thirty maybe. Maybe not that old. He wondered if she slept naked. Six.

He composed himself on his little black ledge between Heaven and Earth, and thought of Jon Voight, thought how Jon Voight seemed stuck, how he took the photograph of his wife and son from his pocket for inspiration only to see it slip through his fingers and fall towards the river below. He thought how Voight forced himself upward again. One more time. This time. The right hand rose again and the left foot launched upwards. For a split second he seemed to hang motionless in mid-air like Tom in a Tom and Jerry cartoon, before the cat realises the ground is no longer beneath him, and plummets to earth with an expression of bemused resignation on his face. Roy's fingers struggled for a grip. Over the ledge. They closed on something. Gripped around it, gripped around the beautiful root and his feet kicked up again and moved upwards to the next hold and the ascent was renewed.

Roy wanted to stop and work out how he had done it, but he had to keep moving, continue the most electrifying ritual ever seen. That was all important. Pursue the sacred vision of the buffalo. Reach the top. Kill the mountain man. Win the Indian maiden. His aching muscles and bleeding fingertips pleaded for respite, but he forced them to go on. Become an Indian chief. Become a man. Easier now. More holds. Hillside turned to rock with many cracks and twists for a warrior's feet and hands. He climbed between two lips of rock onto the grass slope beyond. He'd made it.

He ran up past the deserted, war-time look-out post, past the skeleton of some other small building. He collapsed by the stone that pointed to Edinburgh and Fidra and the Bass, lay on his back exhausted, looked at the sky and laughed quietly to himself. If this were a film, he thought, the helicopter carrying the cameraman would rise above him, spiralling at it went, to show him lying there, victorious, on his summit, with the world spread out around him like a blanket on the ground. had to grab hold of some protruding root to pull himself up. He got to his feet. The sun struggled to break the chill of early morning, but Roy took off his shirt, pulled an imaginary arrow from an imaginary quiver, laid it across an imaginary bow and shot the mountain man.

He ate a hearty breakfast of eggs, bacon and sausages. His father, mother and Stephen were going to Dunbar, but he remained behind. He read on his bed and slept a little. He was awakened by the throbbing in his fingers and lay watching the wispy clouds through the window, moving slowly across the sky. Everything in the house was quiet. At last he rose and crossed the landing to the lounge to see the time on the little clock on the mantelpiece. He did not see Mrs Roberts sitting silently in the alcove, reading. It was her legs he finally noticed, caught in the spotlight of sunshine. Her khaki skirt was pulled up three or four inches above the knee to reveal curvaceous, bronzed and naked limbs.

'Hello,' said Roy.

She turned and smiled.

'Where are you off to today?' she asked.

'My parents have gone to Dunbar.'

'But what are you doing?'

So, he told her about the Law, and climbing the north side, and his bleeding fingers. She asked to see. And she held them firmly and gently, and he thought, crazily, she might be about to kiss them. She did not.

The Roberts family were from Glasgow and Mr Roberts had taken the children to Edinburgh for the day. She was planning to go for a walk and asked if Roy wanted to join her. They took their swimsuits and walked to the open air pool. They changed in the little cubicles around the pool and handed in their baskets of clothes at the counter. Mrs Roberts dived into the water without a moment's hesitation. It was freezing. It was always freezing. As she pulled herself out Roy's eyes clung to the curve of her bottom beneath her black one-piece swimsuit as she sat on the side. Her black one-piece swimsuit followed her body like a second skin. The sun was caught in the droplets of water on her thighs and arms.

The guest house was silent as the grave when they returned. It did only bed, breakfast and evening meal and would remain silent until nearer tea time. The stairs creaked as Roy and Mrs Roberts climbed them. They sat in the lounge with only the sound of twittering birds and the pompous, self-important ticking of the clock. Mrs Roberts said she was going to write postcards. Roy said he should buy some. She said she had some spare, they were in her room.

'Come on,' she said.

There was no reason for him to go to her room with her. She could easily go and fetch the postcards. There was no reason however for him not to go to her room. They went to get the postcards. He had never seen her smoke before, but a packet of cigarettes lay beside her make-up on the dressing table. There was a double bed and single bed and a cot. The beds were all made. Roy sat on the double bed. Mrs Roberts held half a dozen postcards in her hand. She said nothing, but laid them on the dressing table beside the cigarettes and sat beside Roy on the double bed.

Her first name was Dorothy, but Roy always remembered her as Mrs Roberts. Benjamin Braddock had his Mrs Robinson. Roy Batty had his Mrs Roberts.

16

Roy was like the last of the Mohicans. He was the last of a proud race. Once they had ruled this land. They gathered in their thousands on Saturday night, lining up to be bathed in holy light and renewed. Now there were only handfuls of them left to carry the torch for the next generation, more in hope than expectation. Cinema-goers were the Mohicans of the 1970s. They had been all but wiped out by television. There were still 31 cinemas in Edinburgh when Roy was born, though many had already closed. The golden age was already over, cinema's treasures looted by television.

Roy regularly stopped to look at the pictures outside the Tudor cinema, tucked away in a back street in Stockbridge, on the way to his grandfather's house. The Tudor closed in 1966, just before England won the World Cup. Because he had never been inside it, its closure did not bother him. There were plenty of other cinemas. By the time they knocked the Tudor down and built flats, he could appreciate they were knocking down more than a derelict building. He could appreciate how much had been invested in terms of emotions and memories. He bought one of the flats.

Roy watched the last film at the Royal with Sonny Crawford, Duane Jackson and simple-minded Billy, who sat at the back. It was John Wayne in 'Red River' and a lot of yee-hahing. On the way out Sonny and Duane spoke to Miss Mosey, who said nobody wanted to go to the picture house and she just could not keep it going anymore. Sonny and Duane had done their courting in the picture house. Life for them revolved around the picture house, the cafe and the pool hall. The pool hall . . . Roy had never been inside a pool hall. He did not even know if Edinburgh had a pool hall.

For Roy, back then in '72, Sonny and Duane's scrubby little town in Texas seemed infinitely more romantic and attractive than the dreich, grey Scottish capital. Its wide, dusty streets, were dotted with pick-up trucks, tumbleweed and characters with names like Sam the Lion. There was country music on the radio and motels instead of guest houses. The world of Sonny Crawford, Duane Jackson and Sam the Lion was a world Roy could enter only through the silver screen.

He bought his ticket for 'The Last Picture Show'. Timothy Bottoms became Sonny Crawford, Jeff Bridges became Duane Jackson, Ben Johnson was Sam the Lion. Roy sat in the seventh row of the Cameo and was transported to Texas in the Fifties, in glorious black and white.

Sam died, Miss Mosey closed the picture show down, Duane went off to join the army and Roy turned up his collar and headed out into the drizzle of a grey November afternoon.

They closed the Tivoli in '73, just after Roy and his family came back from the last holiday in North Berwick. His father had not been well, but he wanted to go with Roy to the very last picture show at the cinema where they had seen Oliver Reed in 'The Devils', the Collinson sisters as 'Twins of Evil' and Paul Newman as the white Apache who gives his life so others can live in 'Hombre'. Roy had felt choked up when Newman died and the sad, haunting theme tune played. He felt that way again as he and his father passed the empty double seats, for courting couples, at the back of the cinema and took their familiar places in the seventh row.

The house lights dimmed and the screen burst into life for the last picture show at the Tivoli. Charlton Heston's spaceship crashes into an unknown planet in outer space. Heston and the other survivors make their way through a wasteland to a forest where they spot what seems to be a tribe of Stone Age humans. A horn sounds and the humans scatter. Armed horsemen appear in pursuit. Except they are not men. For this is 'Planet of the Apes'. Of course Roy and his father knew the basic outline of the film. There were ape masks and bubble gum cards in the shops when Roy was still at primary school. Roy even knew that the novel written by Pierre Boulle was the inspiration for 'Planet of the Apes' and knew Boulle also wrote the book that inspired 'The Bridge on the River Kwai'.

Roy did not know the biggest shock of 'Planet of the Apes' comes at the end. Heston escapes and stumbles across the desert, wondering how he can get back to Earth only to find, poking out the sand the top of the Statue of Liberty. The realisation dawns that this is Earth, these primitive men are the descendants of humanity, atomic warfare has devastated the planet, man has returned to his original savage state, and the apes have taken over. Of course if Heston had been a bit sharper he might have sussed it was Earth from the fact that the apes spoke English, but he probably put that down to the old cinema convention that in British and American films everyone speaks English. Whether they are from Germany or Jupiter, it makes no difference.

'What did you think?' asked Roy.

'It was a bit far-fetched,' said his father, 'but quite good,' which was the highest compliment he ever paid any film. 'Let's go and get our chips.'

The following summer Roy trekked out to Portobello, where his grandparents had gone on holiday to enjoy the sea air, sit on the beach and walk along the prom. For a long time Portobello tried to ignore the demise of its tourist business and the funfair and cinema continued as normal. Now the

George was closing with a double bill of 'Shaft in Africa' and the western 'Catlow'. Roy had never been to the George before and stood on the pavement across the road and studied it like a painting. He considered it one of the most beautiful cinemas he had ever seen, an elaborate, late Thirties building, like a child's drawing, incorporating towers, sharp angles and semi-circular curves, the odd isolated window here and a whole column of little Rennie Mackintosh-type windows there. The stone work seemed to continue like a chimney beyond any other point on the building simply to accommodate the name 'George'.

'Shaft in Africa' was the third film about jazzy, hip black private eye John Shaft, immortalised by Isaac Hayes's jazzy, hip, black theme song.

'Can you dig him? Right on.'

Even the title of this second sequel suggested they were beginning to struggle for inspiration, reminding Roy of the Biggles books on which he had spent his holiday money one summer, but not actually read. 'Biggles in Africa.' 'Biggles in the Orient.' 'Biggles Flies South.' Think of a destination and the story will follow. 'Biggles Crosses the Garden to the Old Wooden Shed in the Corner'. 'Shaft Walks North Towards the Shop Where He Buys His Groceries'. 'Can you dig him?' Well, let's just say it was easier to dig Shaft in Harlem than in Ethiopia.

Shaft's original appeal was not so different from that of Philip Marlowe or Sam Spade, decent guys living largely anonymous lives by their own particular moral codes and finding it tough keeping body and soul together. But by the second sequel Shaft seems to have an international reputation. He is kidnapped by an Ethiopian emir who is really a good guy and just wants him to track down the slave-traders who are stealing his people.

In 'Catlow' Yul Brynner does not stray too far from his familiar turf, continuing to do what he had done in a string of other films, looking tough, riding about, shooting guns, being bald. Brynner would take this to the absolute limit in

'Westworld' when he played a robot version of his character from 'The Magnificent Seven'. 'Catlow' appeared to be a dry run.

Two weeks later the Astoria, a 1,200-seat brick cinema in leafy Corstorphine, closed with 'Magnum Force', which Roy had originally seen with Alison Westwood. Roy and his father used to go to the Astoria together sometimes. 'Magnum Force' was his father's sort of movie, but he was in hospital. Roy went by himself and the next day he told his father the story of the young vigilante policemen thwarted by Clint.

'Dirty Heroes' and 'The Tenth Victim' were obscure Franco-Italian productions and the latter was already almost ten years old when it arrived as supporting feature on the final programme at the Salon in November 1974. 'Dirty Heroes' starred Frederick Stafford from Hitchcock's 'Topaz' and Adolfo Celi from 'Thunderball'. It was not the most stellar of casts, but Ennio Morricone composed the music. The film was about a group of cons, in the US army, during the Second World War, sent on a secret mission behind enemy lines. Although Roy had still never seen 'The Dirty Dozen', he knew enough about it to recognise the story under a slightly different title. There was action and explosions and there was the satisfaction of that holy communion between viewer and screen, in the darkness of the cinema, that is there, for all real cinema fans, no matter what film is playing.

He emerged from the Salon's last picture show and, as he headed up towards the east end of Princes Street, he remembered that last retreating view he had had of Debbie not so long ago. Debbie was gone and now the Salon was gone too. The Astoria, George and Tivoli had all screened their last picture shows. He sighed then smiled at the recollection of 'Dirty Heroes'. He would tell his father about it next day.

He didn't know his father was already dead. Sonny and Duane had been in Mexico when Sam the Lion died. Roy had been at the Salon watching 'Dirty Heroes' when his father

122

succumbed to the cancer that had been eating away at him for the last two years of his life. Roy had known it was coming and Roy's mother assured him his father had had a good life, 60 years of it. They should remember the good times, she said.

They went to the funeral parlour, where his father lay in his coffin. Roy wore black, as usual. They all wore black. Roy had never seen anyone in a coffin before, except Dracula. His father looked very peaceful. He still looked jolly even in death, like Santa having a sleep before his deliveries. A small family group gathered and waited. And waited. An attendant came in, looked round the room, and nodded. The cemetery was not far, a 15-minute drive. Fifteen minutes before the funeral service was due to start Roy's uncle decided he had better find out when the undertakers intended to set off. Soon. The hearse was just coming. Any minute now. They hoped. It was on its way.

'Where is it?' asked Roy's uncle.

'Ah,' said the undertaker, 'well . . .'

The Battys went to the funeral parlour and sat with the body. The hearse went to the Battys' house to collect the body, four men in black, with an empty hearse and an empty limo, hammering on the door, wondering if the occupants were too distraught to answer.

Roy, his mother, his brother and his uncle climbed into one vehicle and the undertakers tossed the coffin into the other. The hearse made it through the lights on the last flicker of amber but the lights turned to red before the limousine passed through, and a van, appropriately enough a butcher's van, screeched to a halt to avoid a collision. By now the hearse was overtaking another car and the limousine followed, speeding over the cobbles of Comely Bank Avenue in hot pursuit. Roy could have sworn all four wheels left the ground, just for a moment, as they flew down the hill on the wrong side of the road. The dramatic car chase over the streets of San Francisco in 'Bullitt' ran through Roy's mind. The drive to the cemetery was quicker.

'I've never been to a funeral where the hearse overtakes other cars,' said Roy's mother.

'It's not normal then?' asked Roy.

'No, it's not normal,' said his mother.

Roy smiled. 'I think Dad would have liked it. It's a bit far-fetched, but he would have liked it.' He chuckled to himself.

It was weeks later that he went by himself to the Playhouse in North Berwick, where they were showing The Magnificent Seven. Again. And he thought he saw his father on the screen. No, he was sure he saw his father on the screen, as one of the Mexican peasants, and he just wanted to be there with him. He missed him. He wanted to be up there, with his dad again. But Yul Brynner stayed Yul Brynner. McQueen was still McQueen, perversely refusing to hand over his role to Roy. And then his father was gone, vanished in the bustle of white pyjamas and sombreros. He thought he had seen him up there on the screen, but it was difficult to be sure because his eyes had filled with tears. They ran down his face and he wiped them away. In the cinema, in the confessional darkness, no one can see you cry.

17

First there is a mountain. It looks a lot like the mountain at the beginning of the Paramount films. Then a figure in a leather jerkin and fedora comes into view, followed by native bearers and a mule, making their way through tropical jungle beneath the mountain. One of them hacks through the vegetation to reveal a hideous face with big eyes, bared teeth and a tongue hanging out. He screams and retreats in horror, though the face is not alive. It is carved in stone. In the trunk of a tree is an arrow. A caption appears over the scene. 'South America 1936'.

First there is a hill. It looks a lot like the Law at North Berwick in East Lothian. Then a figure in a leather jerkin and fedora comes into view, followed by a single, black, female bearer, with a haversack on her back and carrying a spade. There is no mule. They make their way across the ploughed field beneath the hill and the dull grey sky. The bearer hacks at the nettles at the edge of the field with her spade to reveal a hideous face with big eyes, bared teeth and its tongue hanging out. She ignores it. It is printed on wet, disintegrating paper, bearing the title 'Beano'. If a caption were to appear over this scene it would say 'North Berwick 1986'.

In South America, the man in the fedora tentatively makes his way into some sort of ancient dwelling. Enormous hairy spiders drop on him. Spikes hurl out of a wall, bearing the corpse of a previous explorer. He swings across a pit, using his whip as a rope. At the end of the trail he finds a fat gold idol sitting on its altar. In an instant he whips it from its perch and replaces it with a bag of sand. He smiles. But suddenly there is a rumbling noise, the stand on which the idol had been sitting begins to sink, and the whole building starts to crumble. Before swinging back over the pit, he throws the idol to his principal assistant, who tries to run off with it and leave the man in the fedora behind. The man in the fedora finds his erstwhile lieutenant impaled on spikes and retrieves the idol, at which point an enormous stone bowling ball, much bigger than a man, rolls down the corridor, gathering speed as it approaches, and the man realises he is the pin. He evades the giant bowling ball and emerges from the building to discover he is surrounded by Indians. He makes a dash for it and escapes in his plane.

Outside North Berwick, the man from the seventh row tentatively makes his way into some sort of quarry by the edge of the field. Small hairless spiders run away from him. Worms are squelched beneath his black welly boots. Spikes hurl out of the fencing bearing the wool from an itchy sheep. He jumps across a muddy puddle, without any artificial aid. At the end of the trail he rakes the ground for an hour or more, as rain turns the earth to mud. He finds a grubby stone. He wipes away the dirt, firstly with his hand and then with a brush he produces from the pocket of his sodden combat jacket. He smiles. Beneath the mud is a clean stone, about three inches long, grey, with little to distinguish it from any other in the field, except its cleanliness.

'What is it?' asks his native bearer.

'A stone,' says the man from the seventh row, pushing his fedora back on his head, all the better to admire his find. Rain drips from the brim of his hat onto his face. 'But not just any stone. It's a Stone Age stone. Look, it's been chipped away to make a sharp edge. It's beautiful.'

Suddenly there is a rumbling noise. It is the sound of a big man in a Barbour jacket standing at the top of the bank. He is clearing his throat to announce that this is his field and he will take the Stone Age stone. The man from the seventh row throws the Stone Age stone to his assistant and tells her to run off with it. An enormous Alsatian dog, which seems, from the explorer's perspective to be much bigger than a man, is bounding down the bank, gathering speed, and the explorer is cast in the role of bone. In her haste his assistant has fallen over and cut her hand on barbed wire. She bursts into tears, like a child. At the sight of his partner's injury, the man from the seventh row grits his teeth and stands his ground. The dog stops, suddenly uncertain. 'Fuck you, dog,' the man screams. The dog whimpers and runs back to its master. The man from the seventh row scrambles up the other side of the quarry, where he finds himself surrounded by sheep. He makes a dash for it and escapes in his ancient little green Mini, which is called Alfie, on account of ALF being the first three letters of its registration. 'And fuck you too, farmer,' his native bearer shouts at the ruddy-faced farmer who only now is reaching the gate.

Indiana Jones gatecrashes a Nazi archaeological excavation in the lost city of Tanis, near Cairo. With the help of the crystal of the sun god Ra he locates the Well of Souls and lowers himself into a buried chamber. The chamber is home to hundreds of poisonous snakes, but it also houses a magnificent golden box, the Ark of the Covenant, the container for the tablets on which God wrote the Ten Commandments. The Nazis get hold of it and open it. They want the power of God. They get it. They unleash terrible swirling ghostly mists and fire that melts the flesh from their bones. Indiana Jones and his sidekick Marion close their eyes. They alone survive the wrath of God.

Roy Batty walks through the imposing entrance hall. Eyes watch him from internal balconies overhead as he makes his way to one of the chambers that branch off the main room. His eyes scan the chamber as he walks. It is the wrong one. He turns. A black mamba flicks out its tongue and rises upwards ready to strike. Roy backs off watching it as he does so. Behind him is a rock python and an anaconda, the largest snake in the world, its name a combination of Tamil words for elephant and killer. Its green body, with black and yellow spots, is as thick as a child's, but four or five times as long. It is coiled around a branch that looks as if it should break under its weight. Its beady eyes follow Roy out of the room.

Roy climbs upwards through the ancient building to a small chamber at one end. At the entrance to the chamber is the black granite statue of a goddess, with bare breasts and the head of a lion. He is alone in the room. He moves along a passageway, aware of the sound of his footfall and his quickened breathing. This is the place. On one side is a row of coffins decorated with intricate coloured paintings of cobras, vultures and fantastic hybrid creatures. The body of a falcon is topped with the head of a ram. Some of the coffins are coloured gold. Cold white eyes stare at him from inhuman faces. On the other side of the passage is what he came for. Another coffin. On it is painted the figure of a woman, with black hair and a white pleated gown. But it is not the coffin of a woman. For the coffin is only about two feet long.

Roy slips a small notebook from his pocket and writes down a description. He hears nothing, but the sound of his breath and the scribble of his pen. Suddenly he is aware of a figure by his side. It is a young woman.

Her hair is short and her skin black as coal, highlighting the whites of her eyes. 'There's a cafe downstairs,' she says, sounding as if she has a bad cold and may be losing her voice. 'You can buy me a coffee.'

'That was how I became an archaeologist,' Roy tells Anna, 'and how I met Jo, in the Ancient Egypt room at Chambers Street Museum.'

'Your wife?'

'Very soon she was my wife,' says Roy. 'She had arrived

in Edinburgh that morning, with the address of some friend of a friend, who was supposed to put her up. But it turned out to be an empty flat. Her parents were Nigerian, but she had spent her whole life in London. She just decided it was time to be somewhere different. She was twenty and she was impulsive.

'She asked me to put her up and she usually got what she wanted. She was going to stay with me a couple of nights until she could contact the friend of a friend or find a place of her own. She stayed eight years on and off.

'Jo had a golden tongue. She could talk her way into anything. She sang for a living. Imagine a female Lee Marvin singing old songs from the movies like "Over the Rainbow", "Ol' Man River" and "As Time Goes By". Well, that was Jo. Smoked like a chimney and drank like a fish. I often wondered what she would sound like if she didn't drink or smoke. Maybe there's a whole tribe of Nigerians who sound like Lee Marvin. I loved her singing and she loved the idea of me being Indiana Jones. The next morning she went out and bought me the hat, and she called me 'Indy' the whole time. At least she did at the beginning.

'We got married two weeks after we met. I was a student and she was singing in hotels, nightclubs and bars. I think she imagined that when I graduated life would be one big foreign holiday. Egypt, India, Crete, Mexico. But the closest we got to Ancient Egypt was the Egyptology room in Chambers Street and watching "Raiders of the Lost Ark" together.

'Indiana Jones got to investigate the Temple of Doom and uncovered a cult of human sacrifice. I was lucky to get a job. I was digging up a lost civilisation, but it was in Whithorn. No, you'll never have heard of it. It's stuck out on a peninsula off the road from Glasgow to Ireland. It was the cradle of Christianity in Scotland and in the Middle Ages it was supposedly a city to rival Paris. But it didn't when we were there. To me it was a lost civilisation but to Jo it was just a village in the middle of nowhere. Old people retired there and young people left as soon as they could. It was four hours' drive from Edinburgh. And it always rained.

'Nobody sang in Whithorn. Not for a living. Not for fun. Jo kept the flat on in Edinburgh, working there, and I would go back to see her at weekends. Or she would come down when she wasn't singing. Sometimes we would work on the dig together.' He paused momentarily before adding the word 'occasionally'.

More often she would sit in the cottage watching videos, though she did not share Roy's passion for films. Films were at best a source of songs for her act, at worst a way of passing the time that involved less effort than reading a book. Roy had always had a video player. Back in the Seventies, when he was earning little, he hired one, a big heavy metal box with big knobs you pushed down for 'Play', 'Record' and 'Stop'. Six months advance rental entitled him to a free video film to keep and he chose 'MASH', one of the very first pre-recorded videos available to the public to buy. When Roy left his first job, his colleagues clubbed together and bought him a single blank video tape which he used to record 'The Magnificent Seven'.

Jo considered films more enjoyable if taken with alcohol, cannabis, coke or amphetamines. Sometimes she took amphetamines when she was helping him at the excavation site and would burrow through the earth like someone in a silent movie. Roy was not sure whether it was better that she come across something of interest or not, for it was not at all certain that a fragment of pottery would survive her excavation.

'Look,' she said excitedly, extracting a shard of patterned glass from the topsoil. It carried the faintest traces of the symbolic markings that proved it once served as a container for the local drink known as Irn-Bru. Once she did find a bit of a Mediterranean wine jar and that fired her imagination for a day or two. But she wasn't really into digging with a trowel. She would rather just go at it with a spade and get it done as quickly as possible.

'We decided to have a baby. Jo gave up her job and moved down to the cottage. But the baby didn't happen. Not at once anyway and Jo always wanted everything at once. She said there was nothing to do in Whithorn and she was going back to Edinburgh. She said I could go too if I wanted, but it had to be for good, not just the weekends. I said I wasn't going back to Edinburgh to be unemployed, with someone who didn't really want me around anymore. So that was that.'

Roy left a few details out. As an atheist, he felt vaguely uneasy about excavating an ancient Christian site. He felt it slightly indecent that he did not share the beliefs of the hundreds of skeletons in the earth around the ruins of the cathedral. Secretly he shared Jo's sense that the dig lacked the excitement that had drawn him to archaeology in the first place. He did not want to dig up the beginnings of his own society. He wanted to unearth evidence of strange cults and ancient exotic civilisations. It seemed that the great days of archaeological adventure were in the past.

In 1871 Heinrich Schliemann had discovered the lost city of Troy, to which Rosanna Podesta eloped with Jacques Sernas and a supporting cast that included Ulysses, Achilles, Agamemnon and Brigitte Bardot. Sernas shoots Stanley Baker in the heel, but Torin Thatcher captures the city after hiding his men in a wooden horse. In 1899 Arthur Evans located Knossos on Crete, where King Minos kept the minotaur, the creature that resulted from his wife's coupling with a bull sent by the sea god Poseidon, whose name was later made famous by Gene Hackman's sinking ship adventure. In 1922 Howard Carter opened the tomb of The Egyptian boy-king Tutankhamun, and in 1981 Indiana Jones found the Lost Ark of the Covenant, unleashed the wrath of God on cinema audiences around the world and inspired Roy Batty's belated entry to student ranks to study archaeology.

Latterly during his stay at Whithorn, Roy had become excited by stories of a local cult that sacrificed virgins. And it happened not 1,000 years ago, but in living memory. Everyone knew someone who knew someone who had been involved, generally the girls who had leapt naked through the fire, rather than those who had been there on that awful day when they burnt a policeman to death. Various places were mentioned in the area and he marked them with a cross on a map. Creetown. Kirkcudbright. Gatehouse of Fleet. He visited the roofless church at the hamlet of Anwoth, with its graves dating back four centuries, decorated with skulls and crossbones. It was here that children supposedly danced around the maypole and learned that it represented the penis. But there was no archaeological evidence.

He and Jo drove from Whithorn to the very tip of Wigtownshire and into the caravan park at Burrow Head. It was deserted. Wind blew over the waves and whipped icy rain into Roy's face as he knocked on caravan doors without response. Eventually a young man in a singlet answered and, with a yawn, directed him to a mound overlooking the sea. He drove as far as he could and then he and Jo got out of the car and walked the last few yards across the land. The wind was so fierce here that it threatened to blow them over the edge and they had to shout to make themselves heard.

'I'm going back,' said Jo.

'No, look,' Roy shouted. 'Look. This is it.'

He was pointing to a square hole in the ground. He stepped towards it, but the wind blew him back a step. He knelt at the hole. It had been partially filled with cement and contained the final remnants of what might have been a wooden stake.

'This is where they did it. We've found it. This is where the cult sacrificed Edward Woodward in the wicker man.'

'It wasn't a cult,' said Jo. 'It was only a film.'

'It was a cult film,' Roy replied.

That was when Roy told her he had the chance of another job and asked if she would come with him. He felt this was what she had been wanting for the past two years; he had taken the necessary steps to make it happen, to move from the erstwhile cultural metropolis in the bottom left-hand corner of Scotland back to the 20th Century. Jo asked where the new job was. Roy said she should be prepared to commit herself to going with him before he told her. She said if he told her where it was, she might go with him. He said that was not good enough. All she needed to do was say that, in principle, she would go with him, and then he would tell her where it was. But she wouldn't. So he never told her. He just went. Without her.

18

The yellow blossoms of the prickly pear, the fiery orange on the tips of the spidery ocotillo and the delicate pink flowers of little spiky cacti sprinkled the dry brown landscape with colour, just as they had in Cochise's time. The shopping centres, gas stations and fast-food joints of Phoenix's urban sprawl ended suddenly when Roy turned his one-way hire car off US Highway 60 at Apache Junction, the very name of which marked a transition from Glen Campbell's America to that of Geronimo, Victorio and Chato.

The road was marked on Roy's map as the AZ88, but was popularly known as Apache Trail. He drew the Ford to a halt at the sight of the empty desert spread out before him. He got out of the car and walked across the blistering earth. A snake slithered across a rock and disappeared into the brush. Saguaro cacti, familiar from Roy's earliest western memories rose to several times his height. The characteristic arms do not branch out from the main stem until the plants are about 75 years old and mature specimens live till they are 200. Perhaps Geronimo had stood beneath this same specimen.

The landscape had not changed in a thousand years.

This was the Apache raiding route, twisting, turning and climbing over the ridges of the rocky desert landscape, from Apache Junction to the ancient Salado Indian cliff-dwellings 40 miles away. The Apache could cover 70 miles in a day by alternating walking and trotting. They would put a pebble in their mouth so it would not dry out. Now Roy was going to join them at San Carlos, one of the best known names in the history of the West, and the history of the western.

The Apache were the most feared and savage of all the Indian tribes. Their very name meant enemy. But Roy had seen 'Broken Arrow'. He knew Jeff Chandler was a man of honour, a man of his word, and that it was the white man who spoke with forked tongue, like the snake on the rock by the car. As a boy Roy wore his mother's bright red headband and a long towel that went inside his trousers, but was arranged so that it hung out at the front and rear. He used lip-stick to draw lines across his cheeks.

The government tried to 'concentrate' the Apache on the San Carlos reservation. 'Take stones and ashes and thorns and, with some scorpions and rattlesnakes thrown in, dump the outfit on stones, heat the stones red hot, set the United States army after the Apaches, and you have San Carlos,' wrote Geronimo's nephew Daklugie. Cheated and tricked by the authorities, the Apache regularly broke out of San Carlos. Geronimo had only 20 warriors on his last campaign in 1886, but ran 5,000 American troops ragged. One officer observed that chasing Apache was like 'chasing deer with a brass band'. San Carlos served the same purpose in westerns as Colditz and POW camps did in war films. It was a place to escape from. Some would rather die a good death than live a bad life on San Carlos.

It was all over when Geronimo surrendered in 1886. His people were officially classified as prisoners of war until 1913. Geronimo sold autographed photos of himself to tourists and became an exhibit at the St Louis World Fair in 1904. He took to wearing a top hat and charged appearance fees, like a film star. One night in 1909 he got very drunk and fell off his horse. He lay out all night in the cold, contracted pneumonia and never recovered.

A hundred years after Geronimo broke out of San Carlos Indian Reservation for the last time, Roy Batty arrived. He had little difficulty finding his house in the town of San Carlos, for it was little more than a few streets of identical grey houses, with cars propped up on bricks alongside the buildings to be cannibalised for spare parts. A child with narrow eyes, olive skin and hair as black as a raven's wing watched him, unsmiling, as he got his cases from his boot. He dumped his luggage and walked over to the cafe. The only other customer was an overweight female officer in the uniform of the Apache tribal police.

Like the child, she watched him silently with dark brown eyes, as he ordered breakfast of coffee, bacon and eggs from a young Apache woman in tee-shirt and cut-off jeans. The policewoman noted the strange foreign accent. San Carlos did not get many tourists. Those who wanted to see Indians preferred the dancing variety at Knott's Berry Farm, where they could also see Snoopy and take in a couple of rides in a morning.

'You the archaeologist from England?' she inquired.

'From Scotland,' he said, nodding.

She extended a plump brown hand.

'Yeah, Scotland, I know. I'm Mary MacDonald. I'm part Scottish too.'

Roy wondered which part exactly.

'Do you know the MacDonalds?'

In the days that followed he regularly breakfasted at the cafe and met the Apache policewoman who called herself Mary MacDonald and told her about the old country. They talked about the similarities between the Indian tribes and the Scottish clans. She was in her forties but had never been farther than Los Angeles. After breakfast she would sometimes drop him at a site where the Apache had camped a century before and he would dig patiently in the earth for anything they had left behind. He found a flute that might have been used by some courting young man and a stone wrapped in buckskin that would probably have been the head of a club. But he was also looking for pottery and artefacts of earlier occupants, tribes that had disappeared, tribes like the Salado, who built the cliff dwellings at the end of the Apache Trail, but the search was proving disappointing.

'Denise will give you salado with your bacon and eggs, Roy, if you ask her nicely,' Mary told him.

Roy reflected that Apache puns were worse than those of his dead father.

He got to know the young Chiricahua couple that lived in the house next door, the parents of the little boy who had watched him so curiously when he first arrived. With them he went to an Apache initiation ceremony. Apache girls would become women in the sunrise ceremony. Roy remembered the drama of Richard Harris being pulled to the ceiling by ropes and pegs in his chest in 'A Man Called Horse'. They followed the dust trail of another pick-up to a clearing where dozens of young women were dancing, not very energetically, in lines; and several hundred onlookers sat around on tail-gates and in deck-chairs, drinking and chatting. The girls were dressed in red and yellow and blue Spanish dresses. The onlookers wore jeans and stetsons and cowboy boots. There was not a headband or bath towel in sight. The initiates were sprinkled with yellow powder and it occurred to Roy that it was easier to become an Apache woman than a Sioux warrior.

Prospector Ed Schieffelin arrived in Apache country in 1877. He was told that the only thing he would find there was his own tombstone. But he struck lucky, found silver and, to rub salt into the wounds of his detractors, called his claim Tombstone. Within a few years the town that sprung up in his wake was one of the biggest between St Louis and San Francisco, with a population approaching 20,000 and a murder rate four or five times higher than that of Los Angeles in the late 20th Century. It was here that Marshall Henry Fonda, with the aid of a consumptive Victor Mature, did his duty, rid the town of the murdering Clantons and made the west a safe and decent place for his darling Clementine to live. It was here Burt Lancaster and Kirk Douglas, DeForrest Kelley and John Hudson, walked tall down the main street. You only had to look at them to know they were the goodies.

The Clanton brothers, the McLowry brothers and Billy Claiborne took part in a brief, bloody gunfight at the corral in Allen Street on 26 October 1881. At the end of a furious, point-blank exchange three men lay dead in the dirt, none of them Earp's. Earp survived to become a Hollywood legend, not just on screen in the shape of Henry Fonda and Burt Lancaster, Randolph Scott, James Stewart and President Reagan, but in real life. For he lived long enough to collaborate on a star biography and to give film-makers a first-hand account of his adventures, and in so doing shape his own legend. His friends included the movie stars William S. Hart and Tom Mix and the director John Ford, who said he filmed the gunfight just as Earp said it happened, even though Old Man Clanton was in Ford's gunfight, whereas in real life he died several months before it happened.

Roy joined the throng in Allen Street, where the saloons and boardwalks have been preserved for the tourists, along with shops selling quality souvenirs at discount prices. Fat men, women and children in jeans and cowboy boots. Every few yards notice boards recorded Who Shot Who, an innovation that had not at that point been copied in South Central LA, which stubbornly refused to acknowledge the tourist potential in murder. At the OK Corral itself nine dummies stood motionless where the gunfighters had stood. They looked like animation figures having a break from filming 'Postman Pat'.

'Kee-ow,' yelled a small Oriental boy, pointing a smoking finger at Wyatt Earp, whose pistol was broken, the remains balanced on his outstretched hand. Out in Allen Street amateur enthusiasts recreated a gunfight, with much shouting, shooting and falling over in the authentic spots where real cowboys died a century previous. They looked mean and unshaven beneath their stetsons and sunglasses.

And a minute or two later they got up and did it again. And the fat men, women and children cheered and clapped.

Nobody really knows how it was. But Roy knew that, given the choice between the Sunday afternoon amateurs, the lifeless dummies, the self-aggrandising old phony who hung around Hollywood spinning yarns, and Henry Fonda standing up for law and order, his dead brothers and his darling Clementine, Roy had to opt for the gospel according to Henry Fonda. In another John Ford film, 'The Man Who Shot Liberty Valance', one of the characters, a newspaper editor, says that when the legend becomes fact, they must print the legend.

Roy was doing archaeological work up at San Carlos, looking for Apache artefacts from the 19th Century, but his principal work was rubbish. He was working with the University of Arizona on the famous Garbage Project, which applied archaeological study methods, not to prehistoric middens, but to contemporary household refuse in an attempt to learn a little about the diet and lifestyle of American people in the late 20th Century.

'Couldn't you just ask them?' says Anna.

'Ah,' says Roy, with a grin. 'That's the point. You can't just ask them. Eighty-five per cent of interviewees in Tucson said that in an average week they had no cans of beer. The rest said they had between one and eight. And nobody had more than that. But their garbage proved that what they were saying was garbage.'

'They were lying?' asked Anna.

'Or else memory did not quite correspond to reality,' says Roy. 'More than half of those in the survey drank more than eight cans in an average week. It didn't work so well at San Carlos. And I think the results were being distorted by my own consumption. So I went home, back to the land of the MacDonald tribe, where the population is happy to admit to drinking eight cans a night.'

'You went back to Scotland?' says Anna. 'And what do you do now?'

139

'I got a job at Edinburgh University,' says Roy. 'I teach archaeology, just like Indiana Jones.'

'You teach history,' says Anna. 'Just like me.'

19

A black cat with a splash of white in the centre of its forehead is lurking at the far side of the lounge as they entered Anna'a apartment, unsure whether to stay because she was about to be fed, or go because a strange, threatening man was coming into her kingdom. She sits there, licking her paws like a child washing its hands before eating, watching Roy.

Roy stands looking out of the window at the silver-streaked, solid, black expanse of ocean and the sky punctuated by the lights on the wing tips of planes full of unknown travellers flying to unknown destinations. And wonders what he is doing here.

Following the wall, and keeping as far from Roy as possible, Tiffany makes her way into the recess which is divided from the lounge by a kitchen unit. Anna feeds Tiffany and then, without asking, brings Roy a plain, heavy glass, classic and functional, containing at least a double measure of Scotch. Is it just his imagination, or does her glass have more in it?

'Macallan,' she says, and knocks back most of the contents of her glass in one.

'Slainthe,' he says and does the same.

It is the overpowering stink of the stuff that he cannot stand, as much as the taste. It always seemed like petrol fumes to him. Or maybe the smell of whisky just triggers some deep-seated psychological nausea, like Beethoven's music does to Alex in 'A Clockwork Orange'. It triggers subconscious memories of when Roy was 16 or 17, the room spinning like a roundabout, ignoring his pleas to get off, the vomit in the gutter, the drilling in his head.

'You don't like Scotch, do you?' says Anna.

He shakes his head sheepishly. 'Not a lot.'

'Well, why not just say so?'

She takes his glass, with what is a combination of a snort and a laugh, and pours the remnants into her own.

'Wine? Chardonnay?'

He says that is fine. She brings it in a tumbler. This is a woman who takes drinking as seriously as Roy used to.

'Put on a CD and if you want anything just whistle,' she says, busying herself in the kitchen with bowls and pans and pasta. . . . 'You know how to whistle don't you? Just put your lips together . . .' She leaves the quotation hanging unfinished in the air.

'Where did you come from?' Roy asks.

'Originally? Winslow, Arizona. Like in the Eagles' song.'

'"Take it Easy",' says Roy.

'You know it?' says Anna, sticking her head round the end of the unit. 'That's where I was born. We moved around a bit in northern Arizona and Utah.'

'What did your father do?'

'He was a cinema manager.'

'A cinema manager?'

'Yeah, a cinema manager. He got into drive-ins just as the customers all got out.'

'You must have had the perfect childhood. All those movies.'

'"Sexy Air Hostesses Get Their Kit Off" and "Kung Fu Dragon Fighters". Soft porn and martial arts. Occasionally we had something like "Midnight Express" for the discerning viewer but my dad wouldn't let me watch them. Everybody else could see them. Across the street there was a mound where you could see the whole film for free. You just couldn't hear the words. But I reckon you could follow the plot of "Sexy Air Hostesses" and "Kung Fu Fighting" without the words. Utah is the Mormon state and the authorities complained that the movies might cause an automobile accident - drivers turning their heads to see the screen as they went by. My father pointed out that you couldn't see the screen from the road, you had to park your car, get out and climb the mound. But they closed the drive-ins anyway.'

Cold sharp Chardonnay mixes on Roy's palette with the fuel from the whisky in a peculiarly potent and not unattractive cocktail.

'Why European history?' he asks.

'I don't know,' says Anna. 'It just happened that way. I got the chance to go to Oxford for a year and they're hotter on their own history than American stuff.'

Roy already knew that she had been to Oxford, for he had just read it on the fly-leaf of 'End of Empire', which he found in one of the plain, unvarnished bookcases that lined the walls. The book was about A4 size and every other page had a picture on it, sketches of slaves, drawings of white men killing black, brown and yellow, photographs of British soldiers 'liberating' the Falklands.

'Anna Fisher was born in Arizona in 1966,' said the short biography, 'and educated at UCLA and Oxford University, England. She lives in Los Angeles and teaches European History at UCLA. She is currently working on a book about the Cold War.'

'And I was always really into British movies. The movies I grew up on were the ones I saw on television . . .'

'End of Empire' by Anna Fisher was sandwiched between William Faulkner and F Scott Fitzgerald, a pretty impressive place to be. He is surprised that she does not separate her novels from her factual books. There is a computer by the window and papers stacked on a shelf behind it and it is there that Roy finds the manuscript about the Cold War, beneath a pair of wire-rimmed glasses, and letters and bills. It is not what he imagined.

'And I loved your Ealing comedies.'

The front cover says simply: 'Ice by Anna Fisher'. He opens it.

'Kind Hearts and Coronets . . .' says the voice in the kitchen.

The first page is a synopsis. 'A young black doctor (Denzel Washington), an eccentric white preacher (Clint Eastwood) and a tough, worldly Irish policeman (Sean Connery) make the final preparations to take a group of juvenile offenders for a camping trip in the Sierra Nevada mountains . . .'

'The Ladykillers . . .'

'The teenage gangster, the junkie, the hooker gather at the community centre. They look up at the sound of a terrible rumbling in the earth. They think "earthquake", but nothing happens. One shrugs.'

'Passport to . . .'

'They set off in their mini-bus. They leave the city far behind and enter the wilderness. There is snow on the high peaks and ice on the lakes . . .'

'To . . .'

'The preacher declares that they will sever all contact with the outside world during their trip and switches off the radio . . .'

'Something like Picardy . . .'

'In a television studio a newscaster reports that there have been unconfirmed stories of an enormous explosion in a nuclear arsenal deep underground in the former Soviet Central Asia. It has registered as an earth tremor all around the world. Experts discuss the likely threat from radiation.'

'Passport to Picardy? No.'

'The ice twists and cracks as it creeps slowly across the countryside . . .'

'Not Picardy. Where was it?'

'The newscaster introduces another expert who says there is evidence that the Earth has been thrown off its axis . . . The world might be entering another ice age . . .'

'I'll swap you that for this,' says Anna, taking the manuscript from him and refilling his glass.

'Pimlico.'

'What?'

'Pimlico, it's an area of London. It was "Passport to Pimlico". I thought you said you didn't know anything about films. Now it turns out you come from a film family and you write film scripts.'

'One script. And no one has seen it, except you. I'm not at all sure about it. I don't want anyone to read it. Not yet.'

She pauses, wanting to tell him more of what prompted the script, though nervous of his critical eye on the script itself.

'I think we're going to see a whole big revival in the disaster movie cycle. There's "Twister" out this summer and there's going to be at least two volcano movies. One stars Tommy Lee Jones and the other Pierce Brosnan, the new James Bond. "Dante's Peak". I think it could be huge. We've had fire, earth and water. Volcanoes. Dinosaurs. What about ice? Just think of the special effects in an Ice Age movie. And Pimlico wasn't an area of London. It was an area of France.'

'"Ice" is cool,' says Roy.

'Freezing.'

'And that's the Cold War book?'

Anna nods.

He asks if he can put something on the video player. He chooses a cassette from the bookcase with four shelves of videos arranged in alphabetical order and slips it into the machine. Anna dishes up creamy tagliatelle with Parma ham and mushrooms into two bowls and fills their glasses to the top.

'What's the movie?' she asks.

'Wait and see,' he says, pressing play and joining her at the table.

'I don't need to wait and see,' she says, lifting a forkful to her mouth. 'I know what it is from the space on the shelf.'

The Paramount mountain then a deserted street in the grey, early, New York morning. A yellow taxi draws to a halt and a woman emerges dressed in a full-length black evening gown, long matching gloves, pearls and sunglasses, her hair stacked on top of her head. She looks at the jewellery in Tiffany's window while eating breakfast of pastry and coffee.

'I know this movie backwards,' says Anna.

'The version where she has her breakfast, gets in the taxi and reverses off down the street?'

Roy used to think he knew it backwards to. But when Audrey Hepburn gets back to her apartment and discovers she has no key and wakes up Mr Yunioshi to let her in, it is not Mickey Rooney playing Japanese, in oversized dentures and heavy glasses, it is Roy. Oh well, he thinks, at least this is one role where he cannot be worse than the original.

'Miss Golightly, I ploh-test.'

Anna and Roy sit silently on the floor, leaning against the same floor cushion, propped against one of the ubiquitous bookcases. Holly Golightly is a former country hick who wants to be a New York sophisticate and manages to get $50 from male admirers every time she goes to the powder room.

'Miss Golightly, remember Pearl Harbour, Miss Golightly. No powder rooms there. Just Tola! Tola! Tola! and then boom.'

Holly says she doesn't care that her rich Brazilian boyfriend has ditched her, she will use the air ticket he bought her and find another wealthy bachelor in Brazil.

'Miss Golightly, Melly Clissmass, Miss Golightly.'

Paul Varjak, the poor writer in the upstairs apartment says he loves her. Holly says it won't work, she won't let him put her in a cage. Like 'Cat', she does not belong to anyone.

'Miss Golightly, you people steal "Seven Samu-lai" and

call it "Magnificent Seven". Is too much, Miss Golightly. I phone for the police, report theft of Akeela Kulosawa masterpiece by funny baldy man.'

Holly gets the taxi driver to stop, and, despite Cat's plaintive miaowing, she turns him out into the rain. The taxi no sooner starts again, than Paul tells the driver to pull over. He tells Holly that people do fall in love but she doesn't have the guts to face the reality of it. He gives her the novelty ring they had had engraved at Tiffany's and heads out into the rain.

Tiffany has ventured from the kitchen and is rubbing herself against Roy's outstretched legs. Anna nudges Roy and points to the cat. 'She never normally goes near any men,' she says incredulously.

After a moment of hesitation, Holly gets out of the taxi too. The rain mingles with her tears as she finds Paul looking for Cat. They find him sheltering in a packing case in an alleyway. Holly tucks Cat inside her raincoat. Holly and Paul embrace, with Cat squashed between them, 'Moon River' playing on the soundtrack. And, with a kiss, Holly acknowledges that she and Paul are indeed after that same rainbow's end.

Roy kisses the tears from beneath Anna's eyes. He sniffs and is forced to wipe his own eyes. 'It's that damn cat,' he says. 'I'm allergic.' She takes his hand and silently leads him to the bedroom. 'I never cry.' They embrace.

Outside, lightning forks across the sky and momentarily illuminates the Pacific. Anna pulls Roy onto the bed and slips her hand under his tee-shirt and into the forest of hair on his chest. Somewhere, hot, red flames jump to devour the dry wood that has been thrown to them. Anna and Roy's bodies twist together. A horse neighs agitatedly and rears on its hind legs. An express train whistles as it disappears into a long, dark tunnel. Above Santa Monica Pier, the black heavens are suddenly lit up again, this time by a starbust of fireworks, red and green and silver. The carousel beneath the fireworks spins around and waves crash on the shore. The fireworks spread and fall, like a flower budding, blooming and dying, throwing off its pretty, coloured petals and decomposing into nothingness, all in the space of a couple of seconds. The carousel slows, the train exits its tunnel, the horse whinnies contentedly and the waves slip away again into the Pacific, leaving a damp patch and a little foam behind them on the sand.

Two figures stand silently looking out of the window. One passes a cigarette to the other. Anna is naked: her arms, legs, shoulders and back are darker than her buttocks, which are taking on the round fleshiness that softens the angles on most women in their late twenties or thirties, though her buttocks are nowhere near as white as the fresh linen sheet that is wrapped around Roy.

'I'll be gone soon,' he says.

'I know,' says Anna.

20

It seems appropriate to watch 'Chinatown' at Mann's Chinese Theatre, if only for the reason that neither has much to do with anything Chinese. In both, China is a state of mind.

After breakfast with Tiffany, Roy and Anna go there, to Mann's Chinese Theatre, to the late morning showing of 'Chinatown'. Anna has never seen it before. Roy has seen it a dozen times and finds something new to take from it every time. Jack Nicholson got the ambiguity of the character just right, the teflon overcoat of cynicism that stops the man from crumbling. Just walk away. You have to just walk away. Every good dick knows that. Don't get involved. But they always do.

Roy thought he might be playing Jack Nicholson's part, the detective Jake Gittes. He is slightly disappointed to see Nicholson on screen in the opening scene in his white suit, smoking a cigarette, drinking whisky, showing Burt Young pornographic pictures. They are pornographic pictures of Young's wife and her lover. Roy is disappointed, and yet relieved, a little, just a little, not because there is any reason to think that he is no longer being sucked into that parallel world of the movies, but because he is not sure what he might have done with the role of Jake Gittes. Leave it to Jack. Don't go singing 'Singin' in the Rain' in a city in the grip of drought.

Jake's second client is a woman in black who smokes her cigarettes, through a long holder. She thinks her husband is having an affair. Jake advises it is better not to know, let sleeping dogs lie. But she wants to know. She says her husband is Hollis Mulwray, chief engineer of the Los Angeles Department of Water and Power. Mulwray is in the news because of his opposition to a new reservoir project. Jake photographs him with another woman and the pictures end up in the paper.

Jake almost gets into a fight with another customer in a barber's shop over the way he makes his living, but the barber defuses the situation with a joke about a man who is tired screwing his wife. His friend tells him he should do what the Chinese do, screw a little and stop, screw a little and stop. So the man screws his wife and stops to read 'Life' magazine, and he screws a little more and stops for a cigarette, and he screws some more and stops. And his wife tells him he is screwing just like a Chinaman. Jake repeats the joke to the guys in his office just as Faye Dunaway walks in, claiming to be the real Mrs Mulwray. Her husband's body is found drowned in a reservoir. Evelyn Mulwray is the daughter of a man called Noah Cross, Hollis Mulwray's former partner from the time they privately owned the city's water supply and the author of the new dam scheme. Noah was played originally by John Huston, director of 'The Maltese Falcon' and father of Nicholson's one time real-life partner Anjelica Huston.

But his part has been taken by Roy, who looks older than normal, with lines running out from the corners of his eyes and taller, though Jack Nicholson is pretty short of course. Roy wears black jeans and a black stetson, like the villain in an old western serial, though he still smokes a big cigar like Huston did. He sticks closely to the script, he just says the lines differently, and adds one or two.

'Water is power, Mr Gittes,' he says in a rich, dry voice. 'The ark was never lost, Mr Gittes. It served its purpose. I dammed the water, I controlled the water, I controlled everything, even the animals. I let them live, you know, Mr Gittes. Two by two, Mr Gittes. And Mulwray? There was no longer room for him on my ark. There were already two of us.'

And he draws on his big cigar, patriarch, cowboy, capital.

'Chinatown' has sucked its director Roman Polanski into the action on screen as well, as a little man with a bow-tie and a knife. Maybe he wasn't happy with some aspect of Jack Nicholson's performance. He sticks his knife up Jake's nose and pulls it straight out again, the quick way, sideways, as a hint that he might be best advised to drop his investigations.

Anna shudders and turns to Roy and notices for the first time the line of scar tissue on his left nostril, white and untanned against the darker surrounding flesh. Her fingers close around his fingers, which are cold as ice. Their faces are lit by the light from the screen. For film noir 'Chinatown' is very bright, all white suits, and white houses, and desert, no shadows, no hiding places.

Jake discovers that Noah has been buying up land. He makes love to Evelyn Mulwray, then follows her and discovers that she appears to be keeping prisoner the young woman whom Jake photographed with her husband. Jake accuses Mrs Mulwray of killing her own husband and imprisoning his lover. She says the girl, Katherine, is her sister. Jake doesn't believe her. She says Katherine is her daughter. Jake slaps her. She says Katherine is her sister and her daughter.

People are not always what they seem. Jack Nicholson had finished shooting 'Chinatown' when he found out that the woman he thought was his sister in real life was his mother. Time and again life mirrors art. And it's not the drink and drugs that fuck your mind. It's not the films that fuck your mind. It's life that fucks your mind, life and death.

Noah is Katherine's father, Evelyn's father, Evelyn's lover, Hollis Mulwray's killer. Jake, Noah and the police are up in Chinatown, where Evelyn and Katherine are hiding. Evelyn shoots and wounds her father and attempts to get away with her daughter. A policeman shoots at the car. It comes to a halt, down the street, its horn blaring. Jake runs over. Evelyn is dead. 'Forget it Jake,' someone says. 'It's Chinatown.'

It's all there. And every time you look at it you find something new, something you had overlooked before, like a case that goes on and on forever. And there is no happy ending, there never can be a happy ending.

'Love never lasts,' says Anna. 'Nothing lasts.'

'You have to see the sequel to find out what lasts.'

'"The Two Jakes"? I never saw it.'

'No one did,' says Roy. 'But it just confirms what we already know. Katherine is in it, her husband is dead. She asks Jake if she will ever get over the pain, if the past ever goes away. He makes some wise crack and she leaves. But he chases after her and tells her that it never does go away.'

Roy's voice is breaking and he struggles to get the words out.

'The past never goes away. You never forget.'

Anna puts her arm around his shoulder. 'You're still in love with Jo, aren't you?'

'Jo?' says Roy, looking as if he has not quite understood who Anna is talking about.

'Jo, your wife.'

'I'm not sure,' says Roy uncertainly, 'that I was ever really in love with Jo, my wife. I wanted us to be a family, but it all fell apart. I'm still in love with Jo, my daughter. Jo was my wife and Jo was my daughter.'

21

Roy could still remember the first time he saw his daughter Jo, a little grey head poking nervously out between her mother's bloody, black legs, with a wrinkled forehead, a worried look in the enormous blue eyes that dominated her face, and the mouth silently opening and closing as if she were talking but someone had turned the sound down. She looked doubtful, as if she might at any moment change her mind and disappear back to where she came from.

'Come on, baby,' said Roy, 'Just a wee bit farther, my wee lovely.'

She looked just like ET. Roy called her ET But her mother did not approve of the nickname. Jo insisted on calling the baby Josephine. Roy pointed out that calling a baby after her mother would only cause confusion. But Jo explained they were not calling the baby after her mother, they were calling her after her grandmother, who was also called Josephine.

'But just for birth certificates and passports and things.

She'll be called Jo.'

Roy said he would have to call the baby ET in order to differentiate between mother and child, but it was just the first in a series of nicknames. Roy settled for calling her Rosebud, after the sledge in 'Citizen Kane'. And it even got that Jo called her Rosebud too. It was one of the few things Jo and Roy ever agreed on after he got back from San Carlos.

He had had no communication with Jo while he was away. At first he missed her but after a month or so the ache and the emptiness he felt at night, alone in bed gradually dissipated. He had mixed feelings about seeing her again after all that time. Eight months. He swithered about phoning first, but all the way back from LA to Heathrow and Kings Cross to Waverley he pictured himself standing in the doorway, and the surprise on her face, and then maybe they would make love with the intensity they had in the early days. Absence makes the loins grow harder. But then what? Half an hour later, when he had poured all his absence into her, then what? He even considered just letting himself in and shouting out from the hall 'Jo, I'm home.' But he decided he had better ring the bell. He wondered if she had grown her hair or put on weight. There was a moment of sweet anticipation as he heard her behind the door.

'Don't look so flabbergasted,' she said. 'It's your doing.'

A week later Rosebud was born, prematurely. She was always small for her age. Her grey skin quickly turned coffee-coloured.

Roy had not known if Jo would want him to move back into the flat. He had not known if he would want to move back. Rosebud changed everything. When she cried in the night it was Roy who got up and fed her, changed her nappies, carried her around the room. It was Roy who rocked her on the couch, singing 'Over the Rainbow' to her, until her eyes flickered and closed and she fell asleep. He eventually dropped off, still sitting on the couch, because he knew that to move would wake her and start the whole cycle all over again.

Rosebud did not cry much. Jo cried more. She lay in bed and sobbed and would not be consoled. Roy cooked her boiled eggs and pasta and took them to her in bed, but she ate little. Someone had told her that she should drink stout to regain her strength and she was drinking eight bottles of Guinness a day. Then she would stop sobbing and lie for hours just staring at the portable television in the corner, not even noticing what was on it, and eventually she would fall asleep. Roy was ready to run between the two, with a bottle of milk to quieten one and a bottle of Guinness to quieten the other. Roy slept on the couch in the lounge, aware of every movement in the little cot beside him and in the big double bed next door.

Jo said she was too tired to even hold the baby. The doctor gave her drugs to help her sleep. She cried less and slept more. As the weeks passed, Roy sang to Rosebud, as quietly as he could. Her big eyes opened wide as she seemed to recognise 'Over the Rainbow' and he made her little brown limbs move in time to 'Singin' in the Rain', pausing after the delivery of each single word in that opening line, to crank up the anticipation, and he jiggled her around the room in his arms to the theme tune from 'The Magnificent Seven'.

Dee-dee. Dee-dee-dee; Dee-dee. Dee-dee-dee-dee; Dee-dee-dee-dee. Dee, Dee-dee. Dee-dee, Dee-dee-dee.

'Fuckin' shut up,' yelled Jo from the next room. 'You're driving me fuckin' mental.'

She appeared in the doorway, her eyes fiery and angry. Rosebud looked at her in silent, open-mouthed surprise. She did not cry, but looked at Roy with a look that said 'What's up with her?' The anger slipped from Jo's face.

'Can I take her?' she said. 'I want her.'

The next day Jo got up, dressed and took Rosebud out to visit one of her friends. Roy told her not to overdo it and Jo told him not to mother her. About a week later Jo moved the cot into her room and told Roy she was better. She said Roy had been wonderful and could go on staying at the flat until he found a place of his own.

155

'I wondered,' he said, 'if maybe I shouldn't just stay indefinitely.'

'Don't be silly,' she said. 'I'm better now. It was just baby blues. All mothers get them. I'm better now. And there isn't room here for you and me and the baby.'

'I suppose not,' said Roy. He got a flat of his own, not far away, still on the Southside. He started work at the university and he looked after Rosebud from Friday night until Monday morning whilst Jo was singing. One Friday Jo was not singing. but Roy went to her flat just the same. Jo made him dinner and they drank a bottle of claret. Rosebud slept whilst they drank another bottle and made love. Afterwards they shared a cigarette but they both knew it was over. Roy got up, got dressed and, without waking Rosebud, he lifted her into her carrycot.

Roy would gallop along the hall and round the living room with Rosebud bouncing up and down on his shoulders, chuckling to herself and slavering over his head. He played 'The Magnificent Seven' to her on the video.

'That's Yul Brynner,' he said, 'the one with no hair. And that's Steve McQueen, the one who says he has never ridden shotgun on a hearse before.'

'Aga banka boo,' she said.

'Ah, Lakota dialect,' said Roy. 'Like in 'Dances with Wolves'.'

'Da,' said Rosebud. 'Da. Dada.'

He taped all the children's films on the television for Rosebud. They watched Disney's 'Alice in Wonderland' together, with its little protagonist thrust into a crazy world of hatters and hares, dormice in teapots and unbirthday parties; a terrifying world with its big nasty queen wanting to cut off everyone's head. Rosebud watched in silence. At the end Roy told her the joke about Bing Crosby and Walt Disney, knowing it would mean nothing to her. But when he laughed she looked at him and laughed, even more heartily.

'Off with head,' she said. And Roy laughed some more. 'Off with head, Dada.'

156

Tears of laughter rolled down Roy's cheeks.

'Off with head, Dada,' she said, over and over again.

She watched 'Alice in Wonderland' over and over again. Whenever the Queen of Hearts ordered a decapitation Rosebud would shout 'Off with head, Dada' in the same brisk, regal tone.

She watched 'Alice in Wunnerlan.' And she watched Disney's 'Nokey-nokey', the story of the wooden boy, with the big, 'normous nose and the wee friend called Jimmy Cricket.

'Nokey-nokey goes where the naughty boys go, Mummy. And he almost turns into a donkey ride. And he gets eaten by a big fish. And he lives happily ever after with his dada.' And Rosebud sang: 'Hi, diddy-dee, actor's wife for me.'

'Children under three not admitted to any performance,' said Roy, reading from the programme as the maroon double-decker bus crawled along Princes Street towards the Filmhouse. The former church had been converted into a twin-cinema to replace the Filmhouse's old basement premises that Roy had gone to as a teenager. 'So if anyone asks you your age you're three, OK?'

'I'm two and three-quarters,' said Rosebud in a tiny voice that held not a trace of her mother's rasp.

'Just say you're three.'

'Three,' said Rosebud, 'quarters.'

'Just say you're three and I'll buy you a tube of Smarties.'

'Actually,' said Rosebud. She often began sentences with 'actually', a habit she had picked up from her grandmother. 'I'm three.'

Nobody asked. They paid their £2, climbed the stairs and sat in two red seats in the middle of the seventh row of Cinema 1. The cinema was less than half full.

'Lot of people,' said Rosebud. The lights dimmed.

'Why dey put the lights out?' she asked.

'Wait and see,' said Roy, wiping her runny nose.

The curtains drew back. All is darkness, but for the

purple writing. Darkness. Stars. An indistinct figure makes it way through a forest.

'Is that Eaty?' whispers Rosebud.

'Wait and see,' says her father.

The figure on screen looks down on a patchwork of lights.

'I think that's Eaty,' says Rosebud.

There is a roar like a lion as a vehicle grinds to a halt nearby. Other vehicles appear, all bright light and violent movement, shattering the tranquillity of the misty night. They seem to encircle the figure.

'It's not too scary, is it?' asked Roy.

In the reflected light he could see Rosebud shake her head without averting her eyes from the screen. Roy took her little hand in his. The figure screams in alarm and Roy could sense Rosebud jump.

'Don't worry,' he said. 'It'll be alright.'

Ferns dance as the figure dashes through them. Torches cut the night air as the men from the cars pursue the little figure. The spaceship takes off and ET is left alone.

Rosebud screamed with Elliot when he discovers ET. ET's dumpy little body reminded Roy of the little figure in the red raincoat in 'Don't Look Now'. That figure had reminded Donald Sutherland of his dead daughter. He pursued the figure through the walkways of Venice. It was not the ghost of his daughter, but a dwarf, who stabs him to death.

Rosebud laughed when ET got drunk and Elliott, who feels everything ET feels, drunkenly frees all the frogs from their jars in his biology class. She watched in silence when ET died and when he came back to life. The few snuffles in the cinema sounded like adult snuffles to Roy. Rosebud watched in silence as Elliott and his friends take ET to a rendezvous with his spaceship, with the authorities behind and ahead of them, and their bikes suddenly take off and fly through the air. ET says goodbye to Elliott and his spaceship takes off, leaving a rainbow in its wake.

Only later did Rosebud ask how the bikes could fly.

'ET had special magic powers,' Roy told her.

'Like the Blue Fairy in Nokey-Nokey?'

'Yes, just like the Blue Fairy in Nokey-Nokey.'

'Why did dose men want Eaty?'

'They had never seen anything like ET before and they wanted to find out what he was.'

'What were day going to do with him? Why did Elliott let all de frogs out? Was Eaty a sort of frog? Were dey going to cut him up like a frog?'

It was not a point Roy had considered, but he was enormously impressed that his little daughter had seen the link and thought it perfectly valid.

'Did Eaty really die or was he just pretending?' she asked.

'I think he was really dead.'

'Why did he die?'

'I'm not sure. I think maybe because there was not the right sort of air for him on Earth... or maybe he was just sad because he missed his friends and family.'

'How did he be alive again?'

'Magic. Like the bikes flying.'

'Will I die?'

'Not for a very long time. But everybody dies in the end.'

'Why?'

Roy thought. 'Well if everybody lived forever there wouldn't be enough room for all the new people.'

'They could make them smaller,' said Rosebud. 'When will I die?'

'Not for a long time.'

'Next year?'

'No, no, not next year, or the year after that, or the year after that. Not for a very, very long time. There's nothing to worry about.' He was going to say that he and Mummy would die first, but thought better of it.

'If I die, can I be alive again?' asked Rosebud.

'No,' said Roy. 'That can only happen in the movies. He said that once people died they were dead forever, but they lived on through their children.'

'And in the movies,' said Rosebud, 'where was Elliott's dada? Where's . . . Mex-ico? Was Eaty going to Mex-ico too? Is Mex-ico where you go when you die? Can we watch Eaty again?

'Do you get people from other planets? Can I phone home and ask Mummy? Is it a true story?'

Breathlessly Rosebud related the story to her mother: 'Eaty's spaceship leaves him behind in a wood. And then Eaty goes to a wee boy's house. And the wee boy is called Elliott. And then Elliott finds Eaty. And they both get a fright.'

She chuckled to herself.

'And then Elliott gives Eaty Smarties and they become friends. And then . . . And then . . . And then Eaty dies . . .'

'I don't think that was a very suitable film to take a two-year-old to,' rasped Jo. 'All that stuff about dying.'

'I'm three,' said Rosebud.

'No, you're not,' said her mother.

'Dada told me to tell people I'm three.'

Jo gave Roy a silent, withering look.

When Roy picked Rosebud up the following Friday, she was accompanied by a large cuddly toy ET which her mother had bought her and with which she slept every night. Roy smiled at Jo and kissed her on the cheek, but she turned away.

Roy and Rosebud went back to the Filmhouse to see the cartoon 'The Land Before Time' about Littlefoot, the orphaned brontosaurus; Cera, the young triceratops; and their little dinosaur friends following the bright circle to the great valley.

'Why did Littlefoot's Mummy die?' asked Rosebud.

'She had an accident.'

'Will I have an accident?'

'No,' said Roy, 'and it's probably best that we don't

mention Littlefoot's mummy dying to your mummy.'

Trips to the pictures became a regular Saturday afternoon outing. Often they would go to the special children's matinee at the Filmhouse. They saw Mij die horribly in 'Ring of Bright Water' and Basil Rathbone die deservedly in 'The Adventures of Robin Hood', dispatched for his villainy by the dashing Errol Flynn. Rosebud dressed in green tights and green tee-shirt, and Roy's mother made her a little green triangle of a hat from felt. She looked more like a leprechaun than Robin Hood, thought Roy, but she was happy. Father and daughter replayed the fencing duel between Flynn and Rathbone with sticks from the park, Roy careful not to catch Rosebud's knuckles and Rosebud swinging so wildly that Roy was forced to employ all the dexterity shown by Errol Flynn to survive unscathed.

During the summer Roy and Rosebud were walking along the path beside the River Almond at Cramond when she dropped her ET doll into the water. It was a drop of about ten or 12 feet. There was a wall, but no steps nearby. ET lay there at the edge of the water looking up for help. Rosebud burst into tears.

'Don't worry,' said Roy. 'It'll be alright.'

'She's dropped her teddy bear into the river,' one passing woman said to another.

'Oh, what a shame,' said the other.

Roy took off his Kickers and his socks, grabbed the rope that tied a small boat to the shore and abseiled down the wall to ET, like Jon Voight had done in 'Deliverance' after he killed the mountain man on top of the cliff. The water was shallow, but the mud looked deep. Without taking his feet from the wall, he stretched one arm over to grab ET, held him up to show Rosebud he was safe and clamped him between his teeth. Rosebud, the two passing women, an old man with a stick and four young boys with bikes were standing looking down at him. With ET in his mouth, he started to work his way back upwards. Hand over hand on the rope, he felt the strain on his arms as he walked up the wall.

He got to the top to hear Rosebud telling the boys that he was her father and he was just like Robin Hood. Rosebud hugged ET. Roy laced up his Kickers.

'You missed it,' the old man with the stick said to another old man, who had just arrived. 'The little black girl dropped her toy monkey over the wall and the young man went down the rope and rescued it.'

'Did he?' said the second man.

'Actually, my dada can do anything,' said Rosebud proudly.

Sometimes they went to the ABC or the Odeon or headed away from the city centre altogether on the 14 bus, towards the city boundary and the UCI multiplex. One death that had been widely forecast was that of cinema itself, but here was Roy making his way to an entertainment centre that housed 12 cinemas in one, making his way to a new generation of cinema with a new generation of cinema-goer. She would get a selection of loose sweets, the like of which Roy remembered constituted the contents of the penny tray at the local sweetie shop when he was a boy.

Rosebud would sit with the bag on her lap as she watched the film, dipping into it only very occasionally. She could even turn her head and drink Coke through the straw in the disposable cup that was wedged in the hole in the armrest, without ever looking away from the screen. No matter what she saw, whether it be Disney's beautiful love story 'Beauty and the Beast'; a cartoon frog as a secret agent in 'Freddie as FRO7'; or a big St Bernard's dog called Chris as a big St Bernard's dog called Beethoven in a film called 'Beethoven', Rosebud would inevitably ask if it was a true story and declare it her favourite film.

Roy began buying up just about everything they had seen together at the cinema when it came out on video, and Rosebud would sit for hours watching 'ET', 'The Land Before Time' and 'Beauty and the Beast'. If Roy sat with her, she might ask him to fast-forward through a dull section of the film or replay a particular scene, especially if it was a song. If she had to go back to her mother's flat in the middle of a film, she would just pick up from where she left off the following weekend. Invariably, when she had watched the second half she would watch the first half again, in a personalised, video-age variation of the Batty family's approach to watching films in North Berwick quarter of a century earlier.

He bought other videos too, old and new films that Rosebud had never seen before. When Roy took her to the cinema, she rarely, if ever, spoke, but in the privacy of their home she would comment on the film as it went along and urge Roy to tell her what was going to happen next.

They watched 'Singin' in the Rain' on video and Rosebud delighted in singing a version of the theme song as she splished and splashed through the puddles.

'I walk down the lane.' Splish. 'To the happy drain.' Splash. 'Dance, Dada.'

And Dada would dance and spin with Rosebud and his big green and white Hibernian Football Club umbrella. He bought her a little plain wooden music box, no bigger than a matchbox. Rosebud would wind the little key and it would start off its twangy rendition of the tune in double quick time, only to fall away at the end when each new note became a struggle. 'I'm . . . sing . . . in' . . . and . . .' and finally it would expire on the note that signalled the first half of the word 'dancin'.

The only time Rosebud ever cried at any movie was at the end of 'Citizen Kane', when they burned the sledge that bore her name.

'He had lots of grown-up things,' she said, cuddling ET. 'But I think what he really wanted was his sledge.'

'Yes,' said Roy. His own Rosebud was still very small, but he realised then that she was getting older, not growing up exactly, but just that she was no longer his baby, but rather his little precocious girl.

'Is it a true story, Dada?'

'Eh,' said Roy, 'well, sort of. Citizen Kane is based on a

163

real man called William Randolph Hearst, and he was very rich and lived in a magnificent castle. It was near where I was working before you were born. One day, I'll take you there, Rosebud.'

Jo could say 'Rose . . . bud', just like Orson Welles does when he dies at the beginning of the film and drops the little glass ball with the snow scene in it. Only Jo could manage that same harsh raspy sound. 'Again, Mummy, again,' demanded her daughter.

Jo painted the word 'Rosebud' on the sledge Roy bought as a Christmas present, and the they went sledging together in the snow in Queen's Park, all three of them on the sledge at once. At least there were three of them on the sledge when they started. Only Rosebud was still on it when it reached the bottom of the slope. Roy and Jo lay laughing in the snow.

'Very good,' shouted a blond man who was watching them. Roy stopped laughing and brushed the dry snow off his jeans and jacket. They walked along, with Rosebud holding her mother's hand on one side, and her father's on the other. Simon, the blond bodybuilder who was Jo's new husband, walked beside them, carrying the sledge.

Roy liked the films at the Filmhouse best, the films that he had seen as a boy, 'Thunderbird 6', 'Dr Who and the Daleks', 'Born Free', and 'The Wizard of Oz'. On the way home they saw a rainbow.

'If we follow it,' said Rosebud, 'we might find Dorothy on the other side.'

So they went to look for the end of the rainbow. It seemed to come down in Princes Street Gardens. But they never found it.

'Actually, it doesn't matter,' said Rosebud.

It began to rain again.

'Come on,' said Rosebud and her voice became musical as she sang the word 'We're', holding the note for what seemed like an eternity, 'singin' in the rain . . .' And off she splashed through the puddles.

22

Anna had seen the film before, both the original version and the director's cut, and she shared Roy's passion for the decaying futuristic vision, for the deadpan poetry of the voiceover narrative and for the film's courage to face up to the fundamental questions about what it means to be human, what it means to be alive, what it means to be real.

'Blade Runner' was a thriller like the Philip Marlowe and Sam Spade thrillers that Bogart used to make. At the same time it was nothing less than a quest for the meaning of life, or at least the meaning of one man's life. Or maybe two. She knew both endings, and everything that came before, but that was not the point. Not this time. There was a clue to what it all meant in there somewhere, and she had missed it.

In the beginning was the Word, and the Word was with God, and the Word was God; and God created Man. And the Word filled the cinema screen and updated audiences. God created Man, and Man, or rather the Tyrell Corporation, created replicants, advanced robots that looked like humans. They were stronger and at least as intelligent as the genetic engineers who made them. After a replicant uprising on an off-world colony, where they were used as slaves, they were declared illegal on Earth. Special police squads were ordered to forcibly 'retire' any replicants that returned to Earth. Policemen were called blade runners.

The screen filled with the lights of a sprawling cityscape, in which towers belched fire into the night sky. Los Angeles, 2019. Fire reflected in a blue eye, perhaps human, perhaps not. A strange little aircraft flitted, like an outsize bug, towards a gigantic pyramid. Rows of tiny, illuminated windows indicated the pyramid's multiple storeys, nevertheless its essence seemed to link this future world with the ancient Mayan civilisation of Central America. Roy remembered the first time he had seen 'Blade Runner' at the Edinburgh Film Festival in 1982, exactly one week after the premiere of 'ET' and several years before his first sight of the ancient, stepped pyramids at the end of a long, hot walk in a jungle clearing in Belize. Strange, he thought, how so much in life connects, so many disparate elements come together, and make some sort of sense in the end.

Inside one of the Tyrell pyramids one man is testing the emotional responses of another in various given situations. He suggests that the latter, Leon Kowalski, finds a tortoise in the desert, turns him on his back and leaves him to bake in the sun. Leon gets upset. The interrogator mentions Leon's mother. Leon gets even more upset. He shoots the questionmaster.

Deckard reads a newspaper at a steamy Chinese fast-food stall on a dark, crowded, rainy street. People walk by with umbrellas raised, some of which have lights built into their shafts - pathetic, half-hearted shafts of light in the vast darkness. Deckard looks tired, washed out by the rain or the strain. He says he is an ex-cop, an ex-blade runner, but he talks to the cinema audience like a private detective, in a slow, deadpan monologue.

A policeman called Gaff takes Deckard to see his old boss Bryant. Bryant needs Deckard. Six replicants have jumped a shuttle, killed the crew and passengers and landed on Earth. One replicant is dead and Bryant needs Deckard to track down the four who are still on the streets. Maybe Bryant just isn't very good at arithmetic, but he seems to have lost a replicant somewhere in his thinking. Deckard doesn't ask where.

In the distant future, long after Harrison Ford finished work on 'Blade Runner', there will be a communication network called the Internet, too hard to explain, but it will buzz with speculation as one computer tells another that the missing replicant is Deckard. But Roy knows there was meant to be a female replicant in the film called Mary, and that she was still in the script when the original dialogue was recorded, but subsequently dropped to save money. So much for metaphysics and the meaning of life.

One of the returning replicants was electrocuted trying to break into the Tryell Corporation. Bryant thought they might try to infiltrate the place by taking jobs there and had a blade runner check new employees. Leon was a new employee.

As Deckard asked Bryant what the replicants wanted from the Tyrell Corporation, Roy asked Anna if she wanted a Coke, which surprised her, because even though she had known Roy for only a matter of hours, already she knew him well enough to know that nothing was ever allowed to interrupt his viewing. Instinctively she said she would get them. She got up from her seat in the seventh row and made her way to the foyer of Mann's Chinese Theatre. There was no one else at the counter and she was gone from the auditorium for only a couple of minutes but she missed the clue. When she came back Harrison Ford was talking to Sean Young in a peaceful, spacious room at the Tyrell Corporation.

Sean Young is the epitome of femme fatale cool, with her dark sculpted suit and her dark sculpted hair and her dark sculpted looks, the sort of woman who promised paradise, but meant trouble, for someone. She said her name was Rachael.

Anna hardly heard. Something was gnawing away at her subconscious. There was something important there that she could not quite remember. But it would come to her. In the end it would come to her. What had been in the scene she had missed while going for drinks? She knew the film well. She remembered some of it: Bryant telling Deckard that the latest replicants were almost human, that all they lacked were emotions. The designers thought they might develop their own emotions in time, but they were not sure what those emotions would be. They did not want replicants taking over the world, so they gave them a built-in termination date. Four years. That was all they had. Four years.

Deckard gives Rachael an empathy test, measuring fluctuation of the pupil and capillary dilation in a blush. He asks her questions about dead butterflies and nude pin-ups. He needs to ask more than 100 questions, a lot more than usual, before he concludes she is a replicant. He realises that she proved so difficult to pin down for the simple reason that she genuinely believes she is human. Tyrell says that they have created whole pasts for the latest replicants.

'Memories,' says Deckard. 'You're talking about memories.'

Anna had memories. She had seen this film before with Brad, who fell asleep somewhere near the beginning, and with Jon, her ex-husband, who didn't. It was really John, but he decided to drop the 'H'.

'Great movie,' she said at the end. She said it to annoy him because she knew that he had hated it. She could tell he was above it by the way he fidgeted in his seat and went for popcorn in the middle, which he would never have done if it had been in French or Russian. He told her it was crap.

'That's your opinion,' she said.

'No,' he said, 'that's a fact. Where is the missing replicant? They don't explain because they don't care about the audience or respect their intelligence, because the film is aimed at innumerate morons.'

'And,' she said, 'what is "Last Year at Marienbad" about? A man who had an affair at Marienbad or Frederiksbad or nowhere? Manicured lawns and manicured people, standing around, casting shadows and posing.'

She liked 'Last Year at Marienbad', but that was not the point.

'"L'Annee Derniere a Marienbad" pushed back the frontiers of cinema,' said Jon. His French pronunciation was perfect, as one would expect from someone who studied Literature at the Sorbonne.

'"L'Annee Derniere" is a metaphysical mystery. Did they have an affair in the past? Is it a memory? Is it a fantasy? Is it a prophecy?'

'Are they replicants?' added Anna.

'You're not going to compare this junk with "L'Annee Derniere a Marienbad",' said Jon, his voice, rising in indignation, as he looked through his wire-rimmed glasses down his long nose at her. It was the way he usually looked at her and the tone he usually adopted.

'You're right,' Anna said, 'I'm not going to compare them. Just fuck off out of my life.' And she walked away towards the subway. He called after her but did not follow.

'You're ridiculous,' were the last words she heard as she left him. She never saw her husband ever again, but he did phone her sister's apartment a couple of nights later to tell her he would take her back if she saw a psychiatrist about her personality problems and her drinking, and to stress how stupid she was for leaving him . . . where would she find someone else like him, a professor of film studies with a good salary? She did not know or care where Jon was now.

Leon sticks his hand into an icy cold tank in the laboratory where they make replicants' eyes. He is with the replicant leader, a powerfully built man - robot - with strong Germanic features, very light blond hair and blue eyes. The replicant leader is played by the Dutch actor Rutger Hauer. Never again would Hauer have such a memorable part, except maybe the Guinness adverts.

'Fiery the angels fell,' he says. 'Deep thunder rode around their shores, burning with the fires of Orc.'

Jon had quoted poetry at Anna all the time, but when

Hauer quotes poetry it has a quite different effect, creating an atmosphere not of intellectual snobbery, but of threat and dread, of imminent apocalypse. Anna hears Roy say the words, under his breath, along with Hauer.

'Who is it?' she whispers.

'Blake,' he replies.

Rachael goes to Deckard's apartment. She has a photograph of herself with her mother to prove she is not a replicant. But Deckard knows her most secret memories, except they are not her memories, they are Tyrell's niece's memories. Deckard shoots one replicant, Zhora, in the back and has to be rescued from Leon by Rachael. She shoots Leon.

Anna imagines the replicant leader is played by Roy. Earlier she had felt she could imagine him in Harrison Ford's role, but this is different. She feels he is much better suited to Rutger Hauer's role somehow. She can see Roy up there on the screen, slightly smaller than Rutger Hauer, but not dissimilar. The only great role Hauer ever had and Roy is taking it away from him. They have the same blue eyes. They have similar blond hair. They have the same lines of dialogue. To begin with.

Somewhere inside the womb of the futuristic Mayan pyramid the replicant leader meets Tyrell.

'And Tyrell created man,' Anna imagines she hears Roy tell Tyrell. She finds it difficult to concentrate on the film on the screen, while a slightly different movie plays in her mind.

'But you got it wrong,' Roy says. 'Four years is not enough. I want my three score years and ten.'

Tyrell tells Roy in great scientific detail, involving DNA, mutation and virus, why he cannot extend Roy's life.

'The light that burns twice as bright burns half as long,' says Tyrell. 'And you have burned so very, very brightly, Roy.'

Roy places his hands upon Tyrell's eyes and squeezes.

'Fiery the angels fell,' Roy murmurs in the seventh row.

'Fiery the angels fell,' Roy says on the screen.

Anna knows Roy never said that in the film, not at that

171

point anyway, not when she saw it with Jon, not when she saw the director's cut with Brad. A shiver runs down her spine as she remembers the scene missed, the clue she missed when Roy suggested a Coca-Cola. Of course. Of course.

23

Roy cut down on wine and eating out and saved his wages, £50 some months, £100 in good months. Rosebud cut down on comics and eating sweeties and saved her pocket money, 50p some months, a pound in exceptional months. They had been saving to go to Hollywood, 'the country where the films come from', ever since Roy started taking Rosebud to the pictures. Yes, she would see Dorothy and Eaty, he told her rashly, though he knew nothing about what they might see in America other than the famous Disneyland rides.

In the summer of '95 they got a train from Edinburgh to London, spent a couple of days with Roy's brother, then flew right through the night to LA. They watched films and cartoons on the individual TV screens built into the back of the headrests in front and Rosebud looked out of the window at the stars. She was looking forward to seeing her 'little brown friend' and Roy was looking forward to a fortnight in the exclusive company of his daughter for the first time. Roy had been talking about going to Hollywood with Rosebud for years, but, when it finally came to making the arrangements, Jo started questioning whether Roy could look after her for a fortnight on his own. Jo worried about crime, muggings and rape. Roy asked her which one of them she thought would get raped.

'The plane might crash,' she said, 'or there might be a bomb on it.'

'The chances of there being a bomb on it are a million to one against,' said Roy. 'So if I took a bomb with us, the chances of there being another bomb on it would be a million times a million to one against. So that's what we'll do then.'

'That's not funny,' she said.

'We've more chance of being struck by lightning than being blown up in mid-air.'

'There might be an earthquake. Los Angeles is famous for earthquakes.'

'We'll be alright then, if we're in a plane at the time, won't we?'

'Look after my baby,' Jo said when she came to the station to see them off, tears in her eyes, 'and phone home.'

'Phone home,' droned Rosebud, holding up her ET doll, and making it wave one hand.

They stayed in the Roosevelt Hotel opposite the Chinese Theatre, where they saw the famous footprints and hand prints. They went to the Movieland Wax Museum, where Rosebud posed for a photograph beside Dorothy, the tin man, the lion and the scarecrow, while tunelessly singing the opening lines of 'Over the Rainbow' and throwing her arms wide to express her joy.

Rosebud looked for all the world like the star of the show, with her colourful, costumed chorus line behind her. Dorothy and co were among the better likenesses. Poor George C. Scott looked like he had been replaced by some unknown in 'Patton'. Rosebud photographed her father beside Laurel and Hardy, but the end-result was another fine mess. The tin man didn't have a heart, the lion didn't have any courage and the scarecrow didn't have a brain, but at least they all had heads; Roy, Stan and Ollie did not have a head between them in Rosebud's photograph. Roy kept it anyway.

They went to Disneyland at Anaheim, stayed in the
Holiday Inn and gorged themselves at breakfast on blueberry
muffins and pancakes with maple syrup, enough to keep them
going throughout the day. While others queued for the
excitement of Splash Mountain, Roy and Rosebud stood in
line for a brief audience with Minnie Mouse in her little house
in Toontown, where all the houses looked like they had been
made from Technicolor jelly. Roy and Rosebud swirled
around in giant teacups at the Mad Hatter's tea party, joined
the Pinnochio ride to Pleasure Island, sailed in Captain
Nemo's submarine and Mark Twain's riverboat. They took a
raft to Tom Sawyer Island, where they ate the fruit they had
kept from breakfast time, and they were scared by the noisy
Pirates of the Caribbean. Roy kept remembering Jeff
Goldblum's best line in 'Jurassic Park', in response to Dickie
Attenborough's comparison between Jurassic Park's problems
and teething troubles at Disneyland. Goldblum pointed out
that when the Pirates of the Caribbean broke down they
didn't eat the visitors.

'It's a Small World' was a boat ride that was more to
Rosebud's taste, a long, slow ride that seemed to take in every
nation on the globe. Roy could not shake the repetitive little
theme tune from his head.

But what Rosebud looked forward to most eagerly was
seeing ET at Universal Studios.

'Eaty,' squealed Rosebud at the sight of the little
creature shrouded in a white blanket in the basket at the front
of a ride designed to look like individual bicycles.

'It's like being in the film,' said Rosebud as they started
through the dark pine forest on their bikes. Lights flashed. A
vehicle screeched to a halt. With a scream of delight from
Rosebud, the bicycles took to the air over the forest and over
the lights of the city of Los Angeles, beyond the end of the
movie, accompanying ET over the rainbow through
constellations of twinkling stars.

'It's like in the aeroplane,' said Rosebud.

They flew through the stars to ET's home planet, where

his special powers and glowing finger are needed to save the world and revive his friends, who are seriously peeky, probably after getting the bill for all his reverse-charge phone calls.

'Look Eaty,' said Rosebud to the cuddly toy in her lap, 'all your little friends'.

ET saves the planet and his friends sing and dance in jubilation. Roy wondered if ET was bringing them any of the beer he had enjoyed during his holiday in LA, though they didn't seem to need it, they seemed to have their own stimulants. ET thanked Roy and Rosebud by name when they got off the ride.

'Again, again, let's do it again,' said Rosebud. And they did it again. And again. And again. All day. Not for Rosebud the state-of-the-art 'Back to the Future' virtual ride. It left Roy slightly motion-sick and Rosebud decidedly bored. She wanted to see ET again. It was all Roy could do to get her to go on the studio tour tram. But earthquakes and flash floods did not compare with ET. It was Roy that jumped when the bus drove alongside a stretch of water and a shark came jumping out of it right beside his open window.

'Can we see Eaty again now?' asked Rosebud, as if she had just been humouring Roy by taking him on other rides.

Rosebud splashed around in her bath at the Roosevelt Hotel that night while Roy lay on his bed sipping a Budweiser in a frosted glass, surfing the television channels until he settled on a report about the forthcoming Oscars, suggesting it was a two-horse race between 'Forrest Gump' and 'Pulp Fiction'. He hoped John Travolta might at least win the best actor award. Suddenly he was aware of a little figure in the doorway wrapped all in white, just like ET, with only a little, mischievous brown face showing.

'Phone home,' she droned, as she had done at the station. Rosebud did a great ET impression. So they phoned home.

'Mummy, Dada took me to where they make the films, and we saw Eaty, and we were on a bicycle that flew over the trees, and it was just like the film, but different, because it didn't stop where the film stopped, and we kept going past the stars to where Eaty lives and . . .'

They were happy days for Rosebud and Roy. He wound up and played her 'Singin' in the Rain' musicbox while she prattled endlessly and expensively on the phone.

24

Deckard jumps but he does not quite make it. He clings desperately to the edge of the building, his grip loosening all the time. The street is far below him. Deckard must kill the replicant, the replicant Anna imagines is played by Roy Batty, the man sitting next to her in the seventh row of Mann's Chinese Theatre; kill him or be killed by him.

Roy is stronger, but it seems he is dying. His right hand is knotting up, twisting involuntarily into a fist. He grimaces as he sticks a nail through the palm of the hand.

'Damn this rheumatoid arthritis,' he says. 'My grandfather had it too. Couldn't play snooker in the end.'

And he lets out a demonic exclamation 'Ha' that is both a laugh and a cry. Deckard carried a gun, but he lost it. Roy carries a white dove. Vangelis's melancholy, contemplative music plays. Roy leaps over the top of Deckard and lands safely on the roof. He is almost naked, his body shiny in the rain.

What does it mean? Anna asks herself. This man beside her who was an archaeologist like Indiana Jones and . . . and . . .

'I've seen things,' Roy says to Deckard, with a certain relish, 'that you wouldn't believe. I've seen sharks, as old as the dinosaurs, swimming in the sea as close to me as you, with rows of teeth like the nail in my palm. I've seen a man's head cut clean from his body with a machete in Africa. I've seen Orson Welles play an old man in 'Citizen Kane', I've seen George Best play football for Hibs and I've seen Glen Campbell play 'Amazing Grace' on the bagpipes. I've seen the sublime and the ridiculous. I've seen life and I've seen death. I was there.'

Deckard squirms as his fingers struggle to keep a grip on the ledge.

'I've looked into the face of fear,' says Roy.

Deckard does not hear him. Life slips through his wet, weak fingers. He loses his grip completely. He hangs motionless for just the briefest moment in time, surrounded by space, by eternity, with the earth far, far below him, calling him towards it; the briefest moment in time, a mere comma in the history of the universe, not even a comma, an atom, nothing. Instinctively Roy reaches out his hand and grips Deckard's wrist, saves his life.

What does it mean? Anna wonders. Who is this man beside her, with whom she has shared so little and so much?

'I've looked into the face of fear,' Roy continues, 'and I've looked into the face of love. I've seen people die and I've seen people live. I've seen a child being born . . .'

Anna sees the man who calls himself Roy Batty up there on the screen in the movie, making up lines as he goes along. There is no doubt about it. She sees him. There. On the screen. The movie in her mind is playing up there on the cinema screen. Such is the power of her realisation of the significance of what she missed. Such is her confusion.

Roy looks away from Deckard. There is a far, faraway look in Roy's eyes.

'I've seen the fiery angels fall, heard the thunder ride around the shores.' He sighs as if about to expire and talks again, very slowly. 'When I die those memories will all be lost

. . .'

Anna knows what comes next, or what should come next. It is etched in her memory from the time she sobbed as she was swept away by the pathos of the replicant's plight and Jon sighed in exasperation at the ridiculousness of a robot's death scene. Roy sits next to her in silence, not moving at all, as if only his shell is there, but the real Roy is somewhere else. She looks at the ghostly face beside her in the eerie twilight that bounces back from the screen.

'Like tears in rain,' she whispers, and she raises a finger to wipe her eye.

'Like tears in rain,' the Roy in the film repeats, gently; and he looks away from Deckard, looks straight at Anna in the seventh row.

What was it Tyrell had said? 'The light that burns twice as bright burns half as long.' And then? 'And you have burned so very, very brightly . . . Roy'. He said that when she saw the film with Roy. He said that when she saw the film with Brad. He said that when she saw the film with Jon. She did not imagine it. Tyrell called the character Roy.

She remembers the detail of the scene she missed when she went for Coca-Cola, the scene when Bryant produces the records of the other replicants who escaped with Leon. She remembers all the details. Zhora, a member of an off-world kick-murder squad. Pris, a pleasure model. And their leader. Rutger Hauer's character isn't just called Roy. She remembers now, clear as day. His name is Roy Batty and it always was. But if he is Roy Batty who is the man in the seventh row, who claims the identity of a character in a film, not even a human character, but a robot who cannot even be sure that his memories are his own?

Harrison Ford is readying himself for the voice-over in which he says that he does not know why Roy saved his life, maybe he just fell in love with life, the idea of life; and Deckard will suggest that all Roy wanted were answers to the fundamental questions about where he had come from, where he was going and how long he might have.

180

'I've looked into the face of fear,' says Roy. 'And I've looked into the face of love.' He says a name. Not Deckard's name, but Anna's name.

Anna gasps. She wants to break away from this game, this fantasy. She wants to return to reality, return to the familiar film with Harrison Ford as Deckard and Rutger Hauer as Roy Batty. She wants to stop imagining Roy Batty being played by the man beside her. But she can't.

'Time to die,' Roy tells Deckard and he frees the white dove, which, soars up into the perpetually wet grey sky, the wet grey sky so like an Edinburgh autumn afternoon. He looks again at Deckard, as if summoning his final strength to pull him onto the roof and save his life. He releases his grip. Deckard falls backwards. He plunges towards the ground, getting smaller and smaller as he falls.

Roy turns round and Sean Young is waiting for him, wearing a fur coat that she might have borrowed from Lauren Bacall or Mary Astor.

'Tyrell lied to me,' says Roy's voice on the soundtrack, 'when he said I had only four years to live. The virus he talked about, the seizure in my hands . . . in laymen's terms that really was just a form of arthritis, or rust, take your pick. I was a new type of replicant with no termination date. Rachael and I were the only two.'

Roy shivers in the cold rain and Rachael wraps her coat around his shoulders as they walk away across the rooftop puddles.

'I don't know how long we will have together. But then again who does?'

Roy and Anna stay there, in the cinema, until the credits are finished and the lights go up. 'What does it mean?' asks Anna in a small, shaky voice.

'It's about loneliness,' says Roy, 'The only characters that feel real emotion and affection . . . and love are the replicants. I think that's why Roy saved Deckard's life.'

'But, he didn't,' says Anna, quietly.

The colour drains from Roy's face. He is not quite sure

what she means. Surely she cannot have seen what he saw.

'Roy didn't save his life. Roy let him fall . . . You let him fall.' She looks into his blue eyes. They have the same faraway look she had seen in the film when Roy Batty talked about what he had seen.

'I think I'm going mad. I meet a man from nowhere, I take him home, I sleep with him . . . I . . . I fall in love with him, damn it. And suddenly I realise he is masquerading as a robot from a fucking science-fiction film, because he can't actually be a character out of a film. Can he?'

Roy shakes his head. Her voice is rising now.

'Who are you? Who are you next? James Bond? Harry Lime? Mel Gibson? Who are you?'

In response to the question the man from the seventh row does something very strange. He unzips his fly.

25

Anna waits with the same confused uncertainty with which she had watched the end of the film. She frowns. There have been some crazy things going on, but . . .

Roy pulls out a brown linen money belt that he has been wearing around his waist. From the pocket of it he produces a little pink booklet, which he hands to Anna. Above a golden lion and unicorn it says 'European Community, United Kingdom of Great Britain and Northern Ireland'. Below the beasts it says 'Passport'.

The passport automatically opens at a page that carries a United States visa. American visas are not like other visas. A rubber-stamp will not suffice for the US of A. No, the United States has embossed, coloured paper visas with all the grandeur and technology of a bank note, over-stamped with an eagle and partially covered in cellophane that is transparent, but if you hold it up to the light you can see golden eagles on the cellophane. US visas take up a whole page to reflect the importance of the country.

Anna is not interested in the visa. She knows he is in America and she fumbles impatiently with the little book. You would think that they would put the passport holder's details at the front. But no, that would be too simple for the British.

They used to put them at the front in the old days when Britons had big black hardback passports that reflected the importance of the British Empire. But now Britain puts the passport holder details at the back to reflect the post-empire backwardness of the country. On the inside back page. And they do not even put the details the right way up.

Anna turns the passport sideways and looks into the clear blue pools of eyes that had mesmerised her in the movie that had just played in her mind, the movie she thought she saw on the screen of Mann's Chinese Theatre, or rather the latter part of the movie she thought she saw there. The picture in the passport is certainly not Rutger Hauer or the Roy Batty that Hauer created, as familiar from posters, video covers, album covers, photographs, the Roy Batty who was an established part of post-modernist culture. The blue eyes that stare out at her are the eyes of the man beside her now.

She glances at the man and then back at the passport, as if checking details like a border guard before permitting entry to her country. There is a pronounced dimple in his chin.

'Batty,' it says, under 'Surname/Nom (1)'. And below that 'Roy'. Roy Batty. Like he said. British citizen. Male. Born in Edinburgh in 1957. Of course it gives an exact date, but the exact date comes no closer to registering on Anna's consciousness than the passport number in the corner. Batty. Roy. British. Edinburgh. What else? Children. Enfants. The figure 1. She wants to see the child. She wants to see a picture of the child. But there is no picture.

Roy seems to read her thoughts. He is taking something from a battered black leather wallet, which she can see at once is a small photograph. But before she can take it her eye is caught by another detail in the passport. This time on a page at the front. A heading that runs sideways across the pink page, a page of swirls that looks like the creation of a bored child with a spirograph.

'Children/Enfants' it says. Why do they put the

passport holder at the back and his children at the front. There is only one child, one enfant, one single line of black print to say Batty, Josephine R, 1/3/89, F. One child. Not even one child. For the page is stamped 'United Kingdom Passport Agency . . . Deceased'.

A thought crosses Rachel's mind.

'What does the R stand for?' she asks, limply. It could be Rachael.

'Rose,' says Roy. 'As in Rosebud.'

Anna thirstily drinks in the air, fills her lungs, and lets out a long, terrible, sad sigh. Without saying anything, she takes the photograph from Roy, takes the photograph from Roy Batty, the Roy beside her in the lobby of the cinema. She looks at Roy's beautiful deep blue eyes but not on Roy, not on a cinema screen, but in the face of a smiling, coffee-coloured little girl, in a red duffle coat, laughing as her swing swings towards the camera, kicking up her little blue wellingtons. She was full of life and laughter and love. You could see it in her eyes and her smile and the way she was. Anna looks again at Roy and realises that they are not, after all, the same eyes. For Roy's eyes are no longer the clear blue of carefree sunny days. They are clouded with the sadness of knowing that he will never again push this little brown girl on her swing, never again see her loving smile.

Anna looks deep, deep, into Roy's eyes and sees the pain. She does not know what to say. She wants to say sorry, but it seems so hopelessly, pathetically inadequate. Her expression remains one of confusion. Her expression says nothing, but asks a question

'How?' Asks it again and again.

Somehow they have made their way from the lobby to the entrance, where she recognises the man in the yellow shirt and shorts and baseball cap.

'Actress Norma Talmadge visited the construction site and accidentally trod in the wet cement,' he says.

'Your name really is Roy Batty,' says Anna.

'Yes, it really is Roy Batty,' says Roy.

'Mary Pickford and Douglas Fairbanks Senior followed her example at the premiere of "King of Kings",' says the man in yellow.

'So the "Blade Runner" thing is . . . just coincidence?'

'I think so,' says Roy. 'More or less. I think it was just coincidence . . . at first.'

'And the greatest stars still come here to record their footprints and handprints in the sidewalk . . . for your enjoyment.'

'And your daughter . . ?' says Anna, and her voice trails away into silence.

26

Silhouettes of buildings. A bell rings. The first words appear 'GCF presents', whatever GCF is. Another logo, Eagle-Lion Distributors, imposed upon a circle, the Stars and Stripes within the upper semi-circle, the Union Jack the lower, and an eagle and a lion on top of their respective flags. Obviously some sort of transatlantic alliance, thinks Anna, significantly, not quite sure if it is real, not quite sure what to expect from this classic movie, this hitherto classic movie.

The roar of a train is heard as the logo fades, and a monochrome picture of a station appears. A locomotive thunders through the station without stopping, leaving a cloud of thick grey smoke in its wake. Milford Junction. The first thumping notes of Rachmaninoff's Second Piano Concerto are heard on the soundtrack as the white lettering of the title fills the screen –

'Sam Peckinpah's Brief Encounter'.

Roy and Anna look at each other. A trip to the cinema was never this interesting with Jon.

Jon had declared 'Brief Encounter' was very French and compared it with a bunch of French movies Anna had never heard of. What would he have made of Sam Peckinpah's 'Brief Encounter?' Anna has a feeling that it is not really going to be Sam Peckinpah's 'Brief Encounter' so much as Roy Batty's.

Another train draws to a halt. A single figure steps down from it. A man dressed all in black, from his stetson to his riding boots. Around his waist a gunbelt and a Colt 45. On his shoulder he carries a saddle. He looks around the empty platform as the train slowly pulls away behind him. The next credit appears.

'Starring Celia Johnson and Roy Batty'.

Both Roy and Anna see Roy Batty as the man in black. She wonders if others in the cinema see him too, and looks around to find out if anyone seems surprised. The cinema is still and faces stare intently at the screen, betraying no sign of anything untoward. Roy does not need to look. He knows that the rest of the audience is watching some dull romance with Trevor Howard.

The man in black crosses the railwayline to the saloon, where a grey-haired woman with a prominent chin is tending bar. With her hair up and her lacy dress, she looks more like a school teacher than a barmaid. Roy's character recognises the big wall clock, with the Roman numerals. He has seen it before, in a little town called Hadleyville, watched it tick around to noon, signalling the arrival of another train in another station in another world.

He strides over to the bar, which is cluttered with cups and small jugs and what look like pastries. He lays his saddle down at his feet.

'Whisky,' he says, in a brisk, no-nonsense tone, looking the woman straight in the eye.

'I'm afraid it's out of hours,' says the woman behind the bar.

The man in black is a man of few words, but he cannot help but comment on the woman's curious accent.

'You're not from Arizona, are you?' he says. 'Or Texas?'

'Whatever do you mean?' she says.

'You have a strange way of talking.'

'I don't know to what you can be referring,' says the barmaid, indignantly.

'I'll have a whisky,' he says, returning to the point.

'Look,' she says, 'I told you it's out of hours, and I'll have to send for Mr Godby if you don't mind your manners and Mr Godby is not a man to trifle with.'

The man in black slips his hand from the bar to rest it on the butt of the Colt at his side.

'Why don't you have a bun' she says, 'fresh this morning, and a nice cup of tea.'

The man says nothing, but his sparkling eyes, so obviously blue even in a black and white movie, never leave her face. She interprets his silence as a 'yes' and hands him a cup of tea and a plate with a bun on it.

'The sugar's in the spoon.'

He looks around, notices a woman with large eyes, a thin face and hair that is parted way over on one side and cascades across her head like a wave on the ocean. She is wearing a cap like a Confederate Civil War cap, but bigger, more flamboyant, more ridiculous. She is reading a book and does not look like the sort of girl you might expect to find in a saloon. He sits at an empty table as far from her as possible, though his gaze is curiously drawn to her by the appeal in her eyes or the slight bitterness and disappointment suggested in the line of her mouth. Or maybe his eyes are simply drawn to her by judicious editing.

The tea is a thin, disgusting brew, the bun stale, and the barmaid prattles away incessantly to her assistant Beryl and an elderly uniformed railway employee, who turns out to be the supposedly formidable Mr Godby. He does not even wear a gun.

The thin-faced woman seems a delicate, fussy type. She probably prefers Rachmanioff to Morricone, reckons the man in black, and is 'happily married' to some drip called Dear Fred, who sits around the house doing crosswords, and has a couple of whey-faced kids who can't carry a simple scene

189

about whether to go to the circus or the pantomime without impaling the words on their cut-glass accents.

He watches the woman with the wave on her head collect her several bags and leave the saloon, only to return, moments later, blinking, complaining of a speck of grit in her eye and demanding a glass of water to 'bathe' it. The barmaid claims to know someone who lost an eye from getting grit in it. The man in black wonders if he should offer to help - he is a doctor - but then decides that he would rather not get mixed up with these people. It starts with a simple act of kindness and it always ends in screaming, gunfire, bloodshed and bodies.

The barmaid suggests the woman pull her eyelid down as far as it will go. Mr Godby says she should blow her nose. The thin-faced woman moans on and on. The man in black can stand it no longer.

'Let me see,' he says, 'I'm a doctor.' He takes the black handkerchief from around his neck and wipes her eye clean. She is prettier close up . . . in an ugly sort of way.

Anna tries hard to see herself as the woman playing opposite Roy, but the image remains resolutely that of Celia Johnson. Anna closes her eyes. She sees nothing, but hears Roy and Celia Johnson. She opens her eyes and sees Roy with Celia Johnson. She cannot see, cannot even imagine, herself as this woman with the skinny face and the wave on her head.

Roy, the man in black, looks straight at the skinny woman with an intensity that makes her go weak at the knees. But then most things make her go weak at the knees. A bell rings to announce an approaching train and he says he must go. Impulsively, rudely even, she inquires where he is going. With his forefinger he points straight ahead. He picks up his saddle, hoists it onto his shoulder and is gone; to catch a train for some unspecified destination, though she knows, full well, it is the train to Leeds.

'Well, I say,' says the matronly barmaid, 'what a card.'

Laura doubts if she will see him again, but a couple of weeks later, on her regular weekly outing to Milford, he walks into the Kardomah restaurant. He is dressed in black, exactly as before, though without the saddle on his shoulder. She is still wearing her Confederate Civil War cap. She invites him to share her table.

'I'm afraid we haven't been properly introduced,' she says. 'I'm Laura Jesson. You're Doctor...? I remember you said you were a doctor that day you saved my life at the station. Doctor...?'

There is that look again, the one that makes her feel all jumbled up inside.

'Holliday,' he says. 'Doc Holliday.'

Laura orders soup and fried sole. Holliday asks for tortillas and refried beans, with a shot of tequila on the side. The waitress looks blank.

'They don't do Continental dishes at the Kardomah,' whispers Laura.

He asks for a steak..

They go to the pictures. She suggests 'The Loves of Cardinal Richelieu' at the Palace, or something at the Palladium, the title of which proves impossible to make out because she sounds like she is talking with marbles in her mouth. But Holliday says 'Stagecoach' is on at the Empire, so they go to see that instead.

'That was lovely,' says Laura, over teas in the refreshment room at Milford Junction station. 'Much better than I expected from a cowboy film. Thank you so much for suggesting it. Claire Trevor was excellent and that dashing young actor who played the Ringo Kid . . . What was his name?'

'Roy Batty,' says Holliday.

'He looked like you,' she says. 'Just a little.'

She tries to engage him in conversation about his work as a doctor. But he says he does not practise anymore, and offers no further details.

'What do you do?'

'I play cards, gamble a little. I ride herd occasionally - though there's not much call for that around Milford Junction

191

and Leeds. Sometimes I work over the border.'

'In Scotland?' she says. 'How exotic. Or do you mean in Wales?'

'Wherever the action is,' he says. 'I rode shotgun on a hearse this morning, with Steve McQueen.'

'Where was that?' she asks, with a look that suggests she suspects he is having a little joke at her expense, though she is not entirely sure.

'Boot Hill.'

She laughs gaily. 'Oh, you are so droll, Dr Holliday.'

'Call me Doc,' he says, rising to go for his train. 'Meet me next week at the Kardomah.'

'I'll be there,' she says, as Rachmaninoff roams over the soundtrack, but she is not sure he heard. He did not appear to need confirmation.

They go boating, she says she loves him, but is not free to love him. She says they must stop seeing each other. She cries and witters on about 'being sensible'.

Be sensible? How can you be sensible when you're a gunfighter in a Noel Coward romance?

He knows one thing. He knows that one day, if he stays, he and Dear Fred must face each other on the street at high noon. But he cannot just ride on, not yet, for one simple reason. He does not have a horse.

At the station, in the darkness of an underpass, he embraces Laura and kisses her. She can provide him with companionship and that sort of thing, until he gets a horse.

The following week she says she did not mean to come. But she is there. What a strange little creature she is, so much more difficult than half-breed girls and horses. They lunch at the Royal Hotel. Laura had not been there since Violet's wedding reception. Holliday tells Laura he has a surprise for her. He has borrowed some transport from a friend. She guesses it is a sports car, one of those showy little two-seaters. But she is wrong. There is only one seat and it is not a sports car. There, at the kerb, outside the hotel, is the saddle Laura remembers from the first time she saw Dr Holliday, in the refreshment room at Milford Junction station. And beneath it is a piebald mare he has borrowed from a friend called Stephen, not Steve McQueen, with whom he had ridden shotgun on the hearse at Boot Hill, but someone called Stephen Lynn.

He has also borrowed Stephen's flat for the evening. Laura refuses to go up to the apartment. Holliday says he will be there if she changes her mind, knowing she probably will. He kisses her at the station, just to make sure, and goes back to the flat to wait. As a card player Holliday has learned patience. She actually gets on the train, before finally jumping from her third class compartment and running back, swept along on a deluge of Rachmaninoff.

Holliday opens the door without saying a word, helps her off with her coat and takes her Confederate Civil War cap. They kiss. She says she must go.

'Look, Laura,' he says, beginning to lose patience. 'I've had enough of your silliness. Let's just get on with it.'

It is at this moment Stephen Lynn appears, a supercilious Englishman, who expresses disappointment in Dr Holliday being in his flat with a woman.

'I think I should leave,' says Laura.

Stephen asks Holliday for his key back. He talks with a confidence, arrogance even, out of place in one so ugly, for he seems unable to open his eyes fully and his mouth is curiously reminiscent of that of a wooden puppet. Holliday proffers, not the key, but the barrel of his Colt.

'No, Laura. It's Stephen who's leaving.'

Stephen had looked only slightly bemused at the discovery of Holliday and Laura. Now he looks horrified.

'Ride, I said,' says Holliday.

'Alright. I'm going. But I'll be back, Holliday, and I'll have the sheriff, I mean the police, with me.'

As he slams the door, Holliday turns to Laura. 'Take off your clothes.'

'Oh darling,' she says, 'turn away while I undress.'

'No,' he says, 'I want to watch.' And he watches her, as

she slowly, deliberately, coquettishly, unbelts and unbuttons her jacket, unzips and slips out of her skirt, peels back one stocking and then the other, and removes an entire lingerie store of white undergarments, until, finally, she stands before him, naked, slim, white as new-fallen snow.

'Now,' he says, 'one more thing. Put the cap on.'

'The cap?' she says, momentarily confused. 'Don't you have eh, um, a, um . . .'

'The Confederate cap. Put the cap on your head.'

She puts the cap back on and they fuck on the carpet. He takes her from behind. It reminds him of the night they drove old Dixie down. Gettysburg. That was one wild night.

Stephen is standing in the doorway holding a small pistol in a shaking hand.

'Now,' he says, 'the tables are turned.' But the confidence has gone from his voice, which is as shaky as his hand.

'No one draws on me,' says Holliday, reaching across the floor for his gunbelt. Stephen's whole arm shakes as if in the grip of an epileptic fit. He pulls the trigger and a bullet smacks into the ceiling. Holliday would have fired first, but for some strange reason he is moving in slow motion, defying the laws of physics as he rolls slowly through the air. Of course! Peckinpah. A decent gunfighter would have got in a second or even a third shot before Holliday fired but Stephen is slow - even without the handicap of slow-mo. In one, single motion, Holliday reaches his gunbelt, draws the Colt and fires a bullet through Stephen's heart, spraying the wall behind him with a fountain of red blood, for the screen suddenly bursts into colour.

'I have to go,' says Holliday, rather unnecessarily.

'But where?' says Laura. 'Where will you go?'

'There's a small town in Mexico advertising for a security consultant. I was head-hunted for the job. It doesn't pay much, but the package includes tortillas and beans. I'm going to take it.'

'Take that bloody Rachmaninoff off the gramophone.

I'm sick of it.' She pronounces 'bloody' very deliberately, as if unsure of the word, not quite certain she can get her tongue around it.

So they go to the refreshment room at Milford Junction station to say goodbye. Laura tries to be brave and not cry or whinge. Holliday says little. Mr Godby is chattering away at the counter, telling the barmaid some story about a man who travelled first class with a third class ticket. He told him he would have to pay the excess and when the villain refused he sent for Mr Saunders who ticked him off proper. It crosses Holliday's mind that he would be doing them both a favour to shoot them, but it is not worth the cost of the bullets. Let them be, he thinks, let them lead their little lives, and if they're lucky they might just end up in an Ealing comedy or something like that. But stay out of Tombstone, Mr Godby, stay out of Tombstone, for you would never last five minutes there.

Laura asks if Holiday thinks they will ever see each other again. Holliday just shakes his head. She says she wants to die. He tells her to pull herself together. The barmaid announces that time and tide wait for no man, portentously. Just then a middle-aged woman arrives, with a dead animal around her neck and her arms full of shopping bags. Her name is Dolly Messiter, an acquaintance of Laura's. She asks Holliday to fetch her tea and he overhears her telling Laura that Phyllis has left her. So not quite the respectable matron she seems, thinks Holliday. He wonders if he hadn't seen her once in the whorehouse in Wichita. Dolly - it certainly sounds like a whore's name. She waffles on about shopping and makes Laura seem the strong, silent type.

Thinking aloud, Laura notes Dr Holliday's politeness and composure; no one could guess what he is really feeling. Holliday thinks, aloud: 'Good. I don't need to listen to Laura's whining a minute longer.'

A bell rings and the station announcer's voice is heard.

'The train now standing at Platform 4 is the 3.10 to Yuma.'

195

Holliday rises and touches Laura's shoulder as he passes. She wonders if he might change his mind and reappear, but she knows that he has gone, and she is left with Dear Fred. Or is she?

'Dear Fred,' she tells him that evening.

'What is it my dear?'

'I have decided to leave you.'

'But what about the children?'

'I'm leaving them too. They're appalling, spoilt brats.'

'Well,' says Dear Fred, 'that Rachmaninoff record is mine.'

'You're welcome to it,' says Laura.

27

Roy always checked the room thoroughly before he and Rosebud left a hotel or motel. As often as not he would find her toothbrush still lying by the basin in the bathroom. Roy checked as usual before they left the Roosevelt, while Rosebud watched the latest Oscar preview on the television.

'Can I see that film?' she asked.

Roy glanced at the set and saw John Travolta and Samuel L. Jackson, in hand-me down 'Reservoir Dogs' suits, talking about burgers. Travolta was claiming that in France they call a quarter-pounder with cheese a Royale with cheese. But surely, thought Roy, they would not actually call it a 'Royale with cheese,' they would call it a 'Royale avec fromage'. Or would it be a 'Royale au fromage'?

'Can I, Dada?' repeated Rosebud.

'What?' said Roy.

'See that film,' said Rosebud, with a slight note of exasperation in her voice.

'When you're older,' said her father. It was a reply with

which she was painfully familiar by now.

'But I will see the hamburger man next week?'

'Well,' said Roy, 'We'll see all the big black cars arriving. And maybe you'll see him getting out.'

They would be back in Los Angeles the day before the ceremony and Roy had promised they would go to the Shrine Civic Auditorium in downtown LA to see the parade of limousines.

'Look, Dada,' Rosebud had said at the sight of her very first big black limousine, shortly after arriving in LA. 'That's a very big taxi.'

They checked out of the Roosevelt and joined the solid flow of cars, coaches and trucks and drove for mile after mile without ever leaving Santa Monica Boulevard until eventually they came to the wide, blue ocean, turned north and headed up Pacific Highway Route One through Santa Monica and Venice. The traffic began to move a little more freely on the eight-lane coastal freeway as it left the urban sprawl of Los Angeles behind and passed oil wells and offshore drilling platforms.

Rosebud was excited because Dada had promised they would stop at the beach somewhere and play with her bucket and spade. She would also get to see the enormous fairytale castle which had been the real-life house of the man whose sledge was called Rosebud. She sat in the back of the car turning the little handle that wound up her music box, and she and Roy sang along as it played 'Singin' in the Rain'.

'I-I-I'm singin'-in-the-rain, Just . . .' And when it wound down, getting slower and slower near the end, Rosebud would wind it up again and again until she was bored.

'When will we be there?' she asked.

All children ask that question on all car journeys. Roy could not answer because he was not quite sure where 'there' was going to be. He had not worked out where to play on the beach, where to stop for lunch, where to stop for the night. He looked at the map and noticed that they had recently passed Point Dume. It might have been an omen, for that was the point at which Rosebud discovered she did not have her Eaty and burst into tears.

Roy stopped the car, opened the boot and searched around in her bag without much expectation. He never normally packed Eaty; Rosebud carried him. The favourite cuddly toy was not in the bag. Roy had checked the hotel bedroom floor, checked every surface, checked under the beds, checked under her pillow, but then he got to thinking that Eaty must still be in the bed, down at the bottom, so that even when the sheets were pulled back he would remain there unnoticed in the dark recesses.

Roy promised to telephone the hotel, and Rosebud's distraught wailing gave way to irregular sobs. But their room back at the Roosevelt had not been made up yet and the clerk asked Roy to phone back in the afternoon. Roy and Rosebud walked along the beach hand in hand, with Roy assuring her that Eaty would turn up again, and they would collect him before they flew home, and she would have him to cuddle on the long flight back to London. Occasionally Rosebud stopped to pick up a little shell or a fragment of a shell, from the beach, dust the sand from it, and put it in the pocket of her red duffle coat.

'Do you promise?' she said.

'Yes,' said Roy, not entirely certain that he was in a position to do so. What if the maids just bundled up the sheets and they went off to the laundry without them ever noticing Eaty, he wondered. And what were his chances of getting another similar Eaty if that did happen? They had looked at toys at Universal Studios, but he couldn't remember what they had. Rosebud was more interested in the ET ride than the ET toys.

'You promise we'll get him back,' said Rosebud with the earnestness that only small children possess. 'Cross your heart and hope to die.'

'Cross my heart and hope to die,' said Roy. 'May the world swallow me up if you don't get Eaty back.'

It began to rain when they left the beach. They had

burgers for lunch, and Roy could not get the concept of a Royale with cheese out of his mind. Rosebud covered her burger in ketchup, Roy ordered chilli with his.

'This is a really good burger, Dada,' said Rosebud and Roy overtipped. When they stepped out from the diner there was a half rainbow bent across the sky. Rosebud wanted to see if they could find the end of it. They drove towards the point at which it seemed to hit the ground, but they never found it.

'We never ever find the end of rainbows,' said Rosebud. The rain stopped, the rainbow faded, but curiously the sky grew darker and the sun disappeared behind clouds.

They drove northwards, not talking much, but listening to the radio, which played a lot of Garth Brooks. Roy switched to another station. A few minutes later Garth Brooks was on that station too.

The traffic became more leisurely as they neared the city of Santa Barbara. Roy was sure Santa Barbara had some connection with 'The Graduate'. Didn't Dustin Hoffman drive down the Pacific Highway in the other direction from Berkley to try to stop Katharine Ross marrying someone else?

White-walled, red-roofed Spanish revivalist villas were dotted across the hillside. They checked into an old-fashioned motel with white stucco walls, and Roy telephoned the Roosevelt Hotel to check whether they had found Eaty. He was asked to hang on for a minute or more while the necessary inquiries were made. Rosebud stood silently, expectantly, by his side, looking up at him with her enormous blue eyes, begging him to say they had found Eaty. But they hadn't.

'All the rooms have been changed and nothing has been handed in,' said the formal, female voice on the other end of the line. 'I'm sorry sir. Have a nice day.'

Roy smiled at Rosebud and her eyes lit up in reply.

'Yes,' he said, 'they've found him.' He could not bring himself to tell her anything else. She jumped up and down in her delight. He would check out the malls for a replacement or phone Universal Studios and ask about ET cuddly toys.

They walked down State Street to the old wooden wharf, where he bought her a strawberry ice-cream from one of the stands. The sky was dark and the clouds pregnant with rain, but Rosebud wanted to walk along the beach. It was wide and empty and she skipped ahead of Roy down by the water's edge. He could hear thunder rumbling across the San Rafael Mountains. A few drops of rain became many, splashing on the sea and thumping into the sand.

'I-I-I'm singin'-in-the-rain' trilled Rosebud, unconcerned by the weather now that she knew that Eaty was safe.

The rain was heavy now and the sky dark; illuminated occasionally by a flash of forked lightning high overhead. A few seconds later the thunder would come.

'Rosebud,' Roy shouted, for his daughter was some way off, 'we should go back now.'

Rosebud danced like Gene Kelly. 'Just singin' . . .' But the the thunder and the wind swallowed most of her words. 'Happy again . . .'

Roy could feel the water running down the back of his neck inside his jacket and dropping from his hair onto his face. Rosebud had stopped ahead of him and was laughing and indicating something. Far out to sea sunshine burst through the darkness and danced on the water. The sky was blue and arching across it was the most perfect rainbow Roy had ever seen, ethereal smears of red, orange, yellow, green, blue, indigo and violet, each colour vivid and distinct. No chance of finding the end of that one. The rain was washing the strawberry ice-cream from Rosebud's cone onto her hand, but even at this distance Roy could see the big happy smile on her face.

The beach lit up brightly for a moment like someone had switched on floodlights. But the lighting was not entirely even all over the beach. It seemed to centre directly on Rosebud, as if she pulled the light out of the sky into herself. The beach darkened again. Rosebud stood looking at Roy for a moment, with a look of surprise in her eyes. The ice-cream fell from her hand and very slowly, as if Roy were watching in slow-motion. Rosebud collapsed onto the sand.

Roy ran awkwardly, almost stumbling across the beach on all fours, but he knew, even then, in his heart, that Rosebud was dead.

He held her lifeless body in his arms. Tears poured down his cheeks, mingled with the rain, and fell onto Rosebud's face, which held a look of confusion.

Roy stood, with his little daughter in his arms. He knew she was dead, but he refused to believe it. He stood waiting for her to say it was a joke, all an elaborate joke that he could not quite fathom. He waited for her to come back to life like ET did in the film. If he waited long enough she would jump down from his arms, with a mischievous little laugh, and continue singing in the rain, as if nothing had happened. She could not be dead.

People did come back to life. It was not just ET and Christ that did it. Ordinary people came back to life too. He lay Rosebud on the ground and pushed at her chest without knowing what he was, or should be, doing. He pinched her nose and breathed into her lungs. He did it again, like he was blowing up a balloon and he thought he could feel her body inflate beneath him. He did it again but when he took his mouth away from hers she just lay there, inert. He simply wasn't any good at practical things, and never had been. He gripped his two hands together, fingers interwoven. He lifted his arms above his head and brought the sides of his hands down together on her chest, not quite as hard as he could, for he did not want to hurt her any more than was necessary. Nothing happened. He pinched her nose and breathed into her mouth again. And again. And again. Nothing happened. He was vaguely aware of people running along the beach towards him and an arm around his shoulder. Then he did not remember anything else. Everything went black.

He woke up aware of sunshine pouring through the

window and the white freshness of linen sheets against his skin. And then he felt a knife slice through his heart and twist in his gut as he remembered what had happened. He had trouble sleeping in the months ahead. Sometimes he did not sleep at all. Sometimes he would wake in the middle of the night drenched in sweat, silently screaming. If he did get to sleep and make it through to morning before waking, he would never wake up thinking about Rosebud. That was the cruellest twist of all. He would wake up without a thought in his head. But it only ever took a second for memories of Rosebud to come flooding back. It was the suddenness of realising all over again that she was dead, of freeze-framing that awful picture of her standing on the beach, in her red duffle coat, with a strawberry ice-cream in her hand and a look of confusion on her face. That was the worst thing of all.

It was like someone had paused the video at that moment, but there was no rewind button with this film. The picture remained frozen for an eternity before giving way to jumbled untidy images of Rosebud's collapse and Roy's hopeless ignorant attempts to blow or pummel life back into her. ET came back to life. If this were a movie, Rosebud would have come back to life. There would probably be a sequel, and another film after that. But this was not a movie. There was no happy ending to Rosebud's story, no resurrection, no spaceship to carry her home.

Roy did not take her home. Jo flew out to join him and they had her buried in a field near the beach.

'To join him' is not the right phrase. It implies an intimacy that no longer existed. Roy did not want to go home, and was surprised when Jo agreed to his suggestion that Rosebud should be buried in Santa Barbara. Jo flew to LA and drove up Pacific Highway Route One, but she never really joined Roy. They were together only in the most literal, physical sense. They sat side by side with the body in a little commercial chapel, but they grieved alone, without touching. Jo did not stay at the same motel and they hardly spoke to each other. When they did speak it was about little practical things. The big things remained unsaid.

Roy sat dry-eyed. He had done his crying over the past few days in the little old-fashioned motel room, where he played the tune on Rosebud's music-box. Its tinny rendition of 'Singin' in the Rain' seemed a forlorn accompaniment in search of a singer whose voice had been stilled. It became slower and sadder as it wound down, it seemed to falter once or twice, but dragged on relentlessly. It strained over the final minute, threatening to expire on every note. It managed the first two notes of the title for the umpteenth time and quite suddenly it was gone. All was quiet, but for Roy's breathing, which thundered in his brain.

'I've seen things that other Roy Batty never saw,' Roy tells Anna. 'Yes, I have memories of my own. But I would prefer his. I don't want reality anymore. There is no point.'

He hesitates for a second or two. Anna knows he wants to say something more, but is not sure how to.

'But I don't have a choice anyway,' he says. 'I'm already dead, dead to this world anyway. I'm being sucked into the world of the movies. I know it.'

He pauses.

'And you know it too,' he adds. 'You've seen it as well.'

There was no funeral service for Rosebud. There was no one else at the chapel except the undertakers. Roy and Jo played 'Over the Rainbow' for her. Before they screwed the coffin lid down, Jo kissed Rosebud's forehead one last time and Roy kissed his daughter's lips. She looked peaceful, as if she were only sleeping, but the sudden, unexpected coldness of her lips made Roy shiver.

'Goodbye, Rosebud,' he said. And he placed her beloved, battered Eaty doll in the coffin beside her. It had turned up at the Roosevelt Hotel after all.

28

'Come back with me,' says Anna, glancing up from her coffee cup into the blue eyes across the table in the lobby of the Roosevelt Hotel. She is met by a look of sadness and instinctively turns her gaze away from Roy towards the palms, in giant terracotta pots, stretching up to the balcony on the first floor. Roy's look is also one of wistfulness at the idea that he and Anna, like Rachael and the other Roy Batty, might have had some sort of future together.

'Where I'm going . . .' Roy says slowly, choosing his words very deliberately, 'you can't follow.'

Anna recognises not just the words, but also the tone, from Bogart's farewell speech to Bergman at the airport in 'Casablanca'.

'Where I'm going I have to go alone.'

Anna's eyes ask the questions that her lips cannot quite form. The words do not come easily for Roy either.

'I let her die, Anna,' he says, his voice confessional, little more than a whisper, drained of all emotion.

'It was an accident, Roy,' says Anna, urgently, for she seems to sense they have so very little time left together. 'It could have happened to anyone.' She reaches across the table and lays her hands on his, noticing how deathly cold they are.

'No, Anna,' says Roy, patiently, like a teacher correcting the work of a small pupil. 'If I hadn't allowed her to run around a beach in a storm she'd be alive today. It's as simple as that. She died because I didn't look after her right. She died because of me.

'It was a year ago,' he says. 'She got a single paragraph in the "LA Times". "Girl killed by lightning", it said. "Forrest Gump" and the Oscars were the front page news. I promised to take her there, to the Oscars. I promised her so very much . . .' his voice trailed away.

'We never even said "goodbye". One minute she was there . . . singing in the rain. And the next. . .

'I don't know exactly what's going to happen. Maybe it's a form of madness. But you saw it too. You saw me in "Blade Runner". You saw me in "Brief Encounter". You know that I'm being sucked into the movies, consumed by the passion that she and I shared. I don't know quite how long I have left, but not long. I'm DOA. But first I have to go back to the beach where she died. It is my field of dreams. If I go there . . . she will come . . .'

They sat in silence for a while, maybe a minute.

'I understand,' says Anna, taking her denim jacket from the back of her chair and fumbling in a pocket for something. 'You have to say goodbye, but maybe then you could come back to me, maybe then you can get on with your life.'

She takes a key from her keyring and hands it to him. He looks at it doubtfully.

'Anna?' chirrups the voice of a tall, slim, middle-aged woman with a golden tan and jewellery to match. 'Anna Fisher?'

Anna forces the key into Roy's palm.

'I haven't seen you for an age.'

Roy slips the key into his pocket.

'Are you still teaching at UCLA? And who is this? I'm Jessica. Introduce me, Anna.'

Anna introduces Roy, while replacing her jacket on the back of the chair and wishing Jessica would drop dead. No, she doesn't mean that. But she wishes she would simply disappear as quickly and suddenly as she arrived.

'Oh, I just love an Irish accent, Roy. Scottish. I should have known. And is 'Braveheart' going to win the Oscar for best picture? I do hope so. I cried at the end when the English killed Mel. But I think maybe 'Apollo 13' will win. It's the patriotic American choice, and I don't think there are too many Scotch in the Academy. Have you seen it, Anna? Wonderful film. Really we should go to the movies together sometime. I would really like to see that other film . . . Oh, what's it called, you know the one with Susan Sarandon and Sean Penn, where she's a nun and he's going to die? Yes, I remember, 'Dead Man Walking'. A cappuccino for me, please, waiter. Anyone else? "Dead Man Walking"? Oh, must you go, Roy?'

'Yes, I'm afraid I must,' he says. 'I have a long way to go and not much time.'

Anna moves as if she is about to rise, but Roy puts a hand firmly on her shoulder.

'Look after yourself, Anna.'

Her mouth is dry. Her fingers dart to the crucifix that hangs around her neck. Something from her childhood stirs within her and she feels a sudden desire to tell Roy that she will pray for him - or maybe it was just Jessica's mention of Susan Sarandon playing a nun. Anna says nothing. One moment Roy's hand is on her shoulder, the next the pressure is gone. She does not turn round, but watches Jessica's eyes as they follow Roy out of the lobby. When they return to Anna's face she knows Roy has gone.

'Was that a key I saw changing hands there?' Jessica asks, leaning forward conspiratorially. She does not wait for an answer, because she knows that it was.

'I'm having an Oscar night party, Anna. You really must come and bring Braveheart with you. Ha-ha. Everyone must come as a character from one of the nominated films, a spaceman or a nun or a Scotchman. That will be easy for Roy. He can just be himself. Ha-ha-ha. I love the Scotch . . . especially on the rocks.' She laughs at her own wit. Anna smiles indulgently.

'I've already promised to watch the Oscars at my sister's,' she says, trying desperately to keep her composure. 'And I don't think Roy will be in LA then.'

On the day of the Oscars Anna does not go to her sister's. She follows Pacific Highway Route One up the coast to Santa Barbara, taking a room at the Motel 6. She walks along the beach, not sure what she might find. In the distance she can see a man and a small child playing with an American football. She feels her stride quicken as she hurries along the otherwise deserted beach towards them.

'This is going to be a high one, Jack,' shouts the man.

Anna slows down again as the boy backs towards her, squinting against the late afternoon sun to follow the ball's flight. Ball, boy and Anna come together in a heap on the sand. The father, a young man in wire-rimmed glasses and grey jogging suit, helps Anna to her feet with a smile and apologies.

'It's alright,' she says, brushing the sand from her jeans. 'No harm done.'

She walks back towards the wharf, taking one final look at the beach before leaving. The father and child are still playing ball in the hazy distance. And for a moment she thinks maybe she sees another man and another child just beyond them, skipping along at the water's edge, the child no more than a red blur. But Anna is looking into the sun, as it dances on the water, creating strange, fleeting patterns. She rubs her eyes and looks again. There is only one man, only one child.

In the solitude of her motel room she watches the Oscar ceremony, her heart leaping when a clip is shown of the English knights charging across the plain towards the Scottish army. Mel Gibson, his hair braided, his face painted blue, urges his men to 'hold . . . hold . . . hold . . .' until the English

208

cavalry are upon them and they lift their staves. As the cavalry are skewered like kebabs, Anna catches just a fleeting glimpse of a man with blue lightning painted on his face, the man she knew as Roy Batty, the man in the seventh row. Anna finds herself holding her breath as Sidney Poitier opens the final envelope of the night.

'Let it be "Braveheart",' she prays. 'God, please, let it be "Braveheart".'

She walks down State Street to Stearns Wharf, past the ice cream stands and onto the beach, which is now deserted. At the water's edge she sits on the sand and looks out to the point where the blue of the sky merges with the blue of the ocean. She sits, just staring into nothingness as the day fades. Out on the water a light blinks at her from a passing ship. It is dark when she gets back to the motel and switches on the television set. Mel Gibson is seen arriving at the Paramount party. She wonders if she might see Roy in the crowd scene there, or maybe alongside his 'Braveheart' co-star as he enters Chasen's, but she does not.

Next morning Anna telephones all the hotels and motels in the Santa Barbara area to ask if they have a guest called Batty. They all say the same thing - none of them has a guest called Batty. Until the last one.

'We did have a Mr Batty,' says the voice, 'a Mr Roy Batty, but he checked out a week ago.'

But that is the Roosevelt Hotel, back in LA, just confirming what Anna already knew.

Every day for a week she walks down State Street and along the beach, she watches the lights on the ocean at dusk, and she returns to the emptiness of her motel room and lies awake in bed for hours thinking. She feels close to Roy here, somehow, or at least comforted by her own anonymity and isolation in an unfamiliar setting, a setting as unfamiliar as Roy Batty.

In Los Angeles Anna telephones police stations and hospitals, asking if they know anything of a Roy Batty. Most quickly confirm they have no record of a Roy Batty, but one hospital administrator comes back on the line to ask if Anna is a relative.

'Yes,' says Anna, hopefully. 'I'm . . . I'm his wife.'

'Just a minute . . .' Anna can feel her heart thumping against her chest.

'No,' says the voice, 'There's been no admission under that name.'

She telephones the LAPD public relations office, claiming to be a reporter, just wanting to check if ever anyone reported their own murder or disappearance to the police.

'How could they do that?'

'Well,' says Anna, 'I don't know. My editor just asked me to check. You know what they're like.'

'Assholes,' says the police spokesperson. 'I've been there too.'

'You said it. But I suppose someone might know they were being murdered if they were being poisoned.'

'Why would they take the poison if they knew it was poison?'

'I don't know, but they might know they were about to be killed or abducted. They had seen the signs - strange people following them, strange things happening. They were powerless to stop it, but they were able to tell the police what was about to happen.' Anna feels she is not explaining this very well.

'No,' says the voice, 'that could only ever happen in the movies.'

29

Los Angeles, March 1997

One year later, Anna scans the showbiz section of the *LA Times*. It seems 'The English Patient', the tale of doomed wartime romance, is going to win the best picture Oscar over 'Shine', the Australian pianist movie, and 'Fargo', the quirky Coen Brothers' thriller with Frances McDormand as a pregnant policewoman. 'Fargo' seems to have been around for a very long time. Anna and Roy almost went to see it together, so it must have been in the cinemas before the last Oscars. They went to 'Blade Runner' instead. What would have happened if they had gone to a film about a pregnant policewoman instead of one about a dying robot who shared Roy's name? Which part would Roy have played? The pregnant policewoman? A smile forms on Anna's lips.

Anna never did see 'Fargo'. She had not been to the cinema since 'Brief Encounter'. It was not a conscious decision. It is true that she did mope around for a while after Roy went away, that she felt disorientated, even bereaved, but lately she had been far too busy to mope.

She sips from the thin elegant glass of Rioja and tucks her legs beneath her, facing the newspaper spread out beside her on the couch. She turns the pages without really registering the contents. These last few months she has felt a new contentment with her life. Her eye is caught by a short item reporting that several cinemas will again be staging a festival of classic movies ahead of the Oscars, following the success of last year's event. She scans the cinema chains' adverts, United Artists, Laemmle, instinctively looking for Mann's Theatres. She has a funny feeling that Mann's Chinese Theatre will be showing 'Blade Runner' and 'Brief Encounter', not that she has any intention of going to see them. Her eye runs down a list of films - 'The Wild Bunch', 'Bonnie and Clyde', 'Out of Africa', no mention of 'Blade Runner' or 'Brief Encounter'. But a little shiver runs down her spine as she reaches the film at the end of the list.

She sighs and takes another sip of wine, no longer looking at the paper, staring towards a poster of 'Braveheart' on the opposite wall, but not seeing it, staring into space, enjoying the moment of respite and the unfamiliar peace. She swirls the wine around in her mouth, enjoying its flavour, before swallowing.

Should she go? It is not her type of film - as if that had anything to do with her considerations. She has never seen it, and yet the idea of it has come to haunt her, because it meant so much to Roy. Of course Jon would have preferred the Japanese original. She can reel off the cast like a contender in a trivia quiz and had read on the Internet that director John Sturges claimed he could turn any film into a western, including 'My Fair Lady', which would revolve around a bet that any loser could be turned into a master gunfighter with the right training. She had read too that the two leading men almost came to blows for real. The young second lead kept on trying to upstage the established star. He had grown up on a farm in Indiana and prided himself on his ease with firearms, while the latter was a Russian of Swiss-Mongolian parentage, had read philosophy at the Sorbonne and came to cinema via the circus. There was an existential quality about his life to which Jon might have warmed, and he would certainly have been impressed by the Sorbonne connection and would have felt it worth reminding everyone that he went there too.

Anna's favourite story about the movie was not something she had read in an article or seen on the Internet, but one Roy had told her, about a little boy and his first visit to the cinema. She must go to the film if only to check if it could be true, if Yul Brynner really does keep his hat on until half-way through 'The Magnificent Seven'.

In Britain wealth and privilege have evolved over centuries into the class system. In Britain wealth is a birthright, in America it is more a question of how much you have in the bank. In Britain the rich, the poor, the upper class, the middle classes, the working class and the workless live in their own clearly defined communities. America is not so organised. In America wealth and poverty co-exist cheek by jowl. One second you can be on Sunset Boulevard with its hookers and billboards and bustle, and the next you turn a corner and you are in a quiet residential street where big houses nestle in the foothills and you can look out from the patio windows over the lights of the plain below, like ET at the beginning of his film.

Up past the Chateau Marmont, the hotel where Clark Gable and Jean Harlow conducted a torrid affair and John Belushi overdosed, stands a whitewashed villa, where a woman who looks a little like a slightly younger, long-haired version of Anna Fisher is sitting at a computer terminal. Music plays loudly in the background, so at first she does not hear the telephone ringing. She turns the volume down and cradles a mobile phone between her shoulder and cheek, while continuing to read the computer screen.

'Oh Anna, hi,' she says, with a note of some surprise in

her voice, turning away from the screen. 'Yeah, I'm great. How's my reclusive sister?'

There is a moment of silence as the caller answers.

'Really? Who with? Oh. Well what are you going to see? Why don't you go see "The English Patient"? Well, at least you're getting out at last. Of course I will. Just drop him off on your way. It doesn't matter how late it finishes, because you can leave him overnight and pick him up in the morning, and that way you'll get a decent night's sleep . . . You could stay here too. OK, but I insist that Roy stays overnight.'

Jenni had been worried about her sister, but less so since the arrival of the baby. She had been desperate to see what the baby looked like. She had only recently married and she and Dave had no children yet. The truth was she had never had anything to do with babies at all, knew nothing about them, except that they were fragile, small and smelly. This would be her first niece, or nephew, the first time she would have a chance to see a baby close-up, over an extended period, an opportunity for a test-drive. She was interested in the baby because it was just that, a baby; she was interested because she might, just might, want to get one of her own; she was interested in it specifically because it was her sister's baby; but she was also interested because it might offer some slight clue as to the mysterious father. What colour would it be? Not just its skin. What colour would its eyes be? And its hair? What would it look like? What would it be like?

It? 'It' turned out to be a 'he', with a tiny penis and enormous balls, which Anna assured her was normal. The first time Jenni saw Roy she readied herself to disguise her disgust at the sight of the semi-solid substances that she had been warned issue continually from a baby's every orifice. She would ignore the puke and the smell and the screaming and the green shit and pretend that he was beautiful. But there was no puke or smell or screaming or shit of any colour, just at that particular moment. And the baby was beautiful.

He was three months old now, but already Jenni had been pestering Anna for an opportunity to look after him.

'You need to get out. Just leave the baby with us for a night.'

She had been reading about babies.

'I've been reading about babies,' she told Anna. 'Ask me something.' And she thought she could even stand the puke and the smell and the screaming . . . and . . . and the shit. 'Go on, ask me something.'

Roy is awake when Anna arrives to turn him over to her sister's care for the night. He lies silently in his carrycot examining Jenni, with his piercing blue eyes and he coos contentedly.

'Like a pigeon,' says Jenni, running her fingers through his blond curly hair.

'He's so gorgeous,' says Jenni. 'Does he look like his daddy?'

Anna smiles.

'Yes, he does.'

This is a breakthrough, but Jenni knows not to push too much.

30

Greasy-haired and unshaven, Eli Wallach leads a small army of mounted bandits into a little Mexican farming village, swept along by the grandeur of Elmer Bernstein's music. Not handsome enough to be a goodie, he struts around in his scarlet shirt and stripy trousers, gesticulating with his arms and bemoaning change in society, shameless women's fashions and the decline of religion. The bandits wear sombreros, the peasants wear pristine white pyjamas. Wallach and his men help themselves to chickens, skins, grain and cigars, and he assures the villagers he will be back for the rest, prompting one of them to run at him with a machete, never a good idea when you are ten or twenty yards away and your opponent has a gun.

A small deputation of villagers, including one who looks curiously like a young Mexican Oliver Hardy, ride over the border to buy guns. They arrive just in time to witness an argument over whether an Indian can be buried on Boot Hill. The undertaker's driver has quit. Prejudiced? The undertaker says that when it comes to getting shot the man is downright bigoted, and there is no one else to drive the hearse.

'Oh, hell,' says a voice off-screen.

The camera switches to a man, with strong, handsome features, a little menacing and almost slightly oriental. He is dressed in a black shirt and stetson and is leaning on a fence. He will drive the hearse, he says. To the sound of slow, threatening drums, he walks purposefully over to the rig. Another man borrows the stagecoach driver's scatter gun and joins him. He is younger, fairer, dressed in light, faded colours, with his off-white hat pushed back on his head. He says he has never ridden shotgun on a hearse before.

Brynner and McQueen. They died years ago, long before Anna went to see the film. But on the screen they live on. They live on, larger than life. The man with the shotgun and the easy charm and the man with the cigar and the suit of black. In 'The Magnificent Seven' Brynner and McQueen achieved immortality. They are Akira Kurosawa's samurai knights relocated in the American West, with guns and horses and wistful talk of Dodge and Tombstone in the days before they became civilised. They are the embodiment of the legend, the myth, of the Wild West in corporeal form - not the way it was, but the way it should have been. Gunfighters who fight for the thrill of the fight, for the adventure, but who manage to make sure they are fighting on the right side nonetheless. Most of all they are a couple of boys playing at cowboys and Indians. The only difference between them and Roy and a million other kids around the world is that Brynner and McQueen had the right clothes, the guns, the horses, the landscape and they had the demeanour to become the legend.

But at the end of the day they are still just a couple of boys playing cowboys, thinks Anna. They are gone now, but their ghosts illuminate the Chinese Theatre. Cinema is the gateway to immortality, the door to another dimension, to another state of being, another plane, life after death. Brynner and McQueen are dead, but every night, somewhere in the world, they still ride the range with the others in the Magnificent Seven.

Senor Oliver Hardy and his friends approach Brynner,

who keeps his hat on even in his hotel room, and they offer him the vacant post of village saviour. They promise to sell everything they own to pay him. Brynner observes dryly that he has been offered a lot for his work, but never before has he been offered everything.

Horst Buccholz - Chico - is the first to approach Brynner about joining up. He has the right clothes - a black hat and a leather waistcoat with silver bits - and he has a gun, but perhaps not the right demeanour. The proud, young, hot-headed Mexican is not what Brynner wants, not yet, though Brynner will be convinced in due course.

The first man hired is Brad Dexter - Harry Luck - though in the public consciousness he is very much the seventh man, the odd one out, the obscure one who was not and never would be a member of that party known as film stars. Harry is convinced that Brynner's story about defending Mexican farmers is a cover for something grander - gold, cattle, maybe payroll.

Brynner and the Hardy boys meet up again with McQueen in the saloon. He has been offered a job in a grocery store as a clerk. He has heard of a job defending a village in Mexico, but cannot find out what it pays. Twenty dollars for six weeks, says Brynner. That is ridiculous, says McQueen. Brynner explains it is the village of the men with whom he is drinking. One of the Mexicans says that they appreciate McQueen's position, and that working in a grocery store is good, steady work. McQueen asks Brynner how many men he has. Brynner raises a single finger. With a look of weary resignation, and a furrowed brow, McQueen raises two fingers in a gesture that is apparently meant to signify that he will be joining Brynner, though it could be interpreted as a comment on the proposed scale of remuneration.

Together they ride out to an isolated homestead where a man named O'Reilly is chopping wood for his breakfast. With a single blow of his axe the powerful figure of Charles Bronson cleaves a log in two. A friend of Harry Luck, he is used to hiring out his services for a lot of money, $600 or

$800 a time. But right now $20 seems a lot.

Waiting for Brynner in his room is a southerner dressed like a gambler, with a white shirt, a black lace tie, grey waistcoat and black gloves. Robert Vaughn, the man who would become 'The Man from UNCLE'. Right now he is Lee. Brynner thought Lee was looking for the Johnson Brothers. In a southern drawl, Lee declares that he found them.

Six. They need one more.

By a railway halt, two cowboys argue over whether 'He can' or 'He can't'. The audience has no idea who 'he' is, or the subject of the dispute. The one who claims 'He can' warns the other to keep his voice down or 'He' might hear. The second one, an arrogant, hectoring man, does not care. He is prepared to bet two months' salary that 'He' cannot do it. The doubting cowhand lumbers over to a long slim figure lying asleep in the dirt, with his back and head propped against the bottom of a fence, and his hat pulled down over his face to shield it from the sun. Long and slim, the figure looks almost liquid; like it is in the process of melting and, as it does so, has slipped down from an upright position to one that is very nearly horizontal.

The cowhand calls him Britt and kicks his boots. The camera switches to a close-up of the prone figure, but the audience still cannot see his face, because of the hat pulled down over it. And yet they see a little of it, a thin face with prominent cheek bones and a dimple in the chin.

He slowly, deliberately, raises a forefinger and pushes his hat back on his head to reveal the slim features and blue eyes not of James Coburn, but of Roy Batty. Anna hardly stirs. She is not aware of ever thinking that she might see Roy again in any film other than 'Braveheart'. If she had tried to rationalise it, she might have expected to see him in Yul Brynner's role in 'The Magnificent Seven' or Steve McQueen's, but somehow she is not surprised he should turn up in one of the other parts. The moment where Britt's features are hidden behind the pulled-down hat is a perfect, teasing introductory scene for him. The character raises a finger and it seems the most natural thing in the world that it is Roy.

The cowhand says he doesn't believe Roy can do what he claims to be able to do. The audience still does not know the nature of the claims. Roy does not answer, but pulls his hat back down over his face. The cowhand kicks his feet again. Roy rises languidly, and without a word lays a blue metal mug on the fence beside him and gestures for the cowhand to stand opposite him, next to a telegraph pole. Roy holds a knife in his right hand, by his side. At a signal from an onlooker Roy throws his knife at the pole and the cowboy shoots the mug off the fence.

Roy retrieves his knife. The cowhand claims he won. Roy says nothing, just coolly, calmly, walks away. The cowhand insists Roy confirm that he was faster.

'You lost,' says Roy, matter-of-factly, walking away once more and settling down in the dust with a fresh cup of coffee. Once more he pulls his hat down over his face. The cowhand stands in front of him, calling him a liar and a coward and challenging him to do it for real. He shoots between his legs and threatens to kill him. They go through the ritual for a second time. By the time the cowhand's gun clears his holster, Roy's knife is embedded in his chest.

Britt is the best there is, with gun or knife, he cares nothing for money, he enjoys only the danger and the competition. But, if he is the best, with whom does he compete?

'Himself,' says Brynner in that cold, matter-of-fact way that he has. Britt uses words even more sparingly. Over the space of two scenes, he kills a man, he turns down the chance to join Brynner's band and then he changes his mind and reappears. And he uses only nine words: 'You lost,' 'Call it,' 'Chris' and 'I changed my mind'. But he invests those words with so much power and authority. He makes Chris seem verbose.

Now we are seven.

The Magnificent Seven ride south to Oliver Hardy's

little village. Chico makes a speech, Steve McQueen bemoans the absence of young women, Harry falls in with the local card game, O'Reilly befriends the children, including Johnnie, a white-skinned, red-haired boy, who is always climbing, climbing trees, climbing up on roofs, climbing to the top of the bell tower of the modest little church. Lee has trouble with his nerves. Yul Brynner talks with the old man of the village. He is not a farmer like the others, or even a Mexican. He is a plump, jolly figure, with a white bushy beard. A central American Santa Claus.

Britt shoots Wallach's scouts, shooting the last one out of the saddle just as he is about to disappear over the hill. Chico proclaims it the greatest shot he has ever seen. But Britt is disgusted with himself: he was aiming for the horse. Chico finds the young women of the village, hiding from the American mercenaries, and he finds romance. And Wallach comes back.

He is confronted by Yul Brynner, Steve McQueen and Roy Batty. Wallach and Brynner trade short, threatening sentences, like boxers finding each other's range. Wallach scoffs at the idea that his band of forty could be intimidated by just three gunfighters. Harry and Lee step forward. Five. And Chico. Six. And O'Reilly announces his presence on a roof. Seven. Wallach is still not impressed. Unfortunately for him he does not know they are not just any ordinary seven, but the Magnificent Seven. He needs food for the winter and they have not solved his problem. Brynner says solving problems is not their line.

'We deal in lead,' says McQueen, and the Seven show Wallach's men a sample of their mettle.

Wallach retreats and regroups. Chico infiltrates his band and passes himself off as one of them. He even manages to talk to Wallach himself, for Chico is a master of disguise: he knows that all he needs to do is put on a sombrero and Wallach will mistake him for one of his band. Chico reports that Wallach's men are starving and will be forced to attack the village again. The villagers are disheartened. There is a defeatist element among them.

Brynner and his men go to attack Wallach's camp, but the bandits are gone. The Seven ride back to the village to find Wallach is already there. He lets them live. He takes their guns, but only as a gesture, and he even promises to return them in the hills outside the village. All they have to do is ride away.

Britt straps on his gunbelt.

'Which way are you heading?' asks Harry.

'Back,' says Britt.

'But they won't even help. They don't want us. You must be crazy.'

'I never got a chance to say goodbye,' says Britt. 'I can't ride on till I say goodbye.'

One by one the others gather around his tall, lean figure, strapping on their guns too. McQueen says he belongs in the village. Brynner tells Lee he does not need to go, that he does not owe anything to anybody.

'Except to myself,' Lee drawls, stepping down from his horse to collect his guns.

As day breaks over the desert landscape, figures move silently through the village. So slim is Britt that he looks like a figure made from twisted wire. With his gun drawn, he takes up position behind a wall. McQueen, it is, who is suddenly confronted by one of the bandits. And the shooting begins.

Brynner races around the village, his rifle blazing. Britt stands firm behind his wall, picking off bandits whenever they show their faces. Chico disappears into a building. There are gunshots and cries from within. A few seconds later he emerges from the other side and rushes off, leaping walls like a hurdler. The old man rushes at a bandit with a machete, no, not a machete, a meat cleaver, and expertly turns a bandit into a side of beef. O'Reilly takes up position on a roof, where he is joined by little, red-haired Johnnie, who throws condoms, filled with water, onto the bandits below.

McQueen goes down, shot in the leg. He pulls himself up, dragging his injured leg behind him. He ties a make-shift tourniquet around it. Harry dies in Brynner's arms, with Brynner assuring him that they were really there for the gold. Lee faces up to his own personal demons, kicks open a door and confronts the bandits within. He steps outside again and just stands there, with his pistol in his hand, waiting to be shot. He pirouettes as the bullet hits him and he goes to make peace with his god. Never again would Robert Vaughn produce a performance to match this one.

Wallach has Brynner in his sights, but the latter, as unexcitable as ever, spots him and shoots him. Wallach turns, spins, falls, bounces, overacting to the very end. Brynner stands over him and Wallach dies with the word 'Why?' on his lips. Brynner says nothing. Some things cannot be explained in words. Some things just are. Brynner spins his pistol and drops it into the holster.

Britt blasts away. He drops to the ground. He seems to be hit. But, no, it was almost as if he knew there was a bullet with his name on it coming. And he drops just before it arrives. He defies his fate, defies his script, and lives on. As the battle ends, just as victory is achieved, O'Reilly becomes the final casualty.

The dust settles. The music slows. Brynner strides. The farmers return to their fields. Johnnie and the other boys place flowers on O'Reilly's grave, beneath a simple wooden cross, one in a row of three. Yul Brynner, Steve McQueen, Horst Buchholz and Roy Batty prepare to leave. But first they go to see the old man.

For the first time in the film Roy seems to hesitate, unsure what to do. The old man throws his arms around him. They look at each other, needing no words to say what must be said between them. The old man's eyes point to the house and Roy walks forward alone. On the floor is a little, coffee-coloured girl, singing to her doll, an ET doll. She is singing 'Over the Rainbow'.

She looks up, wide blue eyes looking out from her dark face.

'Dada,' she shouts and she races towards him. He

catches her and spins her round. For the first time he smiles.

'I'll look after her,' says a voice from the doorway. 'I promise, Roy.' The old man is a dark shadow against the brightness of the Mexican day.

For a long time Roy just squeezes his daughter to his breast, as if he fears that if he relaxes his grip she will disappear. Tears run freely down his cheeks. From his pocket he produces a little box and gives it to her.

'Dada, I wondered where that had gone,' she says with glee, turning the handle to produce a twangy rendition of 'Singin' in the Rain'.

With one finger, Roy pushes his hat back on his head.

'Grandad will look after you now,' he says.

She looks up at him.

'Bye-bye, Dada,' she says. 'See you later.'

'Adios, Rosebud,' he says, and he walks out without looking back.

The others are already mounted. Seeing the watering of Roy's eyes, Brynner asks if he is alright.

'Aye,' says Roy. 'Of course. It's those damn cats again.'

On the edge of town they stop. A young woman looks forlornly after Chico. Bynner nods to him and says 'Adios'. Chico rides back to where the women are making flour from maize. He unstraps his gunbelt and joins them.

Only three of the Seven remain on the little hill at the edge of town. They exchange looks.

'It's time to say goodbye,' says Brynner to Roy. 'Your trail leads in a different direction.' Roy nods. Brynner and McQueen turn their horses and Roy watches them go. He rides towards the camera and then past it or over it or through it, but anyway he too is gone.

The camera cuts to a shot of the old man and the little girl standing hand in hand. The words 'The End' appear over a shot of Brynner and McQueen riding off together. They died long ago. But there they are, up on the screen, larger than life.

Anna searches in her bag for a tissue. Finally she summons a single, whispered word, issued through stifled sobs.

'Goodbye.'

31

As Anna digs down to the deepest recesses of her bag for her keys, she realises that the familiar music she heard in the stair is coming from behind her own door; familiar because she was hearing that music only an hour ago, the swell of Elmer Bernstein's violins sweeping the Magnificent Seven to their destiny. She is sure that she did not leave the television on and she knows that housebreakers do not normally watch television, not even when 'The Magnificent Seven' is showing. Her hand is shaking slightly and she has difficulty getting the key into the lock.

Obviously little Roy would not settle at her sister's house and they have had to bring him home to more familiar surroundings. She shouldn't have left him for the night. How ironic that 'The Magnificent Seven' should be playing on television. And would Roy be 'watching' it or was he asleep in bed?

As soon as she enters the room she sees that the film has reached the scene where the cowboy challenges Britt to pit his knife against the cowboy's speed on the draw. The long, slim figure of Britt lies asleep on the ground with his head propped against the fence and his hat pulled down over his face. The cowhand kicks Britt's boots. Britt slowly, deliberately, raises a forefinger and pushes his hat back on his head to reveal the thin, almost emaciated features of James Coburn.

'Hello,' says Roy, emerging from the kitchen, with a Budweiser in one hand and a glass of whisky in the other. 'I hope I didn't startle you.'

He hands her the whisky and she knocks it back in one.

'Of course you startled me,' she says. 'You disappear for a year and then one night I come home and you're drinking my beer and watching a western on the television, as if . . . as if . .'

Words fail her.

'Not just any western,' he says. 'You look well, Anna.'

They stand there facing each other, Anna clutching her empty whisky glass, Roy holding the bottle of Budweiser at his side, as if they are playing out some weird parody of Britt and the gunfighter on the television. The cowboy collapses with Britt's knife in his chest and Anna goes to refill her glass. When she returns she notices for the first time that Roy has removed a picture from the wall. He is perched on the couch, with the remote control in his hand. Laid on the armrest at the other end of the couch is the picture.

'He looks just like his father,' she says.

Roy looks up and his eyes follow her gaze to the photograph of the little, chubby-cheeked baby in an all-in-one blue suit, staring doubtfully at the camera. Draining her second glass of whisky, Anna realises her hand is still shaking.

'I called him after you.'

'What?' says Roy. 'Britt?'

'No, Roy, Roy. You are Roy Batty, not Britt whatever his name is.'

'Yes,' says Roy, as if he had not considered it before. 'I am Roy Batty.'

He flicks the channel control. 'Chinatown' is playing. 'Chinatown', with Faye Dunaway and Jack Nicholson.

'I've been away,' he says, 'I had to go away.'

He changes channels again. Dustin Hoffman is trying to order a hotel room for his liaison with Anne Bancroft, but seems unsure of his name when it comes to registering.

'I had to say goodbye,' says Roy.

Anna nods.

'I know,' she says. 'I know all about the old man.'

'Blade Runner' is moving towards its climax on the television. Harrison Ford's grip is giving way. He is about to plunge to the street below. Rutger Hauer reaches out an arm and saves him.

'I'm back now,' says Roy, talking to Anna, but keeping one eye on the television. 'I think I'm better now.'

'Have you come to stay?' asks Anna.

'With you?' he asks. She nods.

'That would be presumptuous of me,' he says. 'I didn't know if you wanted me to come back and stay. But . . . but the way back . . . It brought me here. And then I saw the baby. I could see his picture on your wall from there.'

He points a finger at the television, which is once again playing 'The Magnificent Seven': Eli Wallach confronts Yul Brynner and Steve McQueen and James Coburn.

'We don't really know each other,' he says.

'Oh, I think we are beginning to,' she says.

Roy flicks the channel on the television again, to 'Blade Runner'. Harrison Ford, battered, bruised, still alive, is musing on why Roy Batty - Rutger Hauer - saved his life, that maybe in the end he loved life more than he ever had before, that all he wanted was to know where he came from and where he was going. And then Ford returns to his apartment and finds Sean Young waiting for him.

Maybe in the end the other Roy Batty, the one with Anna, realised that he too loved life too much to let it go. Or at least thought it worthy of another chance. Maybe he found some answers in the movies, about where we come from and where we are going.

Anna knows where he is now, and will not let him slip through her fingers again.

'I don't know how long we'll have together,' she says. 'But then again who does?'

And on the television Harrison Ford's voice-over echoes Anna's words.

'We don't need to know all the answers all at once,' says Roy. 'Let's just take it a step at a time.'

They embrace and they kiss, and as they do so Roy aims the remote control at the television. His head is turned away from it and his eyes are closed. He intends to turn it off, but somehow it switches once more to another channel.

As their bodies mould together and their tongues touch, Roy is hardly aware of the solemn beat of a side drum on the television and the words 'Franko VR, death by hanging'. He can feel the beat of Anna's heart against his body as someone, far away, announces solemnly 'Jefferson RT, death by hanging'. He does not look up, but he begins to wonder.

'Posey S, death by hanging.'

Roy's eyes blink open and he squints towards the television.

'Wladislaw, T.'

He recognises the face beneath the green army cap immediately. It is that of an old friend. He had been with him until an hour or two ago. It is that of Charles Bronson, none the worse for dying in 'The Magnificent Seven', though facing an uncertain future yet again.

'. . . death by hanging.'

The camera switches to a close-up of a man dressed in a shirt and tie and overcoat in various shades of green and brown. An officer. Lee Marvin. An aerial shot shows that he is inspecting a row of men in an exercise yard. A row of men. One, two, three, four, five, six.

'Anna,' says Roy. Seven, eight, nine, ten, eleven, twelve. A row of twelve men. 'It's "The Dirty Dozen". I never did see it.'

229

Gently she takes the control from his hand and switches the television off. With a smile she looks into his blue eyes.

'I'll buy it for you on video,' she says, 'and you can watch it with your son when he's old enough. Come on. Let's go get him.'

For a moment the room is silent, before a voice hesitantly toys with a few notes.

'Doodle-doo-doo,' it sings. Little drops of piano music begin to fall around the singer's vocal doodling.

'Doodle-doo-doody-doody.'

Then Gene Kelly bursts into a rendition of 'Singin' in the Rain' that is full of life, joy, hope and a determination to be happy even when it pours. The singing doesn't come from the television, or anywhere in particular. It is just there - the soundtrack of life. Roy pulls Anna to him and they kiss again. Roy thinks of his daughter playing with her grandfather somewhere a long way away, somewhere over the rainbow, and he thinks of the son he is yet to meet. Gene Kelly declares that the sun is in his heart and he is ready for love. Roy and Anna's bodies entwine. They are as close as they can be without falling over. No, they are even closer than that. They do fall over, onto the floor. Forced apart by the tumble, they start to laugh. Suddenly big, bright red letters appear superimposed across them. They spell out 'The End'.

But, we know, it is just the beginning.

Another chapter...

Soul Music

32

There was a knock on the door and David looked up without hope or expectation, but as his gaze dropped from Johnny's sun-browned face to his big, calloused hand a smile began to form on his lips. It was just a slight, involuntary curl at the corners of his mouth, as if he had forgotten how to do it, and in truth David had not smiled for some time. Johnny held a pair of tan-coloured cowboy boots at his side, the thumb and fingers of his right hand disappearing inside them. Without a word, he tossed them to David on the bed. The boots had pointed toes and fancy stitching on the sides. However David looked not at the needlework but at the souls of the boots. David was not good at spelling, never had been, and in his mind boots had souls, just like people. He stroked those souls, like he might stroke a little puppy, and he smelled the newness of the leather, as rich and evocative as Ben E. King singing Stand By Me. Johnny was a country and western man, but David loved those old Atlantic soul records.

That was about the only thing his father had left behind – a box of Atlantic soul LPs. His mother told him Da had gone off with some cheap Proddy hure from the club and left her with Pat, Marie, Teresa, Peter, Tommy and David and four quid on the mantelpiece to bring them up. Ma said that was just like the stingy bastard that he was, he couldn't even leave a fiver. But David knew something terrible must have happened to his da. He might have walked out on him and Ma, on his brothers and sisters, but he would never have left

231

Ben E. King, Aretha Franklin, Otis Redding and Wilson Pickett behind. Da would never let anyone touch those records. But David would sit at his feet as Ben E. King reassured them that, even though the land was dark, he would not be afraid as long as they stood by him. It was one of the very few times when his father seemed at peace. But if any of the weans, or even Ma, broke the sanctity of his communion with the music, Da would batter them worse than ever.

When Da left, Ma gave the records to David even before she told him Da was gone. David kept the records in the box, thinking his Da would be back anytime for them, and a month went by, maybe more, before he played them. The first track he played was Ben E. King singing Stand by Me. While the other bairns in the block played Bay City Rollers records and tied tartan scarves round their arms he would wrap himself in the warm embrace of Ben E. King. They called him weird. Once Tommy broke one of his fingers because he refused to say the Rollers were better than Ben E. King, pulled it back on itself, but David refused to utter the lie, pulled it back farther, pulled it through the excruciating pain until David heard it snap like the wish-bone in the turkey Da got from a man at the club for Christmas. When the wish-bone broke he wished for a pair of new shoes. When his finger broke he wished Tommy was dead. Tommy broke his records too, one by one. And his ma said it was a good thing they were broken and told David to take them to the rubbish chute. He used to like putting things into the rubbish chute, clamping the door closed on them, and listening to them hurtle downwards to oblivion. But there were tears in his eyes that day when he opened the chute door, and dropped the pieces of vinyl onto the metal shelf with all the solemnity of a priest. It was his first funeral. And the last time he cried. David was eight years old, but he never cried again.

He never cried at his second funeral. Sunshine offered a cruel illusion of warmth that day, but the trees were bare and the grass was encrusted with frost when they buried Tommy. David's teeth chattered in the cold. Maybe he was too numb to cry for the elder brother knocked down while playing football, by a car that never stopped. His ma saw it happen from the kitchen window, but the driver was never traced. Anyway, that would not have brought Tommy back. There were hundreds at the graveside – neighbours with black ties round their necks and cloth caps in their hands; uncles with beer bellies and red whisky noses, made still redder by the cold; and unfamiliar aunties who smelled of nicotine, ran their hands across his crew-cut head and said how much he reminded them of Tommy. Of course he reminded them of Tommy. He was dressed from head to scuffed toe in Tommy hand-me-downs, had been for eight years. The only thing in the world he had owned that had not been Tommy's was that box of broken records. Now the records and Tommy were gone. And all Tommy left behind were his clothes, a few battered soldiers and toy cars that had belonged to Pat and Peter before him, some Combat comics, an atlas he had nicked from the local library and a scratched 45 of the Bay City Rollers singing Shang-a-Lang as they ran with the gang. David looked up Bay City in the atlas and wondered what Scots boys had been doing in Texas. And he asked Marie what a roller was. She said rollers kept bowling greens flat. He thought maybe that was what Les McKeown and Woody did in Texas, but Marie just laughed and, when he told her he was going to go there when he grew up, she told him he was weird.

David always got a new pair of shoes at the end of the summer holidays: that is he always got Tommy's old shoes at the end of the summer holidays; they were new to David. But Tommy was gone and David was fast outgrowing Tommy's last pair. His ma said he was growing faster than any of the others and she did not know where his next shoes would come from. She tried him in Peter's castoffs, but they came off when he ran. She told him he would have to make do with the pair he had for a while longer. But his toes were crumpled and crushed, the nails on one dug into the flesh of the next, and his socks were stained red when he took his shoes off.

His ma borrowed a Stanley knife from Mrs Connolly along the landing and carelessly cut the leather toe out of each shoe. "They'll fit yi now," she said. "And if yi lose an eye, we'll have an eye-patch ready for yi an' aw." And she put one cut-out piece of leather over her eye and cackled, a moment of rare and ineffective humour. Much funnier was the sight of David in his cut-outs. The other boys guffawed when they saw him, and they laughed again when he doubled over in agony after kicking the heavy leather football in the park. The headmaster sent "a note" to his ma. She told David he would be getting new shoes after all.

"New shoes from a shop?" he asked.

"Aye, yi daft wee bugger," she said, "though I don't know who's going to pay for them. No' yon snooty headie onyways." One day after school they got the No 37 bus from the scheme to Princes Street, sitting upstairs at the front, where they had a good view of the castle, up on its ancient rock, and the gardens below it. His mother held his hand and told him not to touch anything as they entered the shop – Grimshaws it was called. His eye was caught by a poster of a young woman in a leather mini-dress and leather boots, sitting on the grass with one arm stretched behind her and the other resting on her crotch. She was advertising boot polish. He just had time to read "The fastest girl in town. Everything about her is leather. Everything about her is fast," as they climbed the stairs to the children's department. The walls were lined with cardboard boxes, a cliff-wall of boxed footwear. On shelves around the store there were black shoes, brown shoes, ankle boots, lacing shoes, slip-ons, shoes with buckles... and football boots. But David's attention was attracted by a strange contraption by the wall. He asked his ma what it was and she told him you put your feet in the bottom and looked in the top and you could see the bones in your feet. She told him not to go near it, so when she went to speak to an assistant he stepped onto the machine, thrust his feet beyond the curtain and pressed his head against the sculpted shape at the top. Everything was black. No feet. No bones.

He looked round and his ma was talking to a fat, old woman with grey hair, with her back to him, so he took the opportunity to return to his previous spot, undetected. They sat in two armchairs while the fat, old woman with grey hair sat on a little stool with an extension where customers would lay their feet. Roughly she pulled one of his bare legs towards her and took off the black gutty he was wearing. "Oh, David," his mother said, in mock astonishment, at the sight of a grey sock, from which a big toe poked, like a rabbit sniffing the meadow before committing itself to emerge into the day. "What are you doing wearing holey socks?" she said. But his other socks would have allowed a whole army of rabbits through. Army? Flock? They had been doing collected nouns but they had not done rabbits. Pack? His thoughts shifted to the words his ma had used. Holy socks. He smiled at the notion of socks blessed by the Baby Jesus. Despite the exalted state of the socks, David was aware of the faint whiff of foot mingling with the faint whiff of the fat, old woman's perfume, as she leaned over David's foot, two heaving bosoms heaving beneath her blue overall. He thought of the fast woman in the leather mini-dress as the assistant attempted to manoeuvre his foot into a wooden frame. "Everything is very scientific these days," she said, pushing blocks in from the side. "It measures width as well as the length, It is called a Brannock gauge you know," she added smugly. David did not know. She nodded at the contraption in the corner. "We've even got a new machine… except it doesn't work."

Blue veins stood out on her legs as she climbed up a ladder and slid a couple of boxes out from the cliff-wall. A weird thing hung from her neck on a cord, like an oversized medallion. She slipped it between David's heel and the plain black shoe she had produced from the first of the boxes, and with one final shove managed to get the foot into the shoe. "How is that?" she asked, prodding indelicately at his toes through the leather.

"Squashy," said David.

"Oh come, come," said the fat, old woman with the

blue veins. David thought of the fast girl in the poster again. "There's plenty of room. Walk about in them."

David walked up and down and returned to his seat. His ma and the fat, old woman looked at him expectantly. 'Well?" said his ma.

"Squashy," he repeated.

"Really," said the assistant, with a level of indignation that might have been merited had he been suggesting her bosoms were squashy rather than his own feet in her ill-chosen shoes. "I think you have plenty room."

But his ma thought bigger shoes would last longer and insisted on the next half-size up.

"With a buckle," said David.

"No buckle," said his ma. "And maybe not Start-rite," she added.

"Oh, Start-rite are the very best," said the assistant, with a mix of indulgence and indignation.

"Yes, well, I'd like to see some that aren't Start-rite."

"Very well. Madam knows best what madam would like, but..." But she thought better of whatever it was she was going to add and returned to the cliff-wall, leaving the original shoes and boxes abandoned on the floor. David's ma approved a pair of plain, black lacing shoes and asked if he wanted to wear them, but David wanted to keep them in the box, all shiny and brand new; and on the bus home he took the box out of its carrier bag several times and lifted the lid to check the shoes in their tissue, occasionally sniffing the rich newness of the leather. A big smile lit up his face. New shoes, my new shoes, he thought, rehearsing the words in his head. And he took the box out of the bag again and lifted the lid, staring in admiration at the dark beauty of the shoes, though they had been the cheapest make in the shop. He ran his fingers along the smooth, pristine, black soul, unsullied by grit and dog crap. "Och, leave them alane," said his ma, adding: "I dinna ken how we can pay for those." And she looked away, out the window, as if she could no longer stand the sight of the shoes.

Lefty and Righty were sitting on his pillow that night, still unworn, and David was sitting on the bed staring at them, thinking "My new shoes", when his ma called out, sweetly, "Davie, come ben the room a meenit." David saw their neighbour Mrs Connolly, with a cigarette in her hand and her yellow teeth bared in a smile that possessed all the warmth of a hungry wolf, and he saw in his ma's hands a pair of old, battered, greying shoes. "Wouldn't yi know it," said his ma, cheerily. "See these. Too wee for Mrs Connolly's Stevie. So she's brought them roond for yi. Thank God, yi didnae wear those new yins – we can take them back the morn." Tears welled in David's eyes, but none fell. He stared at Mrs Connolly. She held the remnants of her cigarette upright, maintaining the column of ash and smiled, yellowly. "Well, whit dae yi say to Mrs Connolly?"

A tear slipped over the lower lid of David's right eye and rolled down his cheek as he pulled on one of the cowboy boots. It was tight and awkward, but at last he got his foot into it and pulled his jean leg down over it. It seemed a shame to cover the fine stitching, but he never did much like the look of jeans tucked inside boots. As he pulled on the second boot, a second tear rolled down his other cheek. David stamped his feet in the boots, a perfect fit – good boots should be tight. He remembered that time he went to see John Wayne in True Grit with Roy Batty at the Ritz Cinema in Rodney Street in Edinburgh. That was a long time ago.

David swept the back of his hand across his cheeks. He looked up at the clock. It was almost six, almost time. "Thanks," he said to Johnny, extending a hand, which Johnny gripped firmly and held for some time, looking David straight in the eye. David's eyes twinkled, but although Johnny smiled, he could not hide the sadness in his own eyes. They had got to know each other well these last few years. Johnny talked about the daughters he was bringing up alone, after his wife left him. He talked about baseball, and American football, and Kris Kristofferson, Willie Nelson, and Johnny Cash, The

Baron and A Thing Called Love. And David talked about Scotland and real football, and Ben E. King, Stand By Me, and he told Johnny about the new shoes he once owned, for an afternoon. Johnny's ancestors came from Scotland. He had always wanted to go there to trace his family tree. He was a MacDonald and family legend had it they came from the mountains up north somewhere. David said he could show him some beautiful places; but, in truth, David had never been to the mountains up north. He gave out a little sigh at the picture-postcard mental image of snow-dusted Munros. But, oddly, the soundtrack that accompanied it was Ben E. King singing Stand by Me – "When the night has come and the land is dark, and the moon is the only light we'll see." David visualised the mountains shimmering in a ghostly, silver glow.

Johnny put a hand on his shoulder. "OK, buddy?" he asked. David stood up, his eyes now dry, a big, happy smile on his face. And all the time Ben E. King sang in his head: "I won't be afraid." Johnny opened the door and stood aside to let him pass. There were others there, waiting. "No, I won't be afraid…" David knew their faces, but did not see them. "Just as long as you stand by me." Johnny put on his cap and he stood by David. There was a moment of awkward, pregnant silence, like that moment when his ma asked him to thank Mrs Connolly for the shoes a long time ago. Except David did not feel the awkwardness or pregnancy of this later moment with Johnny and the others. He was not even aware of the silence, for Ben E. King still played in his head. Johnny, who stood at his shoulder, filled his lungs with air, drew himself up to his full, and considerable, height, and shouted. "Dead... Man.. Walking...." Each word was distinct and clear and echoed down the empty corridor, bouncing off whitewashed walls and uncarpeted floor. And the little party began its little journey to the room at the end of the hall. And in David's mind he could still hear Ben E. King singing "I won't be afraid, No, I won't be afraid." But in the foreground a thought was forming. "Dead man walking, aye," he thought, "but a dead man walking in brand new boots. Brand new boots with new, clean souls." He knew all along how to spell soles; he just preferred soul. He crossed himself and he smiled again, one last time, at the thought of his fancy new boots and the idea of a new, clean soul.

The story continues…

Hommage

33

Arthur sat in the park in the chilly sunshine of a late spring afternoon and stared off towards the hills, a few miles away, a natural boundary for the city's northern expansion, still dusted with a late fall of snow, like icing sugar. His grandchildren Daniel and Marc were playing on the grass, chasing each other round a tree, with loud shrieks of horror and delight. Round and round they went. Daniel somersaulted forward. In doing so, he never lost his stride, and Marc still could not catch him. Only when they deserted their tree and raced towards Arthur did their elder's gaze waver from the hills. He had been far away, with Captain Boulle, dead and buried almost 40 years ago. A little tear formed in the corner of Arthur's eye at the memory of his friend, but he quickly wiped it away, with a swift irritated movement, and he smiled at Daniel and Marc. They noticed not the fleeting drop of moisture in their grandfather's eye, nor his smile, nor even his presence. They were too wrapped up in the business of their game, birling beneath him once and heading back towards their tree, screaming as they went. Daniel did another triumphant somersault, landing smack upon his feet and continuing to run. Daniel liked somersaults and it seemed he could run and somersault all day without pausing for rest. These days all Arthur did was rest, and watch, and remember. A little girl in a bright red jacket stood some small distance away pointing Daniel out to the old man and woman who accompanied her.

The woman held her hand. The man smoked a pipe. The little girl was much the same age as Daniel, and the man and woman were probably her grandparents. Grandparents, like Arthur.

Arthur was old now, and he never remembered a time when he somersaulted. Even if he had done so, there would have been no little girl to appreciate his feats of athleticism with smiles of encouragement. Things were different these days. Things were different for Daniel and Marc. They were a part of this. They were born here and France had always been their home. They grew up with the chill and the people with their light skins. Daniel and Marc's faces and hands were hardly darker than those of the little girl and her guardians... much lighter than those of Captain Boulle, whose hide had been burned by years under a tropical sun. The word skin hardly seemed appropriate for something that had the texture of rhinoceros and was covered by wiry, grey hairs that seemed to stretch from his ankles to the crown of his head. Not that many people ever saw the crown of his head, for Captain Boulle always wore an old sea captain's cap. It must have been white once, but that was before Arthur knew him. Now it was a deep shade of yellow, with a black brim.

Arthur looked from the little girl to his own hands. He stared at the back of them and sighed. They were black, like the night or the brim of Captain Boulle's cap. But they were not cold like the night. Not yet. With quiet deliberation, he stretched ten fingers in the direction of the hills. They were a little stiff these days, but still warm, and through them coursed the same blood that flowed through the veins of Daniel and Marc and the little girl. He became preoccupied by dirt trapped beneath a finger nail and forgot about Captain Boulle. Some days Arthur remembered Captain Boulle and some days he forgot. He was getting old.

Captain Boulle was already in his fifties when he met – or rather saved – Arthur. Of course Arthur was not called Arthur then. His parents had called him Ham. But Captain Boulle did not know that, and Ham could not tell him – he was only a baby. And Captain Boulle knew nothing about babies. Captain Boulle was born in Marseilles. He grew up on the dockside and ran away to sea at 14, on a cargo ship sailing under a flag of convenience for the Far East. He called the baby Arthur because he once sailed with a man of that name, or so he told Arthur years later. Captain Boulle knew nothing about babies, but he knew all there was to know about the sea, he knew about fighting and drinking and smuggling. He ran guns in a leaky, little cutter, from North Africa to Spain, which was the nearest he had got to returning to France. When Franco won, Captain Boulle turned his back on the sea, just as he had turned his back on the country of his birth. He spent much of the Second World War in Casablanca, before travelling south, overland, and yet always seeming to end up in a port. His journey came to a temporary halt in Bissau, where every morning he would walk to the docks and check out the ships. He would share milky coffee and rum and tales of the sea with men of all nationalities who drifted in and out of the little Portuguese colony. With the passing of the months, his tales grew fewer and his intake of rum heavier. He became quite taciturn, content just to listen, or just to sit and sup and not even bother to listen. Latterly he sat alone, without the need for company. It was only when a returning captain remarked on Boulle's absence that they realised no one had seen or heard from him for weeks. Captain Boulle seemed to have disappeared, seemed to have turned his back on humanity.

A wind of change was blowing through Africa when Ham was born, a violent storm that left much devastation in its wake. Ham was born into a country caught in the grip of civil war and famine, the tightening grip of insanity, where men hungered not for food, but for blood. He was born in the forest, with the sound of gunfire in the distance. His family hid from the guns, and were reduced to living on berries and roots. He did not remember much about his family. But he remembered his mother's milky smell enveloping him as he clung to her breast and drifted off into sleep in the clearing. And he remembered being woken by a terrible explosion in his ear. He remembered the screams and remembered men with guns spewing fire and death. Blood splattered the leaves and branches of the trees. Bodies fell lifeless on the ground. His family had no guns. His father grabbed a stick to use as a club and threw himself towards the nearest soldier, knocking him over. As the soldier fell, a volley from his rifle cut through the forest canopy. With a horrible yell, another soldier released a burst of gunfire that riddled both Ham's father and the first soldier, and they danced one desperate, bloody tango macabre as the falling leaves showered down green upon their black and reddening bodies. With a choked sob that mixed incomprehension, shock and dread, Ham turned to his mother. The breast that had so recently supplied him with milk was torn open and smelled so very different now.

The forest grew suddenly still again. The rest of his family had fled through the trees. The soldiers too were gone. Everyone was gone. Almost everyone. One soldier remained. Ham looked into his eyes as the man levelled his rifle at Ham's head. An eerie, unnatural laugh issued from lips flecked with saliva, and a bloody red finger tightened on the trigger. Instinctively Ham covered his eyes, not wanting to look into the face of his killer. There was a moment when time stood still. The moment seemed to last forever. Perhaps Ham's life might have flashed before his big, expressive, dark eyes, behind his hand, but he had had no life, there was nothing to remember. He would have cried, but in reality there was no time, for the moment of quiet lasted a mere microsecond before the clearing echoed with one final explosion.

When Ham took his hand away from his eyes he saw the body of the soldier lying dead on the earth some feet away and a dark figure standing over him, in shadow, the figure of a huge white man in a torn cotton shirt with short sleeves that exposed heavily muscled arms, one bearing a tattoo of an anchor, the other the words "Vive la France". He also wore a yellowing sea captain's cap.

243

Captain Boulle lived alone in a one-room shack, with a thatched roof, far up the river. He did not encourage visitors and weeks went by in which he said little to Ham, though he fed him mashed bananas with a little milk from the goats he kept. "Arthur," he said, pointing to the little orphan. "Your name." And then he repeated it once "Arthur", as if to say that even a fool would know it by now, though, truth be told. "Ach," said the old seadog when Ham – that is Arthur – merely smiled in response to his christening. At first Captain Boulle gave Arthur a spoon with his bananas, but Captain Boulle used his fingers, so there was never any incentive for Arthur to use cutlery, though he learned quickly to use other tools and helped Captain Boulle construct a little cot in a corner of the shack in which Arthur slept. Or at least he handed Captain Boulle the hammer when he called for it. But these days Captain Boulle's favourite implement was his pen. He sat at the bare table and wrote in lined hardback jotters, while Arthur either watched or wandered down to the river to play on the little canoe Captain Boulle kept tied there.

Once every month or so they would set off early in the morning and canoe down the muddy river for many hours to a little town, where Captain Boulle would buy food and provisions. They stayed in a dirty, little hotel overnight, sometimes for two or three nights. If it was one of those rare times when the hotel had beer, Captain Boulle would stay on and sit in the garden with half a dozen glasses ranged in front of him. When Arthur was older he would sit with his own glass. And local people would come and talk. Arthur enjoyed listening. His pleasure and affection were reflected in his open, expressive features and in the twinkle in his happy eyes. Arthur felt safe with Captain Boulle and enjoyed his conversation. More and more, with each glass he drained. Captain Boulle looked after him, and he would help him, sometimes even carry him, back to their room. As Captain Boulle laid him on the bed, Arthur puckered his lips and kissed him on the mouth. Captain Boulle laughed.

One day, near the shack, Arthur was playing at the

edge of the forest when something dropped suddenly, heavily, from a tree, screamed at him and bared its teeth, challenging him to fight. He did not know the word for it, but it was a chimpanzee. He turned and ran with the chimp in half-hearted pursuit. There were sounds in the night that frightened Arthur – monkeys, cats and things to which he could put neither name nor image. They were merely sounds without shape, whose meaning could only be guessed. In response to one deep growl, he leapt from his cot, darted across the room and straight under the single grey sheet that covered Captain Boulle. Arthur placed an arm around the captain to check he was there in the darkness, though the moonlight shone through the curtainless window and the sheet rose silver in a huge mound above his bulky form. Always, after that, they slept together, sharing the warmth of each other's bodies in the cool winter nights.

There was nothing Arthur liked more than evenings sitting outside the shack, talking or not talking, mostly not talking, just listening to the sound of the jungle. There was plenty beer last time they were in town and Captain Boulle loaded so much into the canoe that it sat dangerously low in the water. One night, all of a sudden, Captain Boulle laid down his glass and announced that they would go to France. At dawn he packed a change of underwear and a spare shirt in his old kitbag and gathered his jotters together and wrapped them in oilskin, and they pushed the canoe out from the bank with a sense of adventure. They sat in the shade of the hotel courtyard and told everyone about their plans. They would get the ferry to the city next day. But they missed the ferry next day. So they sat in the courtyard and drank more beer instead. There would be another ferry in a week. Then they would go to France. Oh, the heads would turn to see two such fine, exotic characters as the old sea captain, returned from the sea, and his handsome young companion from Darkest Africa. They would take a house by the sea and watch the ships sail by. They would have croissants for breakfast, for there was nothing Arthur liked better. They might even sail once more, upon the Mediterranean, sail right into Marseilles, go and see the apartment building where Captain Boulle was born.

But it never happened. Next morning Captain Boulle was dead.

Arthur could not go back to the shack by himself. Instead he stayed around the hotel for a while and was popular company with the guests, though hardly his former happy self. The hotel owner gave him Captain Boulle's cap, expecting him to wear it, but he never did. He kept it in the back room he shared with the handyman, and looked at it every day. He missed Captain Boulle, his company and his talk, and he realised he would never see Marseilles. One day a white man came and took Captain Boulle's jotters, and Arthur left with him. The white man took Arthur on aeroplanes, through the skies, to a faraway place, which was much, much colder than Africa. Arthur finally made it to France and they even took him to Marseilles and photographed him there, outside the apartment building where Captain Boulle was born, holding Captain Boulle's book My Life with Arthur.

Arthur has lived most of his life in France now, much longer than Captain Boulle spent there. It was hard adjusting to a new country, a new life, new people. There were days when he just sat and thought about Africa and felt homesick, sick for a home that no longer existed, because it was Captain Boulle's home, and Captain Boulle was gone.

Charlotte distracted him, Charlotte interested him, Charlotte shared great times with him. She was equally at home tumbling head over heels in the grass or dining under mean, disapproving eyes at some tea party, where the tea was served in a cup rather than a mug. Arthur had never seen a cup and saucer till he came to France. But like Captain Boulle, Charlotte too is long gone now. They had three children together however, and now there were grandchildren. There were no invitations to tea parties anymore. There just did not seem to be tea parties anymore, though it was the scent of food that finally brought an end to Daniel and Marc's game of tig and attracted them back towards the house. Arthur took one long last lingering look at the snowy hills in the distance. He was getting old and he doubted he would see another snowfall. He felt stiff as he rose from his seat, but life returned to his limbs as the scent of croissants wafted into his nostrils. That would be from the cafeteria, it would not be for him. Oh well, never mind. He would go and see what was on the menu tonight. He heard a shout that sounded a little like "Rosebud" and the little girl could just be seen as a distant figure in red, hurrying after her grandparents.

Arthur sighed and descended the climbing frame. He gripped the rope and swung across the ditch to the house. Isabelle, their young keeper, was dishing out bananas to the other chimpanzees, but she did not mash them like Captain Boulle had done. Before eating, Arthur went to his cage to get Captain Boulle's cap. For some reason, Arthur always liked to have Captain Boulle's cap with him at meal times.

Sometimes She'll Dance

34

Sam Murdoch was probably one of the greatest novelists of the 20th Century, though he only ever had two novels published. For years he pestered publishers with his work until one finally accepted the thumbed and battered manuscript of Wallace. It appeared in 1942. The story of William Wallace's struggle to free the Scots from foreign oppression caught the mood of the times. It was an enormous success, though perhaps the English were too eager to see parallels with the situation in Europe at that time to recognise the irony that they were the oppressors in the book. Murdoch adapted it as a screenplay, which was filmed in Hollywood the following year. In 1944 he won an Oscar for best script and his second novel Sometimes She'll Dance was published. It was a huge commercial and critical success. Reviewers fell over each other in their praise. At least one reckoned he could even be in the running for a Nobel Prize after the next book. And perhaps he might. Murdoch's lifestyle at that time was such that it certainly suggested that the Nobel judges could not hang about or they might lose their candidate.

But there never was a next book. Murdoch basked in the limelight and he went to Paris not long after the liberation. They had heard about him but few could have read his books. Yet he was treated as if he personally had been responsible for the defeat of Hitler. He was rich and famous and he drank his way around the globe.

Then in 1947 he disappeared. The press eventually

tracked him down, living on a mountain in a remote part of his native Scotland and the public instantly took this great man to their hearts again. He had returned to his native land, for only there would he find the peace to produce his next great novel. But whereas he had previously courted the newspapermen and willingly posed for photographers, he now refused all interviews and pictures. The public understood. They respected his wish for solitude (even if the press did not). They knew that a man such as Murdoch needed peace to find the inspiration for another Wallace. But there was no other Wallace, no second Sometimes She'll Dance, not even a screenplay, for which he had been promised an unprecedented sum. He wrote nothing. He never again published a single word. The two novels he had written continued to sell very well. But the man who wrote them receded into myth and mystery, an enigmatic literary genius, the hellraiser who tired of the world. He saw hardly anyone. There were reports that he owned vicious dogs and that he chased reporters from his property with a shotgun blast above their heads. And all this just seemed to fuel the public appetite for his books.

My mother never met him… and she was his daughter.

Murdoch met my grandmother in London in 1943 at the premiere of Wallace. Leda Turner was 27, the daughter of a clergyman, a Cambridge blue-stocking and film critic of The Observer. I know little else about her except that for a few months she shared a flat in Camden with Murdoch and that she gave birth to my mother. I read in a biography of Murdoch that he would boast at drunken gatherings, in front of Leda, that he had always wanted to "fuck the press" and now he had, though unusually he had no detractors among the press, at least not at this time. The inevitable "reassessments" eventually followed, but they said more about the ambitions and failings of individual critics than they did about their subject. I have a few cuttings of articles written by Leda. She wrote with wit and insight, and yet no praise was too high for Wallace, not the slightest criticism to be entertained. Murdoch left Leda when she was pregnant, never saw her again and never set eyes upon little Helen Turner, who was to be my mother. He sent Leda money for the child. Leda died the year before I was born but Murdoch did not go to the funeral. He did not even send a wreath, though he sent a cheque to Mother when I arrived. He sent a thousand pounds. Mother returned it and said that no amount of money could buy forgiveness. An unauthorised biography came out. It sold rather well, but the author did not seem to have much access to Murdoch's close friends, or maybe he just did not have close friends.

We never heard from him again after the money was returned. And for me Sam Murdoch was just a name on the library shelves till five years ago, when on my 16th birthday, October 26 1983, Mother told me Sam Murdoch was her father.

She told me that he may be a great writer, but he was also a drunkard, a boor, a womaniser and that he had left Grandmother when she was pregnant. She told me he had not sent a wreath to Grandmother's funeral and she told me about the money he sent when I was born "to ease his conscience". I hated him. I vowed that I would never read any of his books and that I would tell all my friends how bad he was. But I told only one friend and then I changed my mind and decided that I would after all read his books, but on principle I took them out of the library rather than buy them and enlarge his fortune.

I thought Wallace was the best book I had ever read. The English ruled Scotland and the Scottish aristocracy acquiesced in the suppression of their own people in return for the favour of the English court and continued wealth and privilege. Wallace, second son of a small landowner, drove the English from his country and became its Guardian, in the name of the exiled King John. But it was an unequal conflict and the English came again and Wallace was captured, taken to London, and hung, drawn and quartered. His insides were ripped out and burnt before his dying eyes. His head was put on a pike above London Bridge, a quarter of his body was sent to Perth, another to Berwick, another to Aberdeen and the last was put in the Newcastle sewers. But within ten years Robert the Bruce had led the Scots to a historic victory at Bannockburn.

I cried for Wallace and against my will for Murdoch, my own blood, who had told Wallace's story and so lovingly told the story of a people fighting for their identity. I asked my mother if she had ever read it but she had not. My father, who was Scottish, said it was "a classic", which he defined as a book you read more than once. And, when Mother was elsewhere, he told me that great writers could sometimes write the most wonderful books and yet could not begin to organise their own lives. My parents are dead now. They were shot by a burglar, but that is not really part of this story.

Sometimes She'll Dance was very different from Wallace. It is about a woman with whom the author is in love. He can never work out why she will only dance sometimes, so in the end he leaves her. I cried again, though I did not understand why he left her, because then both he and she were unhappy. They wanted to be together and yet he left her.

I read the biography of Murdoch. When he left school he went to work for a local newspaper in Stirling, not far from the scene of Wallace's greatest victory. He was remembered as a lively young man, a reliable worker. For ten years he tried to get his fiction published before Wallace was accepted. He had a rule that after his work had been rejected by three publishers he would destroy all copies and start on something new. Wallace was accepted by the third publisher to whom it was offered.

To those who knew him best in his teens and early twenties he spoke of little else than his ambition to become a novelist. As his mid-twenties passed without any success, he would talk when drunk ever more despairingly of his need to have his work published. When Wallace came out, he quit his job, left his girlfriend and his friends and moved to London.

During the war he went to Hollywood to make the film. There was even talk of him playing the title role, though that never happened. He was remembered as a handsome man, who could be good company, though he did not suffer fools gladly and insulted everyone during his frequent drinking bouts. There was mention of Leda Turner in the biography and how he deserted her. But she merited only passing mention along with other flings in America and England, France and Greece, where he drank in bistros, tavernas and bars till the early hours. Everyone said he was proud and arrogant and selfish. When he grew tired of a lover or a drinking friend he would move on and make new friends and as Europe's greatest novelist it was not difficult to make new friends, of a sort. Drinking buddies might be a more accurate description.

He came back to England for a while and embarked on unprecedented binges. He was the greatest and he let everyone know it, and when they agreed, he ditched them and went looking for new people to tell of his greatness. Eventually he tired of the adulation, tired apparently of everything fame and fortune had to offer and went off to live with the only person, according to his biographer, that he had ever truly loved, himself. No one could accuse the writer of hagiography. The book was what might be termed in the trade "a hatchet job". I think it was because the writer seemed so determined to present Murdoch as some sort of devil incarnate that I began, despite myself, to feel some sympathy for him.

And ever since he tired of his celebrity status he had stayed alone on that mountain in a remote part of Scotland. Arrogant, proud, selfish, they said. And I recalled my mother's words that he was a drunkard, a boor and a womaniser. But I remembered too the integrity, the nobility and the pain of Wallace and the heart-breaking enigma in Sometimes She'll Dance. Over the years I read them again and again – "classics" – and when I started working and set up home by myself I finally came to terms with the fact that the great Sam

Murdoch was my grandfather. It was no longer a notion, a sort of fantasy thought which just so happens to be true. It was a hard fact, which I accepted. I came across a newspaper interview with Leda in which she revealed that neither of them knew she was pregnant when he left her. He had been slighted on that point, she said. He left in January, when the snow was on the ground, and my mother was born in September. She thought he would probably have left anyway, but it was important to set the record straight.

I did not understand the man and slowly a desire to meet him began to take hold in me. He saw virtually no one, but I was his grand-daughter, Perhaps he would be as curious about me as I was about him. I dismissed the idea. He was a great writer who had turned his back on the world, a world where everyone was curious about what had become of the author of Wallace and Sometimes She'll Dance. I was nobody. He had shown no curiosity in seeing my mother, so why should he want to see me. And then I began to think that the fact that he had never seen Mother and knew absolutely nothing about me might arouse his curiosity.

His address had been published in articles in the press, so I drafted a letter saying I was his grand-daughter and asking if I might visit. I drafted and redrafted it. And then finally I wrote a version in which I omitted the fact that I was his grand-daughter and simply presented myself as an aspiring writer trying to find her way in the world. That was the version I posted, along with a photograph and a humorous short story I had written about the Gods on Mount Olympus and Zeus's attempts to keep his family in order. I jumped out of bed at the quiet thud of letters falling on my mat in the morning. But there was no reply. A second week came and went, and a third. I did not really expect a reply. Why should he reply to me, presenting myself not as his flesh and blood, but as a stranger, when he had turned his back on the world for so long? Two months went by and I prepared to forget the whole thing... and then a short note arrived: "Can you come the weekend after next? Please let me know if that's

OK. Look forward to meeting you, Sam Murdoch. P.S If not suitable, suggest some other date." I replied by return that I would arrive late on the Friday night. I took ten days off from my job as a sub-editor on The Times and flew to Glasgow on the Thursday.

It was my first visit to the land of my ancestors. I felt as if I was on another continent early next morning as I began the six-hour train journey to Morar, the second last stop on the West Highland Line. I felt as I had not felt since I was a small child, beginning a great adventure. This was Scotland, land of my ancestors, land of Wallace and of Sam Murdoch. I took out Wallace to read it for the umpteenth time, but it remained unopened on my knee. My concentration alternated between studying the grey picture of Sam Murdoch on the book's cover and the changing scenery outside. Sam Murdoch looked arrogant, or maybe just self-assured. His jaw was firm and his features craggy. He looked hard and yet his eyes were light (I had read that they were blue) and his eyelashes seemed unusually long for a man. It had struck me before that his description of Wallace's features was very much a self-portrait. The train wound past snow-dusted mountains and cold, blue lochs. I conjured up a cliché of clansmen, clad in tartan, claymores in hand. I read intermittently. The scenery became wilder. The train crossed the desolate Rannoch Moor, 400 square miles of peat tarns, streams and boulders. Only the railway crosses the vast wilderness. I saw a deer pick its way across the surface in the distance. I must have dozed a little for I came to with a jolt in Fort William where I had to change trains. I leaned out the corridor window as we left the town and Ben Nevis seemed to swell larger and higher above it the farther away we got. The scenery on the second half of the journey was perhaps even more awe-inspiring than on the first. I could understand why Sam Murdoch would want to live in countryside like this. The train curved round a spectacular viaduct with a splendid view of a Jacobite monument and a long loch stretching off into the distance. Eventually we descended to the sea and sight of some of the

Hebrides.

I got off at Morar, a hotel and a few houses by the water. I fell in love with it at once. I ate lunch and left my case in the hotel and climbed a hill which afforded a view of the village, and on one side the sands, the sea and the islands in the background, and on the other the deep loch and the high, rolling hills. Oh, how like the man who wrote Wallace to want to live here. I saw no one as I walked along the magnificent white sands on the opposite side of the bay from the hotel. I wished it had been a month or so earlier and I might have been able to swim in the sea. I left the beach and climbed between rocky hills and back down to the road which I could follow back to the hotel. All my worries seemed left behind in London, that other world, where I lived with my boyfriend, mainly because I had never quite summoned up the energy to move out. I wished that I could spend the rest of my life here. In the Highlands. Suddenly I felt a curious affinity with him, Sam Murdoch. I felt as if I was about to meet a friend, whom I had not seen for a long time, yet one with whom I shared a certain bond. Any uneasiness I had felt had gone, at least for the moment. I wondered how often Sam Murdoch walked through these scenes, if he had pictured Wallace climbing that hill with his army behind him. It was teatime when I got back to the hotel and I had a delicious salmon steak from the loch before collecting my case, asking directions and setting off on the final part of my journey. It was about two miles along the road round the loch.

As I walked towards my meeting with Sam Murdoch after all these years, I wondered what to say after hello, what we would have to talk about, and whether I should tell him I was his grand-daughter. I do not know why I did not tell him at the outset, why I held back. At least that is what I told myself. Did I know even then how the story might end? I really don't know. I was glad that I had planned to spend the afternoon walking rather than going straight there, for at least that gave me one topic for conversation. I could see the house on the hillside long before I turned up the road that twisted up towards it through the pines. It was a large, white building of two storeys. The sun had just gone down, the time which in Scotland is called gloaming. A light was already on in one of the downstairs rooms, then I realised that a figure was coming down the drive to meet me. I had an urge to turn and run. The figure walked quickly and carried what looked like a staff. He was perhaps smaller than I had imagined, but strikingly upright. "Good evening," he shouted from some way off. I was slightly surprised by the brogue. I don't know why or what I might have expected from a man who had lived so long in these parts. I stuttered a hello. Before he had reached me he extended a hand of welcome. I took it and felt a strong, dry grip, as they might say in some cheap romance. He took my case and asked about my journey. I told him I had stopped at the hotel for something to eat. He said he had expected me earlier and had prepared dinner but not to worry. In my defence, I reminded him that I had said in my letter that I would arrive after dinner. He said nothing further. We climbed the wide, wooden stairs, beneath the heads of stags. He showed me to a room and asked me to join him downstairs in the lounge when I was ready. For a moment or two I sat on the candlewick bedspread. A musty smell hung in the air. I did not know what I had expected but somehow this did not match my expectations. I thought he was probably shoveling my dinner into the bucket. Why did he prepare dinner for me when I said I would come after dinner? My spirits perked up when I saw the glowing coal fire in the living room. Sam Murdoch sat by it reading Treasure Island. He put it down as soon as I entered. "I'd always wondered what books authors read," I said, stupidly. He smiled. "Just the same books as everyone else." He motioned me to sit in the vacant armchair facing his by the fire. His eyes were the most striking blue and his lashes were long indeed. But his features had softened. His hair was now grey, but still thick and long, down over his collar. He wore an open-necked shirt and blue jeans. I could see he was studying me too. He asked if I wanted a drink and I asked for a whisky.

"Anything in it?" I shook my head. "When in Scotland do as the Scots do." He gave me the whisky but took nothing for himself. "Are you not having one?" I asked. "No, I rarely drink now," he said. "It never agreed with me." I smiled at the memory of so many stories. Sam stared into the fire. When he noticed my glass was empty he refilled it but said nothing. "What should I call you?" I asked him. "Sam," he said without emphasis and another conversation died. He seemed bored with me and I wanted to leave. My eyes wandered round the room and noted the bookcases. Every shelf was full and there were stacks of books on the top. On the mantelpiece half hidden by a cactus plant, and covered in dust, was the Oscar he had won for Wallace. He continued to stare unwaveringly into the fire with an expression that discouraged further communication. He seemed happy enough with me when I first came downstairs, but now he seemed to have finished with me. "I expect you must be tired after your journey, don't let me keep you up." I finished my drink and rose to go, disappointed and defeated. But as I reached the door he called after me: "Gaia, thank you for coming. Stay as long as you want."

Over breakfast he suggested a walk I might enjoy to a hill with a cairn on top of it. I had hoped he might suggest we walk together but he did not. I asked if he would like to come, though I thought he would say no. His blue eyes lifted from his book and seemed to harden, as if at the impertinence of the question. "I would love to, if you can be bothered with an old man slowing you down," he said. "You're not old," I shot back instinctively. I felt I had made some sort of inroad and determined to pursue it as we walked. I told him how much I admired Wallace and Sometimes She'll Dance and asked him why he stopped writing. "I had nothing more to say," he replied. "I wrote two books I was happy with. And that was all I had."

"And was it all so disappointing? Was the world so contemptible that you wanted to turn your back on it all?" I asked.

He bent to toss a stone into the loch. "We have our own monster here called Morag," he said. He looked far across the loch, as if searching for something on the opposite shore. "I didn't turn my back on the world," he continued. "I ran away from it. It frightened me. I thought they would find me out – expose the fraud. I was just a daft laddie who got in too deep." He turned to look at me. "Then, I thought 'The party's over, it's time go home.'"

"Do you believe in God?" I suddenly blurted, surprising myself as much as him. "I believe in him," he laughed, "but I'm not too sure he believes in me." He raised his eyes to the heavens. "Zeus, have you forgotten me?" There was no reply, so he turned to me again. His sad blue eyes were those of a cheeky child. "My father was a priest, you know. But I think God is in us all. We call on God, we call upon ourselves. Maybe I don't believe in me."

"I didn't know your father was a priest." I realised the remark must sound a little strange. I had met him for the first time only yesterday and here I was expressing the strongest surprise that I did not know all about his father. I had read many articles about him and never seen any mention of it. "No, they don't know everything," he said and we went home to dinner. He made broth and haggis, turnips and potatoes. He seemed to think it was a big joke to give a Sassenach visitor haggis. He had one glass of Talisker with the meal. He noticed my inquisitive gaze and my subsequent blush at being caught.

"I was once a famous drinker. But not now. It ate away at my soul till there was only the littlest bit left and then I said enough. Well, actually I said enough every time I awoke with someone drilling in my brain and my stomach threatening to come up through my mouth and my mind all messed up with the horrible vapours of whisky or brandy. It was taking away my thinking, It was part of the world you thought I turned my back on. The only way for me to survive was to run away… but now and then I do like a wee reminder of what it was I was running away from."

His grand language made light of it all, but I realised that behind the grandiose words was an honest statement of fact and I realised the famous arrogance was all a front, had always been a shield to hide behind. All next day we walked together, round the loch, along the sands and over the hills. We sat for a long time and looked over the Atlantic to flat-topped Eigg, Skye and farther out Rum. Sam said Eigg always reminded him of the plateau in Conan Doyle's The Lost World, where dinosaurs still lived.

After dinner we walked into Morar. There was a ceilidh in the village hall. He encouraged me to join in the dancing, which I did, while he stood and watched, with a glass in his hand. "You dance well," he said. I urged him to join me, but he refused, time and again. "I don't dance," he said, "not any more." Finally I persuaded him to join me, in a Strip the Willow of all things, and he birled me around with the energy and grace of a 21-year-old.

The moon danced on the loch as we walked back towards the lodge where the stags looked down on us disapprovingly as we noisily invaded their domain. He invited me to share a nightcap and the time seemed right. I told him I was his grand-daughter. He said he knew, had always known, from the moment he saw my picture, a picture that immediately reminded him of a woman he had known a long, long time ago. He turned to look into the fire, his brow knitted in thought and he let out a long sigh. "For years the only thing in the world I wanted was to see my daughter and then to see my granddaughter and at last the wish of an old man has been granted. God does believe in me."

"I don't know how much you know," he said. "I wanted to go to Leda's funeral but I did not think I would be welcome. I had left her, left her with a child, I did not think I had a right to show grief. It might look like self-pity. For that reason I did not even send a wreath. When you were born I still felt a duty so I sent a little money to Helen but she sent it back. I could understand why. When Helen died..." His words trailed away into a pained silence.

"But why didn't you go and see my mother when she was born?" I cried. "Why did you let time build up all these barriers?"

He turned from the fire and his eyes seemed to melt to tears, the tears of a young man grown old. "Leda didn't want me to. I didn't even know she was pregnant until I read in the newspapers that she had had the baby. By then Helen was three months old. I pleaded with Leda but she would allow me to see Helen only if I came back and married her. I don't expect you to understand. I'm not sure I do myself but I did love her in my own way and yet somehow I knew I could not go back to living with her, so I never saw my daughter."

"I guess we all love in our own way," I said to show I felt for him, yet not knowing what the words could mean. We were both silent. I knew he could never have lived with Leda again. It was already too late. At last I thought that perhaps I was truly beginning to understand.

"Did...," I began. "Did Leda dance?" He faced me, his blue eyes strong and young again. He smiled. "Yes," he said, "she danced. She was a very good dancer." "She was my muse, my Terpsichore, my Erato, my Calliope, all in one. Leda... She danced" He paused. He laughed and added "But only sometimes, only sometimes."

He came over to me and gently laid a hand on my shoulder.

"Forgive me." I shook my head. "There's nothing to forgive. We all love in our own way." I kissed him on the cheek and he felt the warmth of another human being for the first time in many, many years. And here is the thing – so did I.

I stayed at Morar with Sam until the last possible hour and then I got the train back to Glasgow. He came to the station with me to see me off and handed me a large, bulky envelope just as I boarded the train. Only after it pulled out of the station did I open the package. It was a typewritten manuscript of a novel entitled The Man in the Seventh Row.

Sam died suddenly a few weeks later but I think he

was happy at the end.

Not long after that I discovered I was pregnant. I finally found the motivation to move out of the flat in London and strike out on my own. I went back to Scotland and took a job in the little hotel in Morar. I had a son. There was no father. I called him Roy. We all love in our own ways. And some of us dance sometimes.

Printed in Great Britain
by Amazon